MAID FOR LOVE

THE MCCARTHYS OF GANSETT ISLAND, BOOK 1

MARIE FORCE

Published by Marie Force
Copyright 2011. Marie Force.
Cover by Rae Monet

ISBN: 978-1467976978

All characters in this book are fiction and figments of the author's imagination.

www.mariesullivanforce.com

The McCarthys of Gansett Island Series

For the late Bob Broz, the "Big Mac" of my childhood.

AUTHOR'S NOTE

My favorite place in the world is Block Island, located twelve miles off the southern coast of Rhode Island. A tiny slip of land with a Great Salt Pond in the middle, Block Island is the place time forgot. You won't find a stop light on the island or a hospital. Internet connections are sketchy at best, and good luck finding a hotel room or a spot on the ferry for your car in the summer if you haven't planned months in advance. What you will find is peace and quiet and beaches and bluffs and quaint shops and a laidback atmosphere that soothes the soul.

The island has played an important role in my life from the time I was a small child arriving on my parents' boat, through a college romance and now as a favorite family vacation spot each summer. I've never been anywhere that inspires me more. Block Island pops up often in my books, so I suppose it was only a matter of time before I made up my own version of the island and set a series there. Thus Gansett Island and the McCarthy Family were born. "Gansett" is a tip of the hat to Rhode Island's Narragansett Bay, one of my favorite places to spend a summer day.

Maid for Love is the first book in a three-part series. *Fool for Love* comes next and Ready for Love completes the first trilogy. A second trilogy featuring Grant, Adam and Evan McCarthy is coming in 2012. I'm also planning a book featuring Maddie's sister Tiffany!

I love to hear from readers! Contact me at marie@marieforce.com.

Welcome to Gansett Island! I so hope you enjoy Mac and Maddie's story. Stay tuned at the end for a sneak peek at Joe and Janey's story, *Fool for Love*.

xoxo

Marie

CHAPTER 1

Madeline Chester retrieved her nine-month-old son Thomas from his crib and checked her watch. She was due at the hotel for the morning housekeeping shift in fifteen minutes. After a diaper change, she handed Thomas his bottle, grateful that he could now hold it himself.

He let out a squeal of delight that drew a smile from Maddie.

"You like that, huh, buddy?"

His pudgy legs bounced about on either side of her hips, and she tightened her hold on him while attempting to tame his soft blond hair. She grabbed the diaper bag, the tote she took to work, retrieved her lunch from the refrigerator and headed out the door. Across the yard, she entered her sister's house through the screen door on the back deck.

"Morning," she called out.

"In here," Tiffany said from the living room where she sat amid three babies and a variety of toys. One of the babies was her daughter, Ashleigh, born just a month before Thomas. The other two Tiffany cared for as part of her in-home daycare business.

Maddie kissed Thomas, whispered that she loved him and plopped him down on the mat with the others. "I'm running late as usual."

"Go ahead. We're fine."

"I'll be back by three."

"See you then."

Tiffany watched Thomas for free during the day in exchange for Maddie taking over the daycare from three to six while Tiffany taught dance classes in her studio under the apartment Maddie rented from Tiff and her husband Jim. The delicate balancing act left Maddie worn out at the end of every long day.

She jumped on her bulky old bike and set off for McCarthy's Gansett Inn on the other side of the island. Checking her watch one more time, she groaned when she saw how close she was cutting it.

From his vantage point in the ferry's wheelhouse, Mac McCarthy watched the bluffs on the island's north coast come into view and felt the vise around his chest tighten. Just the sight of the island where he grew up made Mac feel confined.

"Never gets old, does it?" Mac's childhood best friend, Captain Joe Cantrell, owned and operated Gansett's thriving ferry business.

"What's that?" Mac asked.

"The first view of the island. Always gives me a thrill to see it appear out of the fog."

"Even after all the times you've seen it?"

"I still love it."

Mac studied his old friend. Time had worn some lines into the corners of Joe's hazel eyes, and his sandy hair was now shot through with streaks of gray that hadn't been there on Mac's last trip home.

"You ever wish you'd done something else?" Mac asked. "Gone out in the world a bit?"

Joe took a long drag off his trademark clove cigarette and flicked the ashes out the open doorway. "Go where? Do what?"

"Those things are gonna kill you," Mac said, nodding to the cigarette.

"No faster than working twenty hours a day is gonna kill you."

"Touché," Mac said with a chuckle.

"Are you planning to tell mama bear about your night in the hospital?"

"Hell no! She'd freak out all over me. That's the last thing I need."

Joe laughed. "What's it worth to ya?"

Mac shot him what he hoped was a menacing scowl. "You wouldn't dare."

"So what happened?"

"The doctors said it was an anxiety attack—too little sleep, too much work, too much stress. They ordered me to take at least a month off to recover."

"How'd your partners take that news?"

"Not so well. We're busier than hell, but they'll handle it until I get back." Mac and his partners owned a company that reconfigured Miami office space for new tenants.

"And your girlfriend? Roseanne, right?"

"My ex-girlfriend. We decided to cool it for a while. And then I got the email from my mother about my dad selling McCarthy's. . . I told my mom I'd help him fix the place up a bit."

"I still can't believe that."

Mac shrugged. "He can't work forever, and none of us want to deal with it."

"How's your sister doing? I haven't seen her in a while."

Despite the nonchalant question, Mac knew there was nothing nonchalant about his friend's feelings for Janey. "Still carrying that torch?"

Joe shrugged. "I've yet to meet anyone I like better."

"She and David are engaged, man. Might be time to move on."

"Maybe." He flashed the grin that had made him popular with the girls in high school—not that he'd noticed after he gave his young heart to Janey McCarthy. "She's not married yet."

"Joe—"

"I'm not going to show up at the wedding in a gorilla suit and cart her off or anything."

Mac studied the expression on his friend's face: staged indifference mixed with wistfulness. "That sounds a little too well planned."

"No worries, I don't own a gorilla suit. I *am* thinking about getting a dog, though."

Mac laughed at that because Janey worked for the island's veterinarian.

Joe steered the one hundred ten-foot ferry past the breakwater to the island's South Harbor port.

Mac watched the town of Gansett come into view—the bustling port, the white landmark Beachcomber Hotel with its clock tower and turrets, the Victorian Portside Inn, the strip of boutiques and T-shirt shops, the South Harbor Diner, Mario's Pizzeria and Ice Cream Parlor where Mac stole his first kiss from Nicki Peterson in eighth grade.

His overriding memory of growing up there was plotting his escape. Once he finally managed to leave, he'd never looked back except for occasional visits to his parents. Every time he came home, he counted the minutes until he could leave again. This would be his longest stay since he turned eighteen and left for college. Mac wondered how long it would take before he was chomping to leave again.

Salt air, diesel fuel and rotting seaweed—the aromas of home—filled Mac's senses and turned his stomach. He hated the smell of rotting seaweed.

"Come on back with me," Joe said.

At the ferry's stern, Mac watched as Joe used a combination of engine power and bow thrusters to efficiently turn the ferry in the tightest imaginable space and back it into its berth. "You make that look so damned easy."

"It is easy—especially when you've done it a thousand or two times."

Once the ferry was docked, they stood at the rail and watched the throngs of trucks, cars and tourists disembark from the day's first boat to Gansett.

"I still spend Friday and Saturday nights on the island during the summer," Joe said as Mac gathered up his stuff. "Come on by the Beachcomber if you feel like grabbing a brew or two."

"I'll do that." Mac shook Joe's hand. "It's good to see you, man."

"Been too long."

"Yeah." But as Mac took a long look at the bustling town of Gansett, he decided it hadn't been nearly long enough.

Carrying his oversize backpack, Mac navigated the crowds on his way to Main Street. He stopped to let a family on bikes pass and continued up the hill, mesmerized by the frantic activity.

To his left, in neat, orderly rows, cars, vans and passenger trucks waited to back onto the nine a.m. ferry for the fifty-minute return trip to mainland Rhode Island. Joe's employees moved like a well-oiled NASCAR pit crew, offloading cargo from the arriving ferry and reloading the next boat. The island relied on the ferries to deliver everything from food to mail to fuel to milk. During the summer, when the island's thirty restaurants and bars operated at full tilt, each ferry brought new shipments of beer, wine, liquor, fresh seafood, potatoes, vegetables and linens.

A forklift carrying a pallet of soda came within inches of running into Mac.

"Sorry, man," the operator called out with a smile.

Mac waved to the driver. He cleared the cargo area and fixed his gaze on the Beachcomber, the iconic building that anchored the town. The quacking horn of a Range Rover painted yellow and tricked out like a duck—complete with a bill affixed to the hood—caught Mac's eye. Laughing at the JSTDKY license plate, he stepped off the curb onto Main Street.

A searing pain stabbed through his left leg, sending him sprawling into the street.

Mac lay there for a second, trying to catch his breath and gather his wits. A young woman was lying next to him, her bike about to be run over by a pickup truck that would hit her next. Mac ignored the burning pain in his calf and leaped up to stop the truck inches from her. He wasn't fast enough to keep the truck from mangling her bike, though.

Mac squatted down to help the woman. Since her top had ridden up in the fall, he noticed her extravagant curves and had to remind himself that she was hurt. She was struggling to breathe and must've had the wind knocked out of her by the fall. He quickly adjusted her shirt to cover full breasts.

"Take it easy," he said. "Don't struggle. That'll only make it worse."

Frantic caramel-colored eyes stared up at him

The impact of their eyes meeting hit him like a locomotive to the chest. *What the heck was that?* Long hair the same color as her eyes fanned out under her head, and blood poured from huge cuts on her knee, elbow and hand. Mac winced, wishing he'd been more careful.

Tears spilled from her eyes.

Mac reached out to brush them away, his fingers tingling as they skimmed over her soft skin.

Her eyes widened, and she seemed to stop breathing altogether.

"Breathe," he said.

Anxious to get her away from the prying eyes of the crowd that had formed around them, Mac slid his arms under her and lifted her from the pavement.

She let out a startled gasp and then a moan as her injured leg bent around his arm. "W-what're you doing?"

"My friend Libby runs the Beachcomber. She's a volunteer paramedic on the Gansett Fire Department. Let's go get you cleaned up. Did you hit your head?"

"No, just my arm and leg." She turned her palm up. "And my hand."

Mac's stomach roiled at the sight of her pulpy hand. "God, I'm so sorry." Still carrying her, he crossed the street to the hotel. "I wasn't looking where I was going."

She struggled against his firm hold. "I need to get to work, so if you could just put me down. Please. . ."

"You can't go to work in this condition. You're bleeding."

"I have to go or I'll get fired."

Her twisting and squirming caused her round rear end to press against his belly, which sent a lurid message straight down to where he lived.

He groaned. "Do you mind holding still?"

"No one asked you to carry me," she retorted, apparently misinterpreting his groan.

"Look, I can't just put you down and send you on your way when you're bleeding all over the place. Let's get you patched up, and we'll see what's what."

"I'll get fired," she whispered, her eyes flooding with new tears.

"Where do you work? I'll call them and let them know you had an accident."

"They won't believe you. They're bastards."

"I can be very convincing." He took the steps leading to the Beachcomber two at a time, ignoring the shooting pain from his own injured leg. The porch was full of people having breakfast, and his passenger turned her face into his chest. At the maître d' stand, he asked for Libby and was shown to her office off the lobby.

"Mac!" Smiling, Libby jumped up from her desk chair. "I didn't know you were coming home!" She glanced at the woman in his arms whose shaft of long hair hid her face. "And bringing a friend. Don't tell me you ran away and got married."

"Not exactly. We had a little accident on the street."

Libby glanced at the woman's leg, saw the blood and went into paramedic mode. "Bring her in here." She gestured to a sofa in her office.

"I don't want to get blood all over your sofa," the injured woman said.

Libby grabbed some towels and spread them out.

As Mac put down his passenger, her breast bounced against his arm, sending another burst of lust coursing through him. Her hourglass figure reminded him of the old pinup girl posters his father had in the garage when Mac was a kid. Betty Boop had nothing on this woman.

With her uninjured hand, she brushed the hair back off her pretty face.

"Maddie!" Libby cried. "What happened?"

Maddie gestured at Mac. "Someone wasn't watching where he was going and knocked me off my bike, which is now totaled."

Libby tied back shoulder-length dark hair and broke out an elaborate first aid kit from under her desk.

Mac hovered in the doorway to the small office. "Do you want me to call your work to let them know you'll be out today?"

"Just tell them I'll be late. I can't afford to miss a whole shift."

No way could she work today, but Mac wasn't going to argue with her—yet. "Where am I calling?"

"McCarthy's Gansett Inn, housekeeping department."

Smiling to himself, he reached for his cell phone and dialed the number from memory. Maddie watched him, a startled expression on her face.

Keeping his eyes fixed on her, he asked for the housekeeping department. "Ethel? Hey, it's Mac McCarthy."

Maddie gasped from the double shock of hearing his name and having antiseptic applied to her gruesome cuts.

He whispered to Maddie, "What's your last name?"

"Chester," she said through gritted teeth.

"Little Mac McCarthy, you devil," Ethel said. "How in the hell are you?"

"I'm great, how are you?"

"Can't complain."

"I wasn't on the island five minutes when I knocked one of your housekeepers off her bike."

"Still causing trouble, I see," Ethel said with her trademark guffaw. "Which one?"

"Maddie Chester. She's with me at the Beachcomber, and she's hurt pretty bad. Libby's patching her up, but I don't think she can make it in today."

Maddie scowled at him.

Ethel released a deep sigh. "All right, if you say she can't work, I'll cover her shift."

"Thanks, Ethel. I'll be over to say hello, but don't tell my mom I'm here. She doesn't know I'm coming."

"She'll be over the moon, honey. Good to have you home."

"Thanks."

"That's not what I told you to say," Maddie snapped the second he ended the call.

"You really think you can clean today with your hand ripped to shreds? Not to mention your arm and leg?"

"He's right, Maddie," Libby said as she covered the ugly wound on Maddie's leg with a large gauze pad. "It'll hurt like heck in an hour."

"Already does," Maddie said with a wince.

Her face had lost all color, her mouth was twisted with pain and Mac hated that he had caused her suffering. Despite her killer figure, an aura of fragility surrounded her, with the notable exception of her hands, which were rough and obviously used to hard work.

"You'll need to be real careful with that hand for a week or two," Libby continued. "It won't take much to cause a bad infection if you get something in those open cuts."

Maddie closed her eyes and tipped her head back against the sofa. "Oh my God," she whispered. "What am I going to do?"

Oh my God, oh my God, oh my God. The refrain played over and over as Maddie pondered the deep load of crap she was in—or rather, the deep load of crap Mac McCarthy had *pushed* her into. From the second she'd looked up to see him leaning over her in the street, he'd seemed familiar to her. But with her injuries demanding her full attention, she'd been unable to put a name to the distinctive face. The nearly twenty years since he'd led Gansett High School to the state baseball championship had transformed him from a handsome boy into a stunning man.

Jet-black hair that curled over his collar, bright blue eyes, broad shoulders, defined pecs. . . After the way she'd ogled him in school, she couldn't believe she hadn't recognized him instantly. No, she'd had just enough time to call his parents bastards before she put two and two together to get Mac McCarthy.

Except for the dark circles under his eyes and the grayish tone to his complexion, the man was utter perfection. She knew from Mrs. McCarthy, who bragged about her five darlings incessantly, that Mac lived in South Florida. You'd never know it to look at him.

Back when he'd been five years ahead of her in school, he'd never even known she was alive. And now, the first time he saw her, really *saw* her, he got a full view of the bane of her existence—her overly large breasts. She wanted to die just thinking about it. Maddie wished she could either disappear or find a way to make Mac McCarthy and his big, hulking presence go away.

She opened her eyes. Still there. Still hovering. Still gorgeous. "You don't have to hang out," she said. "I can take it from here."

"I'll see you home."

"That's not necessary."

"It's my fault this happened—"

"*I* hit *you*."

"Because I stepped in front of you."

"You got hit by the bike, Mac?" Libby asked, turning to him. "Let me see."

Mac turned his leg to show a huge bruise forming on his calf.

Both women gasped.

"It's nothing." Mac stood and put his backpack on. "If you're ready," he said to Maddie, "I'll take you home."

"And how do you plan to do that?"

"I'll carry you."

"What if I live on the other side of the island?"

"I'll get a cab."

"I don't need you to take custody of me! I'll figure something out the same way I always do."

Mac leaned in so his face was inches from hers. "You're injured because of me, and I'm going to help you. Now, we can do this the hard way or the easy way. What's it going to be?"

The air crackled between them as they stared each other down.

"You've got a lot of your mother in you, huh?"

He glowered at her. "Now you're just being mean."

"I've, ah, got to get back to work," Libby said. "Come in for lunch while you're home, Mac."

"I will. Thanks for your help, Lib," Mac said without looking away from Maddie.

When they were alone, Maddie said, "You think just because you're a mighty McCarthy everyone has to do what you say, don't you?"

"I don't know what my family has done to piss you off, but since I haven't lived here in almost twenty years, I'm pretty sure it has nothing to do with me."

She attempted to cross her arms in impatience and grimaced at the pain that radiated from her elbow. For a brief, sickening second, she wondered if she had broken it. Then it finally gave way and bent the way it was supposed to. All she could think about was how much money this lost day of work was going to cost her, if it didn't cost her the job itself.

"What's it going to be? I can stay right here all day." He leaned against the edge of Libby's desk. "I'm on vacation."

Oh! He's so sanctimonious and infuriating! "Fine! If you have some sort of macho need to see this through to the gruesome finish, you can take me home, but for the love of God, take me out the back door so I'm not any more of a public spectacle."

"Fine."

"Fine."

Mac scooped her up and gave her a moment to get her injured arm and leg settled. "Okay?"

"Yeah," she said, releasing a long deep breath.

While she once again hid her face against his faded yellow T-shirt, he carried her through the lobby and out the back door. He smelled of sporty deodorant and laundry detergent, and his steady heartbeat echoed in her ear. Too bad he was a McCarthy. Otherwise, she might be tempted to forget about her no-men-ever-again policy.

Maddie directed him through a series of pathways behind the buildings that made up downtown Gansett.

"I used to play cops and robbers with my brothers back here."

"I used to drag trash bags heavier than I was to the Dumpsters when my mother worked at these places." She let her gaze travel up over the strong column of his neck to focus on his jaw, which seemed tense. Maddie wondered what it would be like to trail her lips along his whisker-sprinkled jaw. . .

He glanced down to catch her studying him. "What?"

Her cheeks heated with embarrassment. "Nothing." After a long pause, she said, "Your leg has to be hurting. Why don't you put me down? I can walk." He surprised her when he did as she asked. The sudden weight on her injured knee sent pain shooting through her, and she cried out from the shock of it.

"Have we proven that you could use a lift?"

A surge of nausea took her breath away. "Yes," she whispered. "Please."

He tucked a strand of hair behind her ear, surprising her again with the tender gesture. "I'm really sorry this happened."

Maddie ventured a glance up at him and swallowed hard, taken aback by his intense gaze. "I know you are."

"I'll make it up to you."

"You don't have to. It was an accident."

"An accident that was my fault." He lifted her carefully and once again gave her a minute to settle her injured limbs before continuing on.

Maddie directed him to her apartment over Tiffany's studio.

"Isn't this the Sturgil place?" Mac asked.

She nodded. "My sister Tiffany is married to Jim Sturgil." As they reached the foot of her stairs, Maddie realized that her purse was still attached to the wrecked bike. "My bag! I never got it off the bike. My wallet, keys—"

"Take it easy." He carried her up the stairs to her door. "I'll track it down for you."

Maddie tried to remember how much cash she'd had in her wallet. Twenty, maybe thirty dollars, but she needed every one of them. "The door isn't locked," she told him.

Somehow he managed to carry her, open the door and get her inside without causing her any additional pain. She watched him take a quick survey of the small space and felt her defenses rise. No doubt he was used to much better, but she refused to be ashamed of the home she'd put together for herself and her son.

His eyes landed and settled on the baby toys stacked in the corner. "You're a mom?"

"My son Thomas is nine months old."

He lowered her to the tattered sofa she'd bought at a yard sale. "Where is he?"

"My sister watches him during the day. Oh God. The kids."

"Excuse me?"

"I take over for my sister at the daycare at three so she can teach her dance classes. She watches Thomas for me, and that's how I pay her back."

"I'll do it."

"*What?*"

"I'll watch the kids for you. How hard can it be?"

"Have you ever even changed a diaper?"

"I'm sure I have. Some time."

"Right. Look, I know you're probably some sort of Boy Scout—"

"Actually, I'm an Eagle Scout," he said with a proud smile.

"Of course you are, but you've really got to go now. Your family is expecting you—"

"They didn't know I was coming today."

Maddie wanted to shriek in frustration. *Why couldn't he get the message and leave me alone?* And then it hit her in a wave of sickening despair. "It's not going to happen," she spat at him.

"What are you talking about now?"

"Get out of my cabinets! *What're you doing?*"

"Looking for some painkillers and a glass." He produced a bottle of medicine and a glass of water and brought both to her.

"Thank you," she muttered after she swallowed the pills. "Now, please, just go, will you?"

But of course he sat on the coffee table, and Maddie prayed the flimsy table would hold his two-hundred-pounds-of-pure-muscle frame. "So what's not going to happen?"

"I know what you're after." She wanted to smack the amused expression off his face.

"And what's that?"

"You think if you're nice to me that you'll get something in return."

Amusement faded to bafflement. "Like what?"

"Don't be obtuse. I know you got a good look out there on the street, so you're hanging around hoping to get your hands—among other things—on Maddie Chester's famous breasts."

He stared at her for a long, breathless moment. "That is so not true."

"And how are you different from every other man alive?"

"When I look at you, the first thing I see are gorgeous eyes that remind me of the way melted caramel looks over vanilla ice cream. They're a rather interesting combination of brown and gold. Your mouth, when it's not twisted with cynicism and bitterness, is so lush and pretty that my personal fantasies—if I had them about you, that is—would definitely be focused there, not on what's under your T-shirt. As spectacular as they may be, I'm more of an ass-and-leg man myself."

Maddie had never been more shocked in her life—or more seduced by words alone.

"Now that we've got that subject covered, let's talk money."

That brought her right back to reality. "What about it?"

"I want to pay for your lost wages."

"Absolutely not." She might be short on cash, but she still had her pride, and no one—especially someone named McCarthy—was going to take that from her.

"You have to let me help you, Maddie. I know you can't afford to miss work."

"That's the least of it! If I miss more than one shift, they'll replace me. They need the job done. They don't care who does it."

"I believe we've established that I have some sway with the owners of the hotel and can prevent that from happening."

"Good for you. That still doesn't get my job done, and it won't help me when they decide who they're keeping for the winter and who gets laid off."

"Then I'll do the job for you until you're back on your feet."

Maddie cracked up. "Sure you will."

"You don't think I can do it?"

She realized he was serious. "You have no idea what it even entails. How can you be so sure you can do it?"

"I'm capable of building a thirty-story structure. I think I can handle cleaning a few hotel rooms."

Maddie studied his supremely handsome face. "All right." What else could she do? She couldn't afford to lose her job, so she had no choice but to let him help her. "Since you seem determined to make it up to me, I accept."

He flashed a victorious smile. "Excellent. Now what about the kids? Could I be your arms and legs there, too?"

"Have you ever changed a diaper? Seriously?"

"No," he confessed, quickly adding, "but I'm a fast learner. If you tell me what to do, I'll do it."

He'd be saving her life if he stepped in for her, but wait until he saw what the summer people were capable of doing to a hotel room. Just the *idea* of a mighty

McCarthy stooping to the level of manual laborer at the hotel his family owned brought a smile to her face. She offered her uninjured hand. "Deal."

He shocked her again when he took her hand and brushed a soft kiss over the back of it. "Excellent. Now, let me go find your purse and see about getting you some lunch."

CHAPTER 2

Mac left his backpack at Maddie's apartment and headed into town in search of her purse. He thought about the hour he'd spent with her and the terrible beating his ego had taken. Not that he was a playboy or anything, but as a rule, he tended to be quite popular with women. He'd never met one so eager to be rid of him. And what could she possibly have against his parents? They ran a decent business and took care of their employees—at least he thought they did.

To be honest, he had no clue how their business—which had grown exponentially since Mac left the island—was run today. However, he planned to find out, and if Maddie's opinion was to be believed, he might not like what he discovered.

Mac wasn't surprised to find Maddie's mangled bike propped against a split-rail fence across the street from the Sand 'n Sea novelty shop. Someone had used the cabbage roses growing through the fence to camouflage the bike. Her purse was still sitting in the basket that hung from what used to be the handlebars. He opened her battered wallet to find a twenty, a five and several ones still tucked inside. The sight of the undisturbed cash filled him with an odd sense of homecoming. In Miami, the purse, the cash and what was left of the bike would probably be long gone by now.

Tucking her small purse into the tote bag, he tossed the mangled bike into a Dumpster and planned to get her a new one.

Twenty minutes later, he returned to her apartment bearing cheeseburgers, fries and sodas. On the way upstairs, it occurred to him that she might be a vegetarian like Roseanne. Mac sighed. He was so tired of difficult, hard-to-please women. Could he, just once, encounter one who ate like a normal human being?

At the top of the stairs, he paused, uncertain as to whether or not he should knock, since she expected him to return. Then, remembering how prickly she'd been earlier, he rapped on the door and stepped into the living room to find the sofa empty.

"Maddie?" He listened for a moment, worried that she might have tried to venture out on her own. "Maddie?"

A muffled sound from behind a closed door caught his attention. He put the food and her bag on the kitchen table and went to the door. Knocking softly, he said, "Maddie, are you okay?"

"Will you please just go away and leave me alone?"

"Why don't you come out here and we'll talk about whatever's bothering you?"

No reply.

"I got you something to eat. Come on out, Maddie."

More silence.

He waited another minute before he knocked again.

The door clicked open, and she stared at him through tear-reddened eyes. Something odd and curious twisted deep inside him at the sight of her ravaged face. In that moment, he realized this was not going to be the stress-free vacation his doctor had ordered.

"Are you in pain?" he asked, alarmed by her distress.

"It's better since I took the pills." She took a step and grimaced.

"Let me help you."

Every muscle in her body tensed as he lifted her. Once she was pressed against him, she relaxed into his embrace. Her hair brushed against his face, and he absorbed the bewitching scent of summer flowers.

"W-what're you doing?"

"Nothing." He snapped out of the trance, carried her to the sofa and sat next to her. "How about you tell me what's got you so upset—other than the obvious, that is."

"Why do you care?"

Good question. "If I hadn't stepped off a curb into your path, you'd be at work rather than crying in your apartment."

"It was an accident. No one expects you to fix everything."

"We've already agreed that I'm going to help you until you're back on your feet, so why don't you start by telling me what's wrong."

As if it was taking too much effort to hold up her head, Maddie leaned it back against the sofa and expelled a long sigh. Her weary resignation tugged at him and made him want to fix her every problem—even the ones that weren't his fault. "I don't know how I'm going to take care of Thomas in this condition," she said in a small voice. "Ever since he came along, I've worried obsessively about losing my job and not being able to take care of him. I never imagined I'd get hurt so badly—"

"I'll take care of him. Whatever he needs, I'll do it."

She turned her head so she could see his face and maybe gauge his sincerity.

Their eyes connected, and Mac again felt the impact ricochet through him. He couldn't look away. Unable to resist the overwhelming urge to touch her, to offer comfort, he brushed the hair back from her tear-stained face and dallied longer than he'd intended when his fingers sank into the fine silken strands.

"I don't want you to worry about anything."

Her eyebrows knitted with confusion. "Why?"

He combed his fingers through her hair, no longer because it was in her face but because he liked the thickness and texture. "I don't know," he said, bewildered by the undeniable pull.

The statement hung in the charged air between them. With every cell in his body fully aware of her, he couldn't recall a single other instance in his life when he'd been as powerfully drawn to another human being.

She licked her lips but didn't look away.

Fascinated by the play of her tongue over her plump bottom lip, he shifted to hide his arousal.

"This isn't going to happen," she said.

"So you've mentioned."

"I'm not interested."

His fingertips skimmed over her cheek.

A sharp intake of breath made a liar out of her.

"Okay," he said. His face hovered half an inch from hers. "Maddie?"

Her lips parted, almost begging him to take what he knew she wanted as much as he did, even if she'd never admit it. "Your lunch is getting cold."

Glancing at the bag on the table, she broke the spell.

An odd twinge of disappointment warred with relief. Just as well. He had no business wondering what it would be like to sink into the lush sweetness of her mouth, to run his tongue over that sexy bottom lip, to see her caramel-colored eyes darken with desire . . .

He helped her get comfortable on the sofa and got up to find plates. "Ketchup?" he asked, glancing back to see her nod. Interesting that the same woman who couldn't tear her eyes off him a minute ago was now having trouble looking at him at all. "I hope you eat meat."

"I'll eat anything."

Mac smiled at the irony. If he wasn't careful, he might just start to like this guarded, closed off, supposedly uninterested woman. "The foil wrappers kept the burgers warm, but the fries are kind of soggy."

"I don't care."

He delivered her plate and sat in a mismatched chair that had been old ten years ago. As they ate in silence, he took a closer look around at the threadbare room. The furniture was worn and battered, but every surface was clean. Other than a few photos of an adorable blond baby posed with another darker-haired baby of about the same age and the toys stacked in the corner, the room contained no further clues to unlock the mystery of Maddie Chester. Who was she? Who'd fathered her child? Where was he now? Did she love him? Did she miss him? Did he help her out financially?

Mac had never been so curious about a total stranger. Well, she was no longer a *total* stranger . . . Since he'd held her in his arms and carried her home, they'd probably graduated from strangers to acquaintances. Maybe by the time he nursed her back to health, they'd even be friends. He glanced over at her to find her expression blank, her eyes fixed on the scuffed wall. Okay, friends might be too much to hope for.

"Who's the other baby in the pictures?" he asked, settling on the safest of his long list of questions.

"My niece Ashleigh. She's a month older than Thomas."

"That'll be nice for them to have someone to play with."

"I guess. If we're still here."

"Going somewhere?"

"I'd like to move to the mainland."

He took a bite of cold potato. "So why don't you?"

"I can't leave my mother. She has a lot of problems, but I dream about getting out of here. Better jobs. A fresh start. No one knows me there."

"Why would you want to live alone with your son in a place where no one knows you?"

She shot him a withering look.

He had no idea what she meant. He'd ask his sister Janey. She knew everything that went on in Gansett.

A knock on the door startled them.

"Maddie? Are you home?"

He got up to answer it. A pretty dark-haired woman looked at him with accusatory eyes. "Jim came home for lunch and saw a man . . ." Her brows furrowed. "Who are you, and what're you doing in my sister's apartment?"

"Come in, Tiff," Maddie called.

Mac stepped aside to admit her, deciding that Tiffany must resemble their other parent, because he saw none of fair-haired Maddie in her. And whereas Maddie's curves were extravagant, her sister had the lean, lithe build of a dancer. At the moment, she resembled a protective panther about to pounce.

Tiffany saw Maddie and let out a gasp. "What happened?"

Mac extended his hand. "Mac McCarthy."

Tiffany just stared at him, and once again, Mac wondered why his name drew such an odd, almost hostile, reaction from the Chester sisters.

He let his hand drop to his side. "We had an accident," he said, filling Tiffany in on the details.

She went to her sister for a closer look. "Oh God, Maddie."

"I know."

"Don't worry," Mac said. "I'm taking care of her."

Tiffany's head whipped around, and the look she gave him could've cut glass. *What was that all about?* "I'll take care of my sister. You can go now."

"I tried that," Maddie said. "He's quite difficult to get rid of."

For a brief instant, Mac thought he saw affection on her face, but it was gone before he could celebrate the breakthrough.

"It's my fault that she's in this predicament, so I'll be covering for her at the hotel and at the daycare until she's able to get back to work," Mac said.

Tiffany looked from her sister to Mac and back again to Maddie. "You can't be serious."

"What else can I do, Tiff? I can't lose the hotel job, and you've got your dance classes. We need the help. I can barely move, let alone take care of four babies."

"How will you care for Thomas?"

"We were just discussing that when you arrived," Mac said.

"You'll move in with us until you're recovered," Tiffany declared.

"Tiff," Maddie said softly, "you know that's not a good idea. The way things are with you and Jim right now, the last thing you need is me and Thomas underfoot."

Tiffany seemed annoyed that her sister had mentioned her marital problems in front of "the enemy."

Mac watched Tiffany's expressive face as she ran through the various options and came to the same conclusion he had—Maddie needed him, and he was going to be there for her. Why he was so determined to help her was something he could ponder after he cleaned up the mess he'd made of her life.

"What does he know about taking care of babies?" Tiffany asked her sister.

"Not much, but I'll be there to guide him."

Tiffany turned to him. "I'll expect you downstairs at three, and if you screw up or hurt her any more than you already have, you'll answer to me. Are we clear?"

Mac refused to be intimidated by a tiny slip of a woman, but damn, she was kind of scary. "Crystal."

"Do you need anything?" she asked Maddie.

"No, thanks. You'd better get back so Jim can leave."

"I'll see you later." Tiffany brushed past Mac and slammed the door.

"Pleasant," he said to Maddie.

"Protective."

"What did I ever do to the two of you?"

"It's not you . . ."

"Then who?"

Her open expression slammed shut faster than the door had. "No one."

Even though she refused to say so, Mac knew that someone in his family had done this woman wrong, and if it was the last thing he ever did, he'd find out who. He had a bad feeling he wasn't going to like what he uncovered.

"Will you be all right for a little while?" Mac asked a short time later.

"Of course." Maddie felt like she could sleep for a year.

"I need to do a couple of things, but I'll be back well before three."

"Okay."

"Do you need me to pick up anything while I'm out?"

"No, thank you."

"You look like you could use a nap. Would you like me to help you into bed before I leave?"

Maddie's face heated with embarrassment. "I, um, I sleep here. The bed pulls out. Thomas sleeps in the bedroom."

"Do you want me to pull it out for you?"

"No, I'm fine."

"All right, then . . ."

He seemed both reluctant and anxious to go. Maddie wondered if he'd really be back. Once he reconnected with his family in their big white house, he'd forget all about his charity case in town. The thought of never seeing him again made her sad and then mad—what did she care if he didn't come back?

"You're sure you'll be okay?"

"Yes! Just go!"

"You're really good for my ego, you know that? I've never had a woman so anxious to be rid of me."

"A little dose of humility might be just what you need."

He flashed her the smile that had no doubt convinced many a woman to part with her panties. The bolt of heat that chased through her surprised and angered her. Maddie had no desire to be another notch on his belt, so why was she wondering what it would be like to be kissed by him, to be held in those strong arms when he was offering more than comfort?

"See you later," he said.

Watching him go, all broad shoulders, cocky arrogance and sure-of-himself-and-who-he-was-in-the-world elegance, she should've hated him. She'd spent most of her life envying—and hating—the McCarthys.

He had grown up with everything she'd ever wanted—a safe, secure home, a large boisterous family, and two parents who seemed utterly devoted to each other and their gaggle of kids. After working for his parents for the last eight years, Maddie had discovered that Big Mac and Linda saved their love and affection for their family, sparing very little on their employees, especially grunt workers like her.

Maddie sat there for a long time, thinking about how it was possible that she could actually be somewhat attracted to a McCarthy, of all people. The thought disgusted her. "I refuse to be like every other female alive who falls swooning at the feet of the mighty McCarthy brothers," she said out loud, as if saying the words might bolster her flagging resistance.

When he'd sat so close to her on the sofa that she could feel the heat of his skin, she'd wanted to run as far from him as she could get. Only a man like him, who thought he could get away with anything, would sit that close a woman he'd just met. That she'd felt so safe and cared for in his presence was yet another reason to be disgusted with herself. He didn't give a damn about her, and she'd do well to remember that lest she be swayed by his irresistible appeal.

As she gritted her teeth and tried to move into a more comfortable position on the sofa, she decided that road rash hurt way worse than broken bones. Even the ankle she'd broken in sixth grade hadn't hurt like this.

Turning onto her uninjured side, she finally found relief from the pulsing pain in her arm and leg. She also discovered that Mac had left his backpack in her kitchen. Much to her dismay, that, too, brought relief.

Mac jogged the short distance from Maddie's place to the town's main drag, looking for a cab. When he saw a beat-up woody station wagon heading his way, he smiled and flagged it down.

"Well, I'll be," Ned Saunders said as he pulled up to the curb and jumped out of the car to greet Mac with a bear hug. "Little Mac McCarthy. Are pigs flying in hell and no one told me?"

Mac laughed and hugged his father's best friend. Since Ned's thick white hair was spiked at awkward angles, Mac deduced that the old man still didn't own a comb. His grizzled beard and tobacco-yellowed smile were just as Mac remembered, even though he'd heard Ned gave up his beloved cigarettes a year or so ago after a cancer scare. He wore a Gansett T-shirt that might've once been red, madras plaid shorts that probably dated back to the first time they'd been in style, and battered flip-flops.

"You look great, Ned. Not one day older than when I last saw you."

His tanned face crinkled at the corners of devilish blue eyes. "Aw shit, boy, y'always were a charmer, now, weren't ya?"

"So my mama tells me."

"Speaking of yo mama, she know yer here?"

"Not yet. That's where I'm heading now."

"Yer travelin light, boy."

"I left my bag with a friend. I'll grab it later."

Ned pushed a pile of discarded coffee cups, paper bags and newspapers to the floor and flashed a sheepish grin as he gestured for Mac to join him in the front seat. "I sure am glad to see ya. Yer daddy's been giving me fits lately, talking about selling the place and retiring."

Mac wished he knew why his father selling McCarthy's saddened him so profoundly. His life, his home, his work were more than a thousand miles away. Why should he care if his parents decided to sell their business?

Mac and his siblings had grown up on those docks, had been weaned on his mother's famous sugar donuts and New England clam chowder in the marina restaurant, had held crab races on the pier and earned spending money working there as teenagers. The place was hardwired into their DNA, and the thought of someone else owning it felt so unbearably wrong.

"You really think he's serious?"

"Got himself an interested buyer and everything. I'd say he's pretty serious."

Mac sighed as Ned navigated the cab through the bustling downtown area on the way to North Harbor. Once they cleared town, the island's bucolic beauty unfolded like a red carpet, welcoming Mac home. Rolling fields of green, stone-walls, saltbox houses with crushed-shell driveways, rows of grapes waiting to be harvested, cabbage roses and jasmine. Mac rolled down the window to let the perfume of home drift into the car.

"No place like home," the older man said with a knowing smile. "Ya ever think about coming back?"

"No way. Things are good in Miami. Business is booming."

"More to life than work, boy. Yer daddy taught you that."

Truer words were never spoken. Somehow Big Mac had managed to run a thriving business that demanded his full attention every summer without sacrificing his family. His five children always knew where they stood with him and that nothing was more important to him than their safety and happiness.

As Mac watched the road to home unfold around him, a sudden and powerful urge to recapture the magic of his childhood overtook him. He wanted to go back to the time before the island closed in around him like a prison. He wanted to go back to those endless summer days of fog and sun and boats and people. The startling realization shocked him to his core and sent his life plan out the window like a piece of paper sucked into Gansett's balmy breezes.

"Ya know," Ned said, "if just one of you kids showed the slightest interest in the place, yer daddy would never sell it."

Mac had no idea how to reply to that, so he said nothing. Approaching his parents' rambling home at the top of the hill, Mac caught his first glimpse of the action below: McCarthy's Gansett Inn, perched on a hill of its own overlooking the marina and busy harbor. Adirondack chairs peppered the hotel lawn, and boats were packed three and four deep against the marina's main pier. After five years away, not one thing about the cluster of white buildings and docks looked different to Mac.

They pulled into the driveway of Mac's childhood home, and he reached for his wallet.

"Don't even think about it," Ned growled.

"Thanks for the lift." Mac shook Ned's hand. "It's good to see you."

"You, too." Ned held Mac's hand longer than necessary. "Ya know, sometimes life puts things in yer path to show ya where ya belong." Ned fixed his eyes on the marina. "Don't miss what's right in front of ya."

Mac had a sudden vision of the lovely but bitter woman who'd crossed his path earlier in the day and was filled with a profound sense that something huge was about to change.

Ned released Mac's hand and smiled at him as if he hadn't just rocked his world.

"See ya 'round," Ned said.

"Yeah," Mac said. "See ya."

He flipped the latch on the gate to his parents' two-story white colonial. Stepping into his mother's rose garden, he took a moment to appreciate the fragile multicolored blooms and intoxicating scent before continuing up the stairs to the wide front porch.

Since none of the year-rounders believed in locks, Mac walked right into the house. "Anyone home?"

Silence and the aroma of potpourri greeted him.

Walking on gleaming hardwood floors, he passed a wall of school photos of the young McCarthy siblings on his way to the recently modernized kitchen that looked out over the marina and North Harbor. Mac remembered his father staring out those windows, taking in every nuance of the goings on below. The employees often joked about Big Mac spying on them from "The White House."

Opening the sliding screen door to the expansive back deck, Mac went outside. The McCarthys had one of the best views of any home on the island, stretching as it did from the town beach on the far right to McCarthy's to the two neighboring marinas, Gansett Boat Works and North Harbor Yacht Club. The other two were known for being far more expensive and exclusive than McCarthy's, which prided itself on a family-friendly atmosphere. At the other end of the big, round harbor, a coast guard station and lighthouse guarded the western entrance.

Even though it was mid-June, the brisk sea breeze still held a bit of chill that was a welcome relief from the stifling South Florida heat. Mac stood there for a long time pondering his eventful arrival on the island and the odd conversation with Ned. He cringed when he thought about Maddie and how badly he'd wanted to kiss her. She made him anxious, as if he was constantly on the verge of saying or doing the wrong thing. Since he wasn't used to being so uncomfortable around a woman, he would deal with it by not spending any more time than necessary with her. He couldn't forget his plan to get back to Miami as soon as possible.

The screen door at the front of the house slammed shut. Mac turned just as his sister Janey came bounding through the sliding door to the porch.

She let out a shriek and launched herself into Mac's arms.

Absorbing the blow, he took a step back to keep his balance, smiling at her enthusiastic greeting. As blonde and fair as he was dark, Janey was seven years younger, but they'd always been close.

Mac put her down and tugged on her sleek ponytail. "How goes it, brat?"

She play-punched him in the belly. "Don't call me that. I'm all grown up, or have you been gone so long you forgot that?"

"To me, you'll always be thirteen with braces. Are you driving yet?"

"Hardy har har. I'm even having sex, but don't tell Mom."

Mac feigned a heart attack. The idea of Janey having sex was way too much for him to handle, even if she was twenty-eight and engaged. "Spare me the gories, please."

Janey grinned. "If you think it's gory, maybe you're not doing it right."

"I'm so not having this conversation with you."

Laughing, she added, "As much and as often as we can."

Mac put his hands over his ears. "Lalalala. How's Dr. David?"

"Starting his internship at Beth Israel," she said with a sigh. "One more year." She punched Mac's shoulder this time. "Why didn't you tell us you were coming?"

"I didn't want Mom going crazy cooking and cleaning."

"She does go nuts when one of the prodigal sons comes home."

"That's because we're special."

"Speaking of special, what's this I hear about you carrying Maddie Chester all over town?"

Mac wasn't surprised that Janey already knew about it. "I knocked her off her bike and hurt her pretty badly. I was helping her home."

"Aww, you're so good. She must've thought she'd died and gone to heaven with hunky Mac McCarthy coming to her rescue."

"Actually, she couldn't wait to be rid of me."

Janey laughed—hard. "Bet that doesn't happen very often." She wiped the laughter tears from her eyes. "You and Maddie Mattress—Mom would blow a gasket."

Shocked, Mac took a step back, as if she'd punched him for real. "What did you call her?"

"You've never heard that?" Janey seemed pained.

"I don't remember her at all. She was younger than me."

"Five years. She was in Evan's class." Janey winced. "Sorry to just toss that out there. I figured you'd heard it before."

"Why do they call her that?"

She rolled her eyes. "Come on, Mac, use your imagination. Rumor has it she kept quite 'busy' during high school. The football team was supposedly very fond of her."

Shock bolted through Mac, pinging around inside him and settling into an ache in his chest. "I don't believe that," he said softly. Nothing in his brief association with her had given him the impression she was loose or easy. In fact, she'd been the exact opposite with him, and he didn't think that was only because of his name. No, there'd been more to it than that.

"Now that I think of it, I haven't known her to be with any guy since school. But when Evan and I were in high school, all the boys were wild about Maddie Mattress and her spectacular boobs."

Mac turned to study the harbor and process the information.

"Don't tell me you didn't notice 'the girls,'" she joked. "They're quite something."

He turned back to her, working to keep his anger in check. Why he was so determined to defend Maddie wasn't something he cared to think about just then. "There's more to her than that."

"You're probably the only guy alive who'd say that after meeting her. I see your honorable tendencies haven't been diminished by your years in Miami."

"What's wrong with being honorable?"

"Not a thing. Besides, you've got bigger problems. Mom's gonna flip out when she finds out you're here. She'll be fixing you up with every unattached bimbo in town."

"*What?* Why?"

"Her grandchild clock is ticking like an atom bomb since Janet provided Auntie Joan with twins. Mom is desperate, and she won't be satisfied until all four of you are married and pumping out the babies."

Just the idea of it gave Mac the willies, but even that unsettling thought couldn't clear away the overwhelming sadness over what Maddie must've gone through. No wonder she was so anxious to move into anonymity off the island.

"How come you get a pass on grandkids?" Mac asked.

"Mom knows David and I are years away from that."

"Where is she anyway?"

"Doing the payroll at the hotel. She'll be home in a little while, or you can catch her there."

"Speaking of babies, what do you know about the father of Maddie's?"

"Not a thing. She refuses to say who it was. Word on the street is that it was Royal Atkinson."

"And people just *believe* that? *You* just believe it?"

Janey had the good grace to look chagrined. "Well, when a person has a certain reputation—"

"Whether it's earned or not."

"When she wouldn't name the baby's father, people speculated. She cleaned Royal's house for years." Janey referred to one of the longest-serving town councilmen. "Suddenly that stopped. A few months later, she started to show. People talked."

Mac shuddered at the thought of pretty, petite Maddie getting it on with rotund Royal and his heaving jowls. "No way."

"You asked. I'm just telling you what people say."

"This town needs to get a life. How can you stand it? Don't you ever get sick of it?"

"Doesn't faze me. As long as they aren't talking about me, what do I care?"

"Poor Maddie." The words fell from his mouth before he could stop them.

Janey stared at him. "She got to you, didn't she? And now you're wondering what it would be like—"

"I'm not wondering anything. I just wanted to know her story."

"You should probably keep your distance, Mac. She's had a lot of trouble in her life. Her mother's doing three months in prison for writing bad checks, and her father split years ago. Her sister was a wild child, too. They're not our kind of people."

"That sounds so snobby. She can't help who her parents are any more than we can."

"We got a lot luckier than she did."

"Which is exactly why we shouldn't throw stones."

She went up on tiptoes to kiss his cheek. "You're too good. Just be careful around her."

He'd already thought the same thing himself, albeit for different reasons. However, much to his dismay, knowing what he did now, he was even more intrigued by her than he'd been before.

"You deserve better than someone who's been around the block a few dozen times."

"You don't even know her."

Janey raised an eyebrow. "And you do?"

While he couldn't argue with that, his gut told him Janey was wrong about Maddie.

"Will you be around for dinner?" Janey asked.

"I've got some stuff to do."

"Come by my place for a beer if you're in town."

"I will."

She hugged him again. "Nice to have you home. I've got to get back to the clinic."

"See ya, brat."

"Don't call me that!" she shot over her shoulder as she went back inside.

Mac rested his hands on the rail and fixated on the harbor. When he woke up in the airport hotel that morning, he'd never heard of Maddie Chester. How was it possible that just a few hours later she was all he could think about?

CHAPTER 3

If the house was his mother's domain, Big Mac ruled over the barn-shaped garage. Linda referred to the barn as "the quicksand," because nothing that went in there to be fixed was ever seen again.

Mac navigated his way through the chaos, batting at spider webs on the way to the back corner, his heart pumping with excitement when he saw the white sheet. Just as he'd left it. A couple of old bicycles blocked his path, and Mac took a quick look to see if either of them would be suitable replacements for Maddie.

Dismissing them both, he said, "I'll get her a new one. That'll make her good and mad." He couldn't say why the idea of making her mad was so appealing, but he liked the spark of life that lit up her caramel-colored eyes when he challenged her.

Tugging on the sheet, he uncovered his first love—an orange Honda 250 motorcycle he'd bought from Ned two months after he got his license. His mother had flipped out—and ripped Ned a new one—but Big Mac had urged Linda to "let the boy be."

The bike was already old when Mac bought it, but with his father's help, he'd lovingly restored it. He ran his hand over the gas tank and came to rest on the leather seat. "What'd ya say, old girl? Still got some life left in you?"

Mac wheeled the motorcycle out of the barn to the crushed-shell driveway and was checking the oil when his mother came up behind him, letting out a shriek that nearly stopped his heart.

"Jeez, Mom." He stood up from the crouch he'd been in and hugged her. She was petite with the same fair-haired coloring Janey had inherited. "You scared the hell out of me."

"Oh," she said, "look at you."

"Don't get all mushy."

"You get more handsome every time I see you." She caressed his cheek, her sharp blue eyes zeroing in on him. "But why do you look so tired and thin?"

He smiled to himself. Her children hadn't called her Voodoo Mama for nothing. "Too much work, not enough fun."

"We'll have to see about fixing that while you're home. How long can you stay?"

"A while," he said, intentionally vague. The McCarthy kids had also learned a long time ago not to give her time for scheming.

"Don't tell me you're taking that old rust bucket for a ride." She shuddered. "I hate that thing. I was always so certain you were going to kill yourself on it."

Mac flashed his most charming grin. "There's not one spec of rust on this bike, and I've got to get around somehow."

"Use my car. I just got it out of the shop. I can walk to the hotel or grab a ride into town when I need one."

Mac glanced at the yellow VW bug convertible in the driveway. "Not in this or any other lifetime, Mother."

"Oh come on! It's not that bad."

"Um, yes, it is."

She let out a gasp. "What in the name of God did you do to your leg?"

"I had a little accident in town." He told her about his encounter with Maddie. "So I'll be staying over there, helping her out with the baby, and covering her shifts at the hotel until she's back on her feet."

"You can't work as a chamber maid! What will people say? You're a McCarthy!"

Had he ever noticed before that his family thought they were better than other people on the island? Had Maddie tuned into that, too? Is that why she had such a beef with his parents? "So what? She can't afford to lose the job, and it's my fault she's hurt."

"She won't lose her job. We'll get someone else to fill in."

"She doesn't want that. I'm taking care of it for her."

"No son of mine—"

Mac held up his hand to stop her. "Just because we own the place doesn't mean we're better than anyone else. I'm filling in for her, and that's the end of it. Do we still have those old sleeping bags with the camping stuff?" Leaving her fuming in the driveway, he went back into the garage and found the sleeping bags right where he expected them to be, zipped into large plastic bags to protect them from mold.

"What're you doing with that?"

"I'm sleeping on Maddie's floor for a couple of nights so I can help her with the baby."

"This is insanity, Mac. What will people say? She has a sister—"

"Who has a family of her own to care for. Don't worry, you'll still get plenty of time to fuss over me while I'm home."

He strapped a sleeping bag to the back of the motorcycle while his mother watched him. Pretending not to notice her frosty glare, he tinkered with spark plugs and connections before straddling the bike to kick-start it. The engine sputtered and died. He tried twice more before it roared to life with a deafening backfire.

Mac couldn't wait to open up the bike on the island's winding roads, just like he used to.

"Where are you going?" his mother hollered over the roar.

"To see Dad and then back to Maddie's. I'll be by tomorrow."

"Mac! *Wait!* We need to talk!"

He turned the bike around and gunned it, sending pieces of crushed shell flying behind him.

"You forgot your helmet!"

Flashing a grin over his shoulder, he pretended he couldn't hear her. Just like old times.

As Mac coasted down the long, winding hill that led to the marina, he was glad he hadn't bothered to cut his hair before he left Miami. The wind rushing through it took him right back to high school, and the wild burst of freedom reminded him of a time before life became so complicated.

His thoughts inevitably turned to Maddie and what Janey had told him. They'd grown up just a few miles apart, but light years separated them. While he'd been the hometown hero, she'd been mocked and ridiculed and God knows what else because of something she could neither help nor change.

"It's not up to you to right all those wrongs," he muttered to himself. But for some reason, he wanted to do just that. She'd stirred something primal in him and touched a part of him he hadn't even known existed. The notion both excited and discomforted at the same time.

Even as he decided he should keep his distance, he knew he wouldn't. In fact, as soon as he said a quick hello to his father, he'd be heading right back to her. Surely the reaction he'd had earlier was the result of the accident and the ensuing burst of adrenaline. Once he saw her again, everything would be back to normal, or at least he hoped so.

Mac zipped into the marina and parked next to one of the Dumpsters.

Thanks to his six-foot, four-inch height, Big Mac's thatch of wiry gray hair stood out amid the chaos on the main dock. Because the word sunscreen was not, and had never been, in his vocabulary, he was already as tan as most people were by the end of the summer. He wore a blue T-shirt with a faded silkscreen of a wide-mouthed bass and bleached-out denim shorts with his trademark boat shoes.

Mac watched his father interact with kids, customers and employees as he shouted out orders and engaged in a series of hand signals to direct incoming boaters while deftly fending off another arriving boat. Big Mac choreographed the scene with the finesse of a dispatcher and the authority of a drill sergeant.

Amused, Mac waited for his father to finish tying up the newcomer. Farther down the main dock, the marina's second-in-command, Luke Harris, wrestled with a throttle-happy power boater who'd put speed ahead of safety and skill.

Luke, a high school classmate of Mac's, had worked at McCarthy's for more summers than Mac could count. Mac watched him corral the out-of-control boat without any damage to the others around it. The crowd on the dock gave Luke a round of applause that earned a scowl from the boat's captain.

Big Mac had turned his attention to a crew of kids he'd no doubt recruited from the boats who were shucking a bushel of corn for the restaurant. He said something that had them all laughing. Pulling a fly swatter from his back pocket, Big Mac took care of the early-season bees that were bugging the kids and returned the swatter to his pocket.

Patting one of the kids on the head, Big Mac turned and noticed his son standing on the sidelines waiting for him. His face lit up with pure joy. Mac's throat tightened as his father made his way across the pier. He loved no one more than the giant of a man who'd raised him with a gentle but steady hand. His father stopped, gave him a measuring once-over and then shook his head as if he couldn't believe his eyes. Behind the dark sunglasses, Mac suspected he'd find tears.

"What a nice surprise," Big Mac said softly, framing his son's face with calloused, work-roughened hands the size of dinner plates. Their father's effusive love had once mortified his sons, but Mac had long ago outgrown his aversion. "What's wrong with you?"

Mac laughed, not one bit surprised that his father could also take a quick look and know something wasn't quite right. "Apparently, I've been burning the candle."

"Well, you look like hell." He slung a thick arm around Mac's shoulders. "Buy you a late lunch?"

"Thanks, but I already ate. I actually have to get back to town." He gave his father a quick recap of what'd happened earlier with Maddie.

"You can't be serious about covering for her at the hotel."

"She can't work for a few days, and she's petrified about losing the job."

"We can see that doesn't happen, son. We're not ogres."

"It's a pride thing. Besides, how hard can it be to clean a couple of rooms?"

Big Mac snickered. "Harder than you probably think. Mom will pitch a cow over this."

"Believe me, I've already gotten an earful."

Big Mac nodded to the bike. "Got the old girl out of mothballs, huh?"

"She's running great."

"I take her out for a spin every now and then to keep her lubed up and ready. Just in case."

"In case of what?"

"In case you come home."

The stark simplicity of his father's statement tugged at Mac's heart. "I'm sorry it's been so long."

"No matter. You're here now. For how long?"

Mac took a long look around at the marina, taking in the peeling paint, the sagging roof on the main building that housed the office and restaurant, and the broken windowpane in the gift shop. Seeing his father made Mac forget all about his vow to get in and get out as quickly as possible.

"As long as it takes."

Maddie slept deeper than she had in years. She dreamed about Mac McCarthy. They were on a sailboat, and he was at the helm. The sun shone down upon them, the warmth cooled by an ocean breeze that powered the sleek wooden boat. He wore only a bathing suit tied low on narrow hips. A light dusting of dark hair covered his muscular chest and rippled abs, forming a tantalizing trail into his suit.

He caught her watching him and smiled, dazzling her with his beautiful face and twinkling eyes. That he—Mac McCarthy, local hero and golden boy—seemed so happy to be with her was nothing short of miraculous.

A nagging voice in the back of her mind warned her to be careful. Surely a man who could have any woman he wanted wouldn't really be interested in her. But no one else was around just now. For however long he chose to stay, he was hers and she wanted him more than she'd ever wanted anything. Knowing he had the power to shatter her did nothing to quell the wave of longing. As if she was outside herself watching someone else, Maddie stood up in the boat's roomy cockpit and went to him.

He slipped an arm around her shoulders and drew her in close. His hand caressing her sun-warmed skin sent desire darting through her.

Maddie looked up at him, the yearning no doubt apparent on her face.

He studied her for a long moment before he lowered his head and brushed his lips over hers in tentative kiss, keeping his eyes focused on hers.

Hooking her hand around his neck, she brought him back for more.

His open mouth came down on hers as if he'd been dying to kiss her forever. He traced the outline of her mouth with his tongue before delving deeper to engage in a fierce duel with hers.

Maddie met him thrust for thrust.

Without surrendering her mouth, he released his hold on the wheel and wrapped his arms around her, bringing her in tight against his instant arousal. The unattended sails flapped in the breeze as the boat foundered.

The desire was so intense, she didn't even care that her breasts were now pressed against his chest.

A moan escaped their joined lips, and Maddie wasn't sure if it came from him or from her. What did it matter?

From outside the screen door, Mac heard the moan and rushed in to find her sleeping—and clearly dreaming. Her hair formed a wild halo around her face. Her lips were pursed and moving.

Transfixed by the sight of her, he dropped the sleeping bag and the extra bandages he'd bought just inside the door and went to her. She moaned again, and he wondered if she was in pain. When her legs fell open and her hips thrust upward, he went hard as stone.

"God," he muttered, worried that she would reopen her wounds if she kept thrashing about. Sitting next to her on the sofa, he put his hands on her shoulders to hold her still. "Maddie, wake up. You're dreaming."

"Mmm."

She has the prettiest mouth I've ever seen. Before he could indulge in a fantasy about what it would be like to press his own mouth to her plump, pink lips, she lifted her hips again.

"Maddie."

She shocked him when she hooked her uninjured arm around his neck and dragged him down to her. What had been a brief fantasy only a second ago quickly became reality as her lips opened under his and her tongue thrust into his mouth with wild abandon.

Mac knew he should stop her—that was, if he could think clearly enough to do anything but hang on for the ride. Besides, if he fought her, he risked hurting her and he'd already hurt her enough. He cupped her soft cheek, and his tongue met her ardent thrusts, feasting on her sweet flavor.

Time seemed to slip away as he gave in to the attraction that had simmered from the second their eyes first met. Immersed in the scent of summer flowers that came from her hair, he had no idea if he kissed her for five minutes or an hour. All he knew was he didn't want it to end—ever.

He knew the exact instant that she woke up and realized she was no longer dreaming. Her body went tense and rigid, and her ardent mouth stilled.

Mac pulled back to stare at her, astounded by the kiss, the emotion, the desire. Brushing the hair off her forehead, he watched surprise, embarrassment, anger and longing dance across her face. The longing caught him off guard and filled him with a brand new kind of desire—to give her everything and anything she wanted.

"What're you doing?" she finally asked.

Mac cleared his throat. "I was trying to wake you up, and you kissed me."

"I did not kiss you!" But then she seemed to realize her arm was still hooked around his neck. Her face flushing with color, she released him.

"Ah, yeah, you did." He leaned in again so his lips lingered just above hers. "And guess what else? You liked it."

"You don't know that."

"I can tell when the woman I'm kissing is enjoying it."

Disgust twisted her pretty mouth into a sneer. "Oh, you and all your experience, *of course* you can tell."

He continued to hover just above her, amused by her disdain. Why did he get such a kick out of pushing her buttons?

Her hand landed on his chest to keep him from getting any closer. "Would you please move? I need to get up."

"And go where?"

"To the bathroom, if you must know."

Rather than get up, he slid an arm under her legs and lifted her.

"Put me down!" She winced from the pain of her sore knee bending over his arm. "I can get there on my own."

"But you don't have to." He delivered her to the door and waited while she got her footing. The agonized look that crossed her face made him ache.

"I'll be out in a minute. Feel free to be gone by then." Leaning on her uninjured hand, she used the wall as a makeshift crutch.

Mac closed the door and waited outside, leaning his head back against the wall in a failed attempt to calm his overheated body while reliving the kiss that had blown his mind. So much for his plan to keep his distance and not get involved. With one kiss, he was already more involved with her than he'd been with any other woman.

The bathroom door opened. "I need to get over to my sister's."

"I know."

Her eyes landed on the sleeping bag he'd left by the front door. "What's that?"

"A sleeping bag."

She glared at him. "No kidding."

"You might need help with the baby during the night."

"You can't stay here. No way."

"I'm not leaving you to fend for yourself and Thomas with one working hand."

"It's not up to you to fix this! I don't know who you think you are, but you're not bombing into my life and barking out orders—"

"I won't be responsible for you dropping your son or something else happening to him because I was clumsy."

"It's not your responsibility! It's mine. I'll take care of Thomas the way I always have—by myself. The last thing I need is everyone in town knowing you're staying here."

The mulish set to her chin amused him, and apparently he did a poor job of hiding it.

"What's so funny?"

"You are when you get all. . ." He waved his hand. "Worked up."

Her eyes spit fire at him. "I am *not* worked up. I'm pissed!"

"So I gathered. Here's the deal—either I can find a place to toss my sleeping bag inside or I'll sleep on the deck so you can tell all these 'people' you're so worried about that I didn't actually stay here. Believe me, I've slept in worse places than under the Gansett stars."

"I want you to go back to wherever you came from and leave me alone."

The emphatic statement hurt more than it should have. "As soon as you're able to care for yourself and Thomas, I'll be gone."

"Are you always this arrogant and pushy?"

Mac thought about that. "Yeah, I guess so."

"It might work with other people, but it does nothing for me."

"Duly noted."

"Now you're making fun of me."

"I am not." He glanced at his watch. "We have to go. I don't need another Chester woman screaming at me. One is plenty."

"Ugh, you're insufferable."

"So I've been told. You might want to change your shirt. There's blood on it."

Shooting him a dirty look, she hobbled to the bedroom.

"Need some help?"

"No!" The door slammed shut.

She might've liked kissing him, but she still didn't want him around.

Maddie leaned against the closed bedroom door. *Oh my God.* Her mind raced at a frantic speed. *I had a sexy dream about Mac McCarthy, and then I all but attacked him. If he's heard what people say about me, now he'll believe it.*

Of course he'd believe it. Why wouldn't he? *Better yet, why should I care what he believes? It's not like he plans to stick around after I recover. He'll be back to his life in Miami, and I'll still be here working for his parents and living my life. He's nothing to me.*

Except, she thought as she wrestled her way painfully into a clean T-shirt, *he seemed to like kissing me.* He'd seemed equally affected by the sensual kiss. She hadn't missed the impressive bulge in his shorts or the heated look in his eyes. Running her fingers through her hair, she caught a hint of his cologne and brought her hand to her nose to breathe in the spicy scent that would now forever remind her of him.

"Stop it," she hissed to her haggard reflection. "The last time you got carried away by a man's empty promises, you ended up a single mother. Don't be a fool again. He'll take what he can get from you and hit the road, just like they all do. Nothing about him is different or special."

Even as she said the words, however, she knew they weren't entirely true. He had already proven he was different by insisting on helping her as she recovered. As for special? She'd have to wait and see, but she would not—*could not*—allow herself to expect anything from him.

She refused to ever again risk her heart for a man, especially one who had the power to crush her while moving on with his own life as if she'd never existed.

Never again.

Hours later, Mac carried Maddie and the wriggling Thomas back up to their apartment. Despite being peed and puked on, Mac had had done an admirable job—with her verbal assistance—of taking care of four babies ranging from nine to twelve months old. To say he'd never changed a diaper before, he'd caught on fast, and Thomas had taken an instant shine to him.

Maddie held Thomas with her good arm while Mac navigated the stairs and play-bit the fingers Thomas put in his mouth. Mac had barely made eye contact with her all afternoon. Was it because of the kiss or something else? Had he heard what people said about her?

Her stomach ached and her palms grew damp. How she longed to be just a regular girl with nothing that made her different, without the suitcase full of troubles she dragged behind her. Sighing, she wished she could somehow lose the suitcase.

"Why the sigh?" Mac asked as he lowered her and Thomas to the sofa.

She ventured a glance up at him to find him watching her.

"Does something hurt?"

My heart. My stomach. My knee. "No."

He scooped up Thomas as if he'd been doing it all the boy's life. "What comes first? Dinner or bath?"

"I can take it from here. Why don't you go visit your parents?"

"Are you going to keep this up all night?"

"Just until you get the hint that I don't want you here."

"You don't? I'm shocked and hurt."

"Shut up."

He shielded Thomas. "Don't talk that way in front of the child."

The look she sent him could've cut glass.

"I'll repeat the question: what comes first, dinner or bath?"

Through gritted teeth, she said, "Dinner or you'll have to do the bath twice."

"Got it." He glanced down at the stains on his T-shirt. "I should probably change first. I reek."

Maddie couldn't help but notice how he held Thomas just right, propped on his hip with a strong arm protectively around him. "You, ah, might want to wait until after dinner and the bath. It can get a little messy."

"This baby thing is not for the faint of heart, is it?" he asked, playfully scowling at Thomas, who clapped his hands.

"Which is why you shouldn't get involved."

"Too late." He flashed a charming smile that made her mad all over again. "Well, all righty, buddy, let's get to it."

Following Maddie's directions, Mac kept up a steady stream of animated chatter that held her son captivated in his high chair. Mac used a variety of voices and hand gestures to keep Thomas's attention as he opened a jar of sweet potatoes to go with the tiny bites of leftover chicken.

"Just put the chicken on the tray," she said. "He eats that with his fingers, but you'll have to feed him the potatoes."

"I can do that," Mac said, making a funny face at Thomas.

Watching Mac's intense focus on the task of wresting spoonfuls of orange baby food into Thomas, she wondered if he gave everything he did the same level of attention. The thought made her body tingle from head to toe.

He glanced at her. "What? Am I doing it wrong?"

Clearing her throat, she said, "No, you're doing fine."

Thomas took advantage of Mac's break in concentration to grab the spoon and fling the orange glob, which landed with a loud splat on Mac's cheek.

Maddie dissolved into giggles.

Thomas followed suit as Mac glowered at him.

"You think that's funny, do you?" he asked, dabbing sweet potatoes on Thomas's nose.

The baby laughed, and Maddie's heart contracted with something strange and foreign and altogether uncomfortable. That's when she realized she could warn herself off this man until the end of time and still find him irresistible, especially when he was displaying such tender kindness toward her son.

"I think I got more *on* him than in him," Mac said when the jar was finally empty. The floor and wall around the high chair resembled a war zone, and both "men" were covered in orange slime.

"See why the bath comes after dinner, rather than before?"

"Your mommy is very wise," Mac said to Thomas as he freed the squirming baby from the high chair. "But you already know that, don't you? Let's hit the tub, my man."

Irritated that she couldn't bathe her son herself, she said, "Just be careful. He's like a slippery eel once he gets wet."

"We'll be fine."

"Don't let the water get too hot."

"I won't, don't worry."

"Towels are in the cabinet."

"We'll find 'em."

She wished she could see them working out the logistics. Instead, she listened to Mac's low voice as he talked to Thomas, who let out an occasional screech or a squeal. Bath time was his favorite part of the day, and she smiled imagining the mess Mac would have to clean up when they were done.

Despite being badly injured, she had smiled more that day than she had in years. It was hard to stay dour with Mac's cheerful, upbeat personality around to lighten things up.

The screen door opened, and Tiffany stuck her head in. "Just checking to see if you need anything."

Thomas chose that moment to shriek.

Tiffany glanced at the bathroom. "What's going on?"

"He's giving Thomas a bath."

Her sister's eyes widened. "Seriously?"

"Listen," Maddie said.

The distinctive rumble of Mac's voice mixed with Thomas's baby patter and some serious splashing.

"Well," Tiffany said grudgingly, "that's nice of him."

"Yes, it is." Maddie wasn't sure why she felt compelled to defend Mac.

"I hope you're not getting all . . ." Tiffany waved her hand. "Caught up."

"Save the sisterly advice. You have enough of your own problems. Stay out of mine."

"Mark my words, Maddie. That guy is trouble." In a hissing whisper, she added, "Remember what Evan McCarthy's friend did to you? Evan knew he was lying and did nothing about it. That's his brother in there. His *brother*. And what their mother did to Mom!"

"Stop! None of that has anything to do with him." Maddie's heart raced at the reminder of a long-ago time she never wanted to think about again. "Now please . . . Go."

After Tiffany stalked out the door, Maddie took several deep breaths to calm down. Her hands shook as the memories from that horrible year of high school came flooding back.

When Mac emerged, dripping wet, from the bathroom holding Thomas wrapped in his Mr. Froggie towel, Maddie forgot all about the past and returned her son's gummy smile. While Thomas had clearly won the battle in the tub, Mac looked awfully pleased with himself even with water dripping from his hair to his face to his soiled T-shirt.

As she watched him bounce Thomas up and down on his hip, Maddie decided that Tiffany was right about one thing: Mac McCarthy was trouble. Big, big trouble.

CHAPTER 4

Maddie talked Mac through dressing Thomas and making his bedtime bottle but insisted she could hold him while he drank it.

Taking one of the boy's pudgy hands, Mac rubbed it softly against his own face. "Gentle hands. Mommy has boo-boos. Be very nice."

Thomas's tiny white-blond eyebrows knitted with concentration as he listened to Mac's instructions. When Mac released his hand, Thomas mimicked the gentle caress to Mac's cheek.

Mac's eyes went soft, and his lips quirked with amusement. "Good boy." He lowered Thomas to Maddie and helped her find a comfortable position before he handed the bottle to Thomas.

"Thank you." Her heart suddenly felt too large for her chest, her skin too tight for her body, her lungs compressed from the effort to draw air. To think that ten hours ago, she'd never met him and now he was feeding and bathing her son with the same care he'd no doubt show his own child. She couldn't process it.

As she held Thomas, Mac cleaned up the mess around the high chair and restored order to the kitchen. Even though he was tall and broad shouldered, he moved with an easy grace. Rippling muscles under a snug T-shirt had Maddie licking her lips and remembering what it had felt like to kiss him. He bent over to wipe the baseboard and his shorts tightened over his taut rear end. Infused with heat that made her skin tingle with desire, Maddie looked away.

"I need to make a quick phone call," he said when he was done. "And grab a shower. Are you sure you're all right?"

Maddie skimmed her lips over Thomas's soft, damp hair. "We're fine."

Mac withdrew his cell phone from his pocket. "Be right back."

She imagined he probably had a girlfriend in Miami waiting to hear from him. The thought filled her with irrational jealousy. Tiffany's warning came rushing back to her. Before she could get too mad with herself for being stupid *and* jealous, Mac returned and stashed the phone in his backpack. He approached them, casting a downward glance at Thomas, who was beginning to doze off. "He's so cute," Mac whispered, smoothing the baby's fine blond hair into place. "And so good."

"He really is." Unnerved by the intimate whisper and the natural, gentle caress he'd bestowed upon her son, Maddie kept her eyes on Thomas. "If I had to go it alone, I definitely got the right kid."

"Why are you? Going it alone, that is?"

After a long awkward pause, she finally ventured a glance up to find his cool blue eyes trained on her. "That's, um, a long story."

He flashed that irresistible grin. "Good thing we've got all night. You can talk to me through the window while I'm sleeping on the deck."

Before she could tell him she didn't talk about Thomas's father—with anyone—Mac grabbed his backpack and shut the bathroom door behind him.

Maddie closed her eyes and tried to calm her racing heart and mind. Nothing good would come of the crush she could feel developing. His attention toward them was temporary, and she needed to remember that. She couldn't let Thomas get attached to a man who wouldn't be around in a few days. The bottle fell from Thomas's slack lips, and he snuggled in deeper. Normally, she'd transfer him to his crib at this point, but she feared she might drop him. She hated to admit Mac might be right about something.

While she waited for him to help her, she kept her eyes closed and listened to him singing Sinatra in the shower. Smiling for the umpteenth time that day, she floated on an unusual cloud of contentment with her baby asleep in her arms and a sexy guy singing in her shower.

Mac opened a bottle of shampoo and breathed in the scent of summer flowers that had captured his attention each time he'd been close to Maddie. Immersed in the fragrance, he imagined her reclined in a field of wildflowers with a daisy tucked behind her ear and a come-hither smile directed at him. In his fantasy scenario, she was relaxed and untroubled. She gazed at him with none of the usual bitterness. He'd like to see her like that—carefree, happy, content.

Just the idea of it sent a surge of desire darting through him that settled in his groin. "Why her?" he whispered urgently into the shower's steady flow. "Why now?" Nothing in his past history with women had prepared him for the day he'd meet one who made him want to step off the treadmill for a closer look, to find out what might be possible.

Maybe it was because the women he usually dated always wanted something from him. When they discovered he'd never been married and had enjoyed a successful professional life, he became doubly appealing to them. Roseanne had been the latest in a long string of women who'd used him to gain a leg up. They used him, he used them and no one got hurt. The hassle-free arrangements had always been just fine with him.

Now he'd found one who needed everything but wanted nothing from him. Yet he wanted more of her, especially now that he'd experienced the soft sweetness of her kisses. He wanted to do things for her because she'd never ask him to the way others always did. The more he gave, the more Maddie would protest, and the idea of fighting with her filled him with anticipation rather than the usual dread of the unfortunate confrontations that ended the arrangement du jour.

When it came right down to it, she wasn't even his type. He tended to go for women who were confident in their sexuality, who gave as good as they got in bed and walked away when it was over without pretending they'd fallen in love. None of those qualities applied to Maddie. Thanks to her remarkable figure, she'd no doubt had a difficult time with men and sex, and if Janey was to be believed, guys had taken advantage of her and then blabbed about it.

The thought of what she must've endured filled Mac with white-hot rage that would've frightened him if he'd been in his right mind. Thanks to fatigue that lingered like a wet blanket, he clearly wasn't thinking straight. Mac McCarthy didn't get "involved." The word wasn't even in his vocabulary. So what was he doing in her shower? Or bathing her son? Or tending to her every need? What the hell was wrong with him?

Let's face it. Sex with her would definitely not be the usual no-strings deal I prefer. The realization caused his burgeoning erection to wither and roused him from the shampoo-scented dream state he'd slipped into. He returned the bottle to the rack and ran a razor over his face before stepping out of the shower. When he heard a sharp knock on the screen door, he wrapped a towel around his waist and went out to answer it.

Glancing at the sofa, he noticed Maddie had dozed off with Thomas in her arms. The sight of them tugged at his heart and made him forget for a second that he was on his way to the door. A second louder knock got his attention.

"Mr. McCarthy?"

"Right. Come in." Mac swung open the door to admit the delivery guy from the Beachcomber who'd brought the dinner he ordered before his shower. "Just put it on the table." Mac found his wallet, grabbed four twenties, and handed over the cash. "Keep the change."

"Wow, thanks."

Mac saw him take a measuring look at Maddie and Thomas on the sofa and then at him in a towel before he headed out the door.

"Did you seriously just answer my door wearing nothing but a towel?" Maddie asked in a sleep-roughened voice.

"Yeah, so?"

"Oh my God." She struggled to sit up while accommodating the sleeping baby. "It'll be all over town in less than an hour that I'm doing Mac McCarthy. That's *just* what I need."

Mac wanted to shoot himself for being so stupid. Needing a second to figure out how to handle this latest challenge, he leaned down and took Thomas from her. Even though he was careful, his fingers still brushed against her breasts, causing her to pull back from him.

"Sorry." He walked Thomas into his crib and settled a light blanket over him. Before he left the room, he combed his fingers through the baby's hair. "Don't be in any rush to grow up, buddy. It's not all it's cracked up to be."

Steeling for a fight, he returned to the living room and stopped short in his tracks. "I'm sorry," he said, moved by her tears. "I wasn't thinking."

"Why would you? No one in this town has ever thought anything less than the best of you."

"I'll make sure people know exactly what's going on here."

Her uneven burst of laughter surprised him. "Gee, thanks. That'll make it all better."

He sat next to her on the sofa. "I'm really sorry. It never occurred to me—"

"What's done is done. You'd think I'd be used to it by now."

Mac had no idea what to say to that, so he thought it best to keep quiet.

"Someone told you, didn't they?"

The soft, weary tone to her voice went straight to his heart. "I don't believe it."

When she looked up at him with caramel eyes still damp with tears, the need to offer comfort overtook his better judgment. He slipped an arm around her and brought her head to rest on his shoulder.

At first she resisted, but he resisted right back. "I don't believe a word of it," he said more forcefully this time as he buried his fingers in her soft, thick hair to keep her head right where he wanted it.

"Why? Because I didn't fall at the feet of the almighty Mac McCarthy at the first opportunity and beg him to have sex with me?"

"For one thing."

The teasing comment earned him a genuine burst of husky laughter, the sound of which was so sexy and so appealing that the breath seemed to get stuck in his throat on its way to his lungs.

"So I've dented your ego, then, huh?"

"Very badly," he replied in a grave tone as he combed his fingers through her hair. He kept waiting for her to tell him to stop, but she didn't.

"I'd apologize if I didn't think the dose of humility was good for you."

So the bitter, world-weary Madeline Chester could also be quite witty. The discovery, on top of all the others, made his heart race. "I'd say the least you could do to make it up to me is to have dinner with me." He gestured to the bags on the table. "What do you say?"

"What's on the menu?"

"I was jonesing for a lobster, so I asked Libby to send over a couple."

Maddie stiffened against him.

"What?"

"It's ripping through town right now that Mac McCarthy is half-naked in my apartment and buying me lobster. They'll be speculating about what he's getting in return."

"Maddie . . ."

"Let's just eat." The laughter of a moment ago was replaced by sorrow. "They'll say what they're going to say no matter what I do. The truth is never a consideration where I'm concerned."

With his finger on her chin, he urged her to look at him. "I never meant to cause you any trouble."

"You started causing me trouble the second you stepped in front of my bike."

"The only part I regret is that you got hurt."

"Stick around. You'll grow to regret a whole lot more than that."

"Is that an invitation?"

She drew back, horrified by the corner she'd painted herself into. "*No!*"

"Sounded like one to me," he said in a playful tone, leaning in to close the distance between them. He could no more fight the magnetic pull than he could avoid taking the next breath.

Her expression shifted from wariness to fear. "Don't."

"Why not?" he whispered.

"Because nothing can come of it."

"You don't know that."

"Yes, I do."

"You make me want to prove you wrong." He brushed his lips over hers, gratified by the gasp that escaped from her tightly closed mouth. "Kiss me the way you did before."

"I w-was asleep. That doesn't count."

Her stammer drew a small smile from him. "You're right. It doesn't. This one does, though." Ignoring the press of her hand against his chest as well as the way her eyes widened in shock and maybe dismay, Mac fitted his mouth over hers and sank into the satiny softness. He moved his hand from her arm to cup her cheek but kept his lips still against hers. He'd made the first move. Now it was up to her.

Mac thought he'd go mad waiting for a sign, a signal, anything to tell him she wanted more. Just when he was about to give up, he felt her uninjured hand on his neck and the first tentative brush of her tongue against his bottom lip.

Green light.

Mac devoured her with sweeping thrusts of his tongue into the sweet depths of her mouth, steeped in her addictive flavor. At first she seemed too taken aback by his ardor to respond, but when her tongue finally tangled with his, meeting him thrust for thrust, Mac fought off the urgent need for more.

Many minutes later, he pulled back from her, breathing heavily, feeling more spent by one sensuous kiss than he normally did from the full act. Opening his eyes, he found hers fixed on him. Unable to process all he saw, he took the coward's way out by burrowing into the smooth column of her neck and pressing hot, open-mouth kisses to her heated skin.

"Mac." She sounded as breathless as he felt.

"Hmm?" At the base of her neck, he found a sensitive tendon and rolled it between his teeth.

She cried out.

"Sorry." Mortified by his overwhelming reaction to her, he rested his head on her shoulder and tried to regain control.

Her fingers sifted through his hair in a soothing caress that made him want to stay right there for a long, long time.

"It didn't hurt," she said after a charged moment of silence.

"No?"

She shook her head, and her fragrant hair brushed against his face, sending another surge of hot-blooded lust to his lap.

Encouraged, he ran his tongue lightly over the same spot on her neck.

A shudder rippled through her. "I don't want to be what you expect me to be," she said softly.

Raising his head, he found her eyes in the encroaching darkness. "And what's that?"

"Easy." Her quiet dignity touched him in places he normally kept walled off and unreachable. "Cheap."

Mac chose his words carefully. "Sweetheart, I've had easy and cheap, and you're neither."

Incredulous, she stared at him. "How do you know that?"

"Gut instinct."

"And your gut is never wrong?"

"Hasn't failed me yet."

"People in town will speak poorly of you if you get involved with me."

"Maddie, I've never once given a crap what anyone thought of me, and I'm not about to start caring now."

"That's easy to say when you've been loved and adored your whole life. You have no idea how vicious people can be."

He dropped another light kiss on her swollen lips. "If it means I get to spend some more time with you, I'd be willing to find out."

"You say that now . . ."

"How about that lobster?"

She held up her injured hand. "I might need some help."

"You got it." He scooped her up and carried her to the table. "After dinner, we'll change the bandages and put some more ointment on those cuts."

"Oh goodie. Something to look forward to."

He grinned at her, enjoying her cutting wit. "Give me one second to throw on some clothes." When he returned a minute later dressed in clean cargo shorts and a Miami Dolphins T-shirt, he leaned down to bring his face in close to hers. "I want you to know that I'm not here because I feel like I have to be."

Her pretty lips formed a surprised O. "No?"

Mac shook his head. "Today has been fun—not the part where you got hurt, but everything since then."

"Clearly, you don't get out enough."

Wiggling his brows at her, he uncorked a bottle of white wine and poured it into mismatched glasses he'd found in her cabinet. He handed one to her and raised his in toast. "Here's to getting out more."

Maddie made him wait an uncertain, breathless moment before she touched her glass to his.

Celebrating the small victory, Mac got busy with the lobsters.

Linda McCarthy paced the length of her wide back porch without noticing the spectacular sunset. She'd succeeded in luring Mac back to the island, but nothing else was going according to plan. If she didn't find a way to get him to come home, the whole town would be talking about *her son* being shacked up with that . . . that woman!

He hadn't given his own mother even an hour of his precious time, but he had plenty of time to spend with a woman most people considered the town tramp. Not that Linda had anything against Maddie. She was a good worker at the hotel and at the house one afternoon a week. However, she wasn't someone Linda wanted to see with any of her sons, especially Mac.

Linda didn't believe in a mother having favorites, but Mac had always been special, a son any mother would be proud of. Watching him pitch his team to the state championship his senior year remained among her fondest memories. When he suffered the injury that ended his professional baseball aspirations, her heart broke right along with his.

And then he picked himself up, refocused on his education and emerged with an engineering degree that led to his current career as the co-owner of a thriving business. Along the way, she'd hoped and prayed he would meet a woman who'd complement and support him as he continued along his successful path.

That certainly wasn't going to happen once the local woman she had in mind for him heard he'd stayed overnight with Maddie Chester. He'd just made his mother's plan to find him a suitable wife on the island a lot harder than it would've been otherwise.

The phone rang in the kitchen. Hoping it might be Mac, Linda rushed inside and groaned when she heard her sister's voice. "Hello, Joan."

"Why didn't you tell me Mac was coming home?"

"Because I wasn't sure which day he was getting here." No way would she admit he hadn't bothered to share his travel plans with her. Joan would take too much pleasure in hearing that.

"Teensy just called. Her grandson delivered lobsters to Mac at Maddie Chester's apartment."

Linda suppressed a groan. Three hundred pounds on her slimmest day, "Teensy" was the island's biggest gossip. If she knew Mac was shacking up with Maddie, everyone else knew, too.

"And get this," Joan said, clearly enjoying the scoop, "Mac answered the door *in nothing but a towel*!"

Linda would kill him. "He knocked her off her bike and hurt her badly. He's helping her until she recovers. There's nothing more to it than that."

"Teensy's heard they looked *awfully* cozy."

When she was finished with Mac, Joan would be next on her hit list. "Honestly, he's been in town for eight hours. What do you think could be happening when she's bruised and bloody from falling off her bike?"

Joan's chuckle infuriated Linda. "Use your imagination. He's a red-blooded man, and she's always willing. A few scabs won't slow her down."

"That's just unkind, Joan, and beneath you." It really wasn't, but Linda had no desire to start World War III with her sister. "Mac is doing an honorable thing by helping her. I don't appreciate you making it into something dirty."

"Don't get pissy with me. I'm not the one who answered the door in a towel."

"I have to go. Big Mac's home, and he's hungry."

"Before you run away, I heard from Josh today. Ellen's expecting again! We're having a regular baby boom in our family."

Linda wondered if a head could actually explode. "Congratulations. That's wonderful. They sure do stay busy, don't they?"

"Lucky for me. Talk soon."

Linda slammed down the phone with a swear word that never usually left her lips.

"Well, good evening to you, too, my love." Big Mac kissed her forehead. "What's got you all fired up?"

"*Your* son! *That* woman and Teensy." Linda banged around the kitchen fixing him a plate of the spaghetti and meatballs she'd eaten earlier. "How could he answer the door wearing only a towel?"

Big Mac plugged his cell phone into the charger and turned back to her. "What's that you said? Teensy answered the door wearing only a towel?" He made a face of supreme dismay. "I just lost my appetite."

"Not *Teensy*! Pay attention, will you? *Your* son answered the door at *Maddie Chester's* apartment wearing *only* a towel! And he's buying her *lobster*!"

"God, what a swine. Where did we go wrong with him?"

"*You don't get it!* It'll be all over town by morning that he's sleeping with her! Then who will want him?"

"Any woman would be lucky to land him."

"No one wants a guy who's been with the easiest girl in town."

"Lin," he said in his disapproving tone. "She's a nice girl."

"With a reputation that would make a porn star blush." Linda plopped his plate down on the table. "I need to fix this. Fast."

"Linda. . . You know how these things always go. Remember when you fixed Sophie's cousin up with Grant when she was visiting LA?"

Linda stared at him, incredulous. "How is that my fault? Sophie failed to mention her little cousin had just been sprung from the psych ward."

"Then there was Debbie's niece, who you sicced on Adam. . ."

"When I asked him to show her a good time in New York City, I never said he should spend the whole weekend in her hotel room. And if *she* didn't know she had chlamydia, how was *I* supposed to know?"

"Of course Tina's songwriting sister wasn't exactly the one for Evan."

"Tina never told me that her sister was more interested in boozing her way through Nashville than in songwriting. But Evan figured it out."

"Not before she puked in his new truck."

Linda scowled at him. "Whose side are you on anyway?"

"Yours, love. Always."

"Coulda fooled me."

"These meatballs are exquisite."

"Don't go using that McCarthy charm on me. I know all your tricks."

"So matchmaking isn't your thing. You have many other talents. Such as making meatballs that melt in my mouth."

"Mac needs a wife. He'll be having babies in his forties at this rate."

"Maybe if you'd been a little sweeter to his friend Roseanne when we were in Miami this winter, he might not be shacking up in town tonight."

Hands on hips, Linda faced off with him.

"What? I'm just saying. . ."

"*She* is *all* wrong for him. I had her number in five minutes. His head was turned by the way she looks, but he'll figure her out soon enough—if he hasn't already."

"Let's face it, babe. There's not a woman out there who'll ever meet your standards for any of those boys."

"That's not true! I want them to be happy. I want them to have what we've had all these years. Is there anything wrong with that?"

"Aww, honey, of course there isn't." He reached for her hand and drew her onto his lap. "But you've gotta let them get there in their own way and in their own time."

"I've tried that, and now I have four sons in their thirties who have no intention of ever settling down and having families. They'll *regret* that later, Mac. You know that as well as I do."

"Maybe so, but they'll be *their* regrets."

"I don't want them to miss out on love." The thought of it broke her heart. "Where would you be today if I hadn't saved you from yourself?"

His big laugh rang through the kitchen. "God only knows."

"See? That's all I want for them, too."

"Promise me you'll leave Mac alone while he's home."

Linda hesitated. How could she promise that?

He drew back from her so he could see her face. "Linda. . ."

"Fine! I'll leave him alone." She intentionally didn't use the word "promise" and made sure he couldn't see the fingers she crossed behind his back.

Mac gathered up the trash bag full of lobster shells and followed Maddie's directions to the garbage cans. He tossed the bag into the can and turned to go back upstairs when the flare of a cigarette lit up the darkness, illuminating Tiffany's face.

"What're you doing hanging around here?" she asked.

"I'm just trying to help your sister."

"I can help her. Why don't you go back where you belong?"

"And where's that?"

"In your big white house overlooking your North Harbor kingdom."

"It's not my kingdom."

"Whatever you say."

"What've I ever done to you or your sister?"

"Not a damned thing."

"So then what's your beef with me?"

"I have no beef with you. I have a beef with guys *like* you who brag to your friends that you had a go with one of the Chester sisters."

"That's not my style."

"What isn't? Having a go with the trashy girls or talking about it?"

"Maddie's not trashy." Mac grew to dislike this bitter, unhappy woman more with every passing second. "Why would you say that about your own sister?"

"It's not me who says it. Did she tell you where our mother is right now?"

"My sister did."

"I'm sure she took great pleasure in that. Did she tell you how my mother got there?"

"No."

"Ask *your* mother about that."

"What does she have to do with it?"

"Ask her." Tiffany raised a handheld baby monitor to her ear. "Talking in her sleep."

"Where's your husband?" Mac had known Jim Sturgil in high school but not well.

"Another good question."

"Look, I don't know why you're so pissed at me—"

"You wouldn't, but if you screw with my sister, you'll deal with me."

Mac had never known two more jaded women. "I just want to see her back on her feet."

"Noble of you. Truly."

"What would you have me do? Walk away and leave her to fend for herself after I caused her injuries?"

Tiffany ground out her cigarette. "I'll be watching you."

"Thanks for the warning."

She left him standing in the dark. He saw her enter her house through the sliding door on the back porch and took a moment to get himself together before returning to Maddie's apartment.

"Did you have trouble finding the trash cans?" she asked.

"No." He skimmed his fingers through hair still damp from the shower. "I ran into your sister."

"What did she say?"

Mac shrugged. "Nothing worth repeating." He debated for a second but had to know. "What did my mother have to do with putting your mother in jail?"

Maddie gasped. "She *told* you that?"

"Is it true? Did my mother have something to do with it?"

Maddie seemed to weigh her words carefully. "It was a combination of things."

He lowered himself to the coffee table, forcing her to look at him. "Tell me."

"My mother passed a bad check at the hotel bar, and yours reported her."

"For a first offense?"

"Third." Maddie's eyes dropped to her lap, her cheeks flushing with embarrassment. "Your mother didn't have a choice."

Mac covered her good hand with his and squeezed. "I'm sorry."

"She's been courting disaster for years now. It was bound to happen eventually."

"And you've tried hard not to make the same mistakes."

"For all the good it's done me. I'm always one step ahead of disaster."

He linked his fingers through hers and was pleased when she let him. "I'm incredibly drawn to you, Maddie."

Her face flushed again. "Don't say things like that. You don't mean it."

"I *do* mean it."

Bringing their joined hands to his lips, he kissed the back of hers and decided not to push the issue. He had a feeling that too much too soon was *not* the way to woo this stubborn woman. "What do you say we clean up those cuts?"

"I was hoping you'd forgotten about that."

"No such luck."

"I'd love to take a shower. I feel gross."

He tucked a shank of honey hair behind her ear. "You don't look gross. In fact, you look quite lovely."

"You don't need to say that stuff to me. It's not going to get you anywhere."

"And where is it that you think I want to be?"

She replied with the scathing look he'd grown quite fond of during their day together.

"Why don't we deal with this thing you're worried about right now?"

"What're you talking about?"

"You think I'm only doing all this so I can sleep with you, right?"

She had the good grace to appear embarrassed by his frank assessment. "It's crossed my mind."

"Then let me put your mind at ease—we won't sleep together until you tell me you want to." When she began to protest, he rested his fingers over her lips. "Until you say these words: 'Mac, make love to me,' I swear it won't happen. I can't promise I won't try to kiss you again, because I really liked kissing you. But anything more than that? It's all you."

"Can I talk now?" she asked.

Mac smiled and removed his fingers.

"I'm not used to people without ulterior motives."

"I'm sorry you've been mistreated in the past, but not all men are lousy pigs."

She studied him with eyes utterly lacking guile, and his heart stuttered in his chest. "They aren't?"

Without breaking the intense eye contact, he shook his head. Reaching out to caress her cheek, he leaned in to kiss her lightly. "I can't resist you."

"Try harder."

"You don't really want me to."

"How do you know?"

"Well, you started the whole kissing phase of our relationship."

"I was asleep! And it's not a relationship."

Mac's grin spread across his face. "What would you call it?"

"An annoyance."

He laughed—hard, which seemed to infuriate her. "Let's table this debate for now and get those cuts taken care of."

"Do we have to?"

"Yep. Ready for a lift to the bathroom?"

"I guess."

Mac moved carefully to lift her from the sofa and carry her to the bathroom. "How do you want to do this?"

"By myself."

He followed her into the bathroom. "You could fall."

She turned and seemed surprised to find him right behind her. Placing a hand on his chest, she stopped him from coming any closer. "There's *no way* you're seeing me naked, so turn around and get out."

Mac put on a pout face. "You're no fun at all."

"So I'm told."

He closed the lid to the toilet. "Why don't you sit and let me take off the bandages."

Eying him warily, she said, "All right, but then you're out of here."

"Yes, ma'am." Mac helped to ease her down and then knelt in front of her to unwrap the gauze. Uncovering the angry, seeping wound on her knee, he winced, and his stomach turned. "God, Maddie." He glanced up at her pale face. "Don't look."

"Okay."

He removed the bandages on her elbow and hand, struck by her stoic courage when she had to be in terrible pain. "I hate that I caused this."

With the fingers on her good hand, she brushed the hair off his forehead.

Staggered by the gentle caress, he looked up at her.

"You're not what I expected."

"No?" He kept his tone light, but the small bathroom became airless.

"From your mother's stories, I pictured you as a real playboy. Different day, different woman."

Mac cringed at the somewhat accurate description. "That might've described me at one point in my life, but not anymore."

"And when did this miraculous change occur?"

He pretended to give that significant thought. "About nine o'clock this morning."

CHAPTER 5

As he left the bathroom, Maddie wanted to believe his interest in her was genuine, but she was still convinced that the minute she was fully healed, he'd forget about her and go running back to his regular life. How could she believe anything else? Every man she'd ever loved had let her down. Why should he be any different? *You're not being fair*, the angel sitting on her right shoulder said. *He's been nothing but lovely to you and Thomas all day.*

Yeah, but he's probably just worried about you suing him for hurting you so badly, the devil on her left shoulder countered.

"Enough," Maddie muttered. Leaning on the sink, she stood slowly and breathed her way through the pain. She managed to remove her shorts, underwear and T-shirt but was stymied by her bra. Her injured hand wouldn't cooperate to release the four tight hooks. Teary eyed from the pain in her hand, she reached for a towel and wrapped it around herself. "Mac?"

"What'd you need, honey?"

The endearment made her swoon with desire. How she wished she could be his honey, but it wasn't going to happen. Having feelings for a man who lived thousands of miles away was foolish and risky. "I, um, I need some help." Just the thought of him seeing the old-lady bra made her feel sick.

"Do you want me to come in?"

Swallowing hard, she said, "Please."

The door opened, and his face went slack at the sight of her in a towel.

"Try not to ogle, will you please?"

"Who's ogling?"

"You are."

He seemed to make an effort to focus on her face.

"Can you, um, unhook my bra? Please?" She watched his Adam's apple bob up and down in the strong column of his throat.

"Sure," he said in a strangled tone.

Maddie turned and let the towel drop just enough to give him access. His fingers brushed against her back, and she gasped.

"Sorry."

"S'okay." She held her breath while he worked on the hooks.

"All set."

"Thank you."

Maddie waited for him to leave, but instead, he pushed the straps aside.

"They cut into your skin."

"Yes." His lips brushed her right shoulder, and she stiffened in surprise. "W-what're you doing?"

"I have no idea."

Sensation tingled through her, making her tremble. "Mac—"

He kissed the indentation on her left shoulder while continuing to massage the other side. "Can I ask you something?"

"If I say yes, will it get you out of here so I can shower?"

"Uh-huh."

"What's the question?"

"Since you hate them so much, do you ever think about having them reduced?"

Turning, she stared at him. "*Seriously? That's* your question?"

"I'm sorry. It's none of my business. I shouldn't have—"

"Every day since sixth grade! I hate them! They've totally ruined my life!"

"So, why don't you . . . you know . . ."

"I don't have health insurance or thousands of dollars."

"I didn't mean to upset you."

"It is what it is." Looking up at him, she said, "May I take a shower now?"

"Yeah, sure." He turned to go. "I'll be right out here. If you need me. Again."

Once the door closed, Maddie dropped the towel and stared into the full-length mirror affixed to the back of the door. Her breasts looked like mini-cantaloupes, her hips were too round and curvy, her belly not quite as flat as it had been before Thomas. Despite backaches, shoulder spasms and a variety of skin issues, she'd learned to live with breasts that developed far too early and gave the teenage boys in her class plenty to obsess about. Some days she wished she could wave a magic wand and wake up with normal-sized breasts. Then maybe every man she encountered would actually focus on her face rather than her chest. A girl could dream.

Maddie stepped into the shower and gasped when the water hit her cuts. Her tears were only partly caused by pain. Just once, *one time*, she'd like to feel like a normal woman who stood a chance at happiness with a man like Mac.

Just once. . .

Mac wanted to shoot himself for asking that question and upsetting her, but his desire to know everything about her had trumped his better judgment. He sighed when he thought about the deep, red grooves the bra straps had left in her slender shoulders. He wanted to give her the money. She needed it. He had it. If only it was that simple.

That he'd give this woman he'd known only one day thousands of dollars without hesitation and expect nothing in return should've scared the hell out of him. Rather, it pleased him to know he might be able to do something like that to make her happy. If she'd let him, that is. A huge "if."

Thomas whimpered, and Mac went to check on him. He found the baby sleeping with his bum in the air, his face pressed to the mattress and his mouth open and moving. Mac fixed the blanket that had gotten tangled under his legs and covered him again. For a long time, he stood there and watched the baby sleep before he reached out a finger.

Thomas tightened his little hand around Mac's finger. The implied trust touched Mac's heart, and his throat tightened with emotion. "I wish I could convince your mom I can be trusted," he whispered.

"Did he wake up?" Maddie said from behind Mac, startling him.

The scent of her shampoo and floral soap filled his senses and sent another surge of lust rippling through him. "Just doing some talking."

"He dreams like I do."

Remembering her earlier dream, Mac extricated his finger from Thomas's grip and turned to her. She wore a robe and had her hair turned up in a towel. He studied her pretty face, wishing he could take her into his arms and kiss her again the way he'd yearned to since the last time.

"You're staring," she said after a long, breathless moment.

"You're pretty. Very, very pretty."

"I wish you'd stop saying that stuff."

"Why?"

"It makes me uncomfortable."

"Because you don't believe it?"

"Because I'm afraid to believe it."

He framed her face with his hands, running his thumbs gently over her face. Her lips formed the surprised O he was coming to love.

"I would never hurt you."

"I'm sure you'd like to believe that."

"Hasn't anyone ever been kind to you, Maddie?"

She thought about that. "My grandmother, but she died when I was seven."

He moved closer, his lips hovering just above hers. "You make me want to do everything for you. Do you know why?"

She shook her head but didn't look away.

"Because you'd never ask me to."

"And others do?"

"Always."

"Even the ones you've loved?"

"I've never loved any of them."

Her expressive eyes widened with surprise. "*None of them?*"

He liked shocking her. "It hasn't been something I've ever had or needed." *Until now,* he wanted to say, but didn't dare. "You seem to be getting around a little better."

"The water hurt, but it loosened things up."

"Let's get you some new bandages."

"I just, ah, need to get dressed. First."

Mac heard her but couldn't bring himself to look away or leave the room.

"Mac."

"Oh. Right. I'll wait for you out there."

"Thank you."

Mac went out to the living room and dropped to the sofa, his hormones working on overdrive. He'd never reacted to a woman quite like this. Figured it had to be one who wanted nothing to do with him. Releasing a short bark of laughter, he marveled at the irony. He'd finally, *finally* found one who sparked more than just his libido and she couldn't care less about him.

Well, he'd just have to change her mind. She wouldn't be easily swayed, but he couldn't let her slip through his fingers without finding out what they could possibly have together.

Maddie eased her way into a tight camisole that somewhat contained her breasts and put an extra large T-shirt over it. She'd learned to play down her considerable assets. Her thoughts drifted to the man waiting in the other room. His steely blue eyes made her itchy for something she'd never wanted before. He looked at her like he wanted to devour her. The feelings he generated in her were bigger and more dangerous than any she'd ever known. He scared the life out of her. If only she could convince him to leave her alone.

She ventured into the living room where he sat with his head back and his eyes closed. Maddie studied his strong jaw, the smooth skin on his neck, the broad shoulders, the muscular chest, the bulge of his sex. Shocked by her own curiosity, she quickly glanced at the hair falling into his eyes, and those perfect, kissable lips . . . What a package. She sighed, hoping for the fortitude she'd need to convince him to go.

"See something you like?"

She jumped, startled by the rumble of his voice. "Of course not."

"Ouch. The hits to my ego just keep on coming." He stood up to his full six-foot-two- or three-inch height.

Next to him, she felt tiny. "If you can't take the hits, there's the door."

His eyes hardened with displeasure. "Let's take care of those cuts."

Now that he'd made her feel not just tiny but small, Maddie lowered herself to the sofa. "I'm sorry."

"For what?" he asked, but he didn't look at her.

"For being nasty."

He shrugged. "I can take it."

"But you don't deserve it. Not after everything you've done today."

He unrolled the gauze and placed it on the coffee table next to the ointment. "I'm being made to pay for every guy who's done you wrong in the past. I get it." Propping her injured leg on his knee, he looked up at her. "Are you ready for this?"

Maddie bit her lip and nodded. Even though he was gentle, she cried out the second the ointment touched her ravaged skin. "Oh, God," she gasped. "That hurts!"

He tightened his hold on her leg. "I know, honey. Just hang in there for another minute."

By the time he finished dressing her knee, she was sweaty, nauseated and on the verge of tears.

Mac reached for her.

She rested her head on his shoulder and focused on his now-familiar scent.

He smoothed his hand over her hair, whispering soft words of comfort. "Better?" he asked several minutes later.

She nodded but didn't raise her head off his shoulder.

"Ready to do the elbow?"

"No," she whispered into his neck as she clutched his shirt with her good hand.

A tremble rippled through his big frame. "Maddie," he said in a raspy voice. "Honey, you're making me crazy. I'm only human."

Had she ever made a man crazy before? Not that she could recall. She liked the feeling of power that came over her. As if it had a mind of its own, her hand traveled from his chest to curve around his neck. Turning her face ever so slightly, she found his mouth warm and willing.

When his big hands cupped her face and his tongue slid between her lips, her brain shut down and all the reasons this shouldn't be happening ceased to matter.

Mac's cell phone interrupted the carnal kiss.

Maddie pulled back from him.

He groaned and tightened his hold on her. "Let it ring."

"It might be important."

"Trust me, it isn't." He tried to kiss her again. "This is important."

She held him off. "You need to get it."

Still groaning, he crawled over to his backpack to retrieve the phone. "What?"

"Mac? What kind of way is that to answer the phone?"

"I'm busy, Mom." He glanced at Maddie, who quickly looked away. Fabulous. One step forward, two steps back. "What do you need?"

"It's all over town that you're answering her door in a towel and buying her lobster."

"So what?"

"Why should you care? You don't live here."

"Is there a purpose to this call, Mother?"

"I'd like to know when you'll be home—here."

He ventured another glance at Maddie, who was doing her best not to look at him. "I'm bringing Maddie and her son Thomas to dinner tomorrow."

"*What?*" his mother and Maddie said in stereo.

"Six thirty good for you? I have to work, so I need time to get back here to shower and pick them up."

His mother said nothing for so long he thought she'd hung up. No such luck. "Six thirty is fine," she said stiffly.

"We'll see you then. Make your famous pot roast, will you? I miss that."

"Anything else?"

"Well, you know I love your chocolate cake."

"You and I are going to have a very long talk, young man. Do you hear me?"

"Are you hearing all that static on the line? Gotta go. See you tomorrow." Chuckling, Mac ended the call, imagining the scene at his parents' house. He felt a little sorry for his father.

"There's no way I'm going to dinner there."

"It'll be great. They'll go nuts over Thomas."

"You can't ask this of me, Mac. I *clean* that house."

"So you can't eat there?"

"You have no clue how things work around here."

"I don't care and neither should you. Now, where were we before we were so rudely interrupted?"

She gave him an arch look. "You were about to put medicine on my elbow."

"That's not how I remember it."

With a gentle push to his chest, she turned her injured arm so he could have access.

"If you want to be that way about it . . ."

"I do."

Mac applied ointment and bandages to her elbow and hand.

"You can't come in here and upend my whole life and then just walk away," she said after a long period of quiet while he dressed her wounds.

Her soft words and the bravery behind them touched him. "I'm not going anywhere."

"You're going back to Miami."

"Not for a while."

"Don't you have a business to run?"

"I'm taking some time off."

"How much time?"

"A month or two."

"That's an awfully long vacation."

He looked up at her. "Can you keep a big secret? One that would freak out my mother?"

"You knocked up some floozy in Florida, and now she's after the family fortune?"

"Very funny. You're just a regular comedienne, aren't you?"

Her unexpected giggle took his breath away. "You should do that more often."

"What? Make fun of you?"

"Laugh. It sounds good coming from you. So do you want to hear my secret?"

Maddie settled back into the sofa, her face still pale from the pain of her injuries. "Yes, I want to hear your dirty secret."

"I never said it was dirty." Mac sat next to her and brought her feet to rest in his lap. "I had an anxiety attack last week. It scared the hell out of me. I thought I was having a heart attack."

Concern radiated from her. "What brought that on?"

"Too much stress, not enough sleep, skipping meals."

"So you're on a forced vacation?"

"I guess you could say that, but I also wanted to see my dad and find out if he really plans to sell McCarthy's."

"You've heard about that, huh?"

"Yeah. It makes me so sad to think of that place belonging to a stranger."

"Well, your dad can't work forever."

"I know." Mac began to massage her feet. Talking to her was almost as much fun as kissing her, and it seemed that he couldn't be near her and not want to touch her. "You have the softest skin."

She tried to remove her feet from his lap, but he didn't let go. "I can't do this, Mac. I don't take these kinds of risks. They don't work out well for me."

"Will you give me a chance? That's all I'm asking for."

"I have to consider Thomas."

"I know you're a package deal."

"I can't think with you sucking up all the space around here."

He flashed her a smug smile.

"I knew that would go straight to your head," she muttered.

"I have to take the compliments where I can get them. You're rather stingy that way." He watched her stifle a yawn. "Let's get you into bed." After helping her to the chair across the room, he unfolded her bed and turned down the covers. "Do you want me to sleep on the porch?"

Maddie thought about that. "It's already all over town that you're answering my door in a towel and buying me lobster, so I guess the damage is done."

"Are you sure? I don't want to cause you any more trouble than I already have."

"Yes, you do."

He couldn't help but smile at her sauciness as he tucked her in.

"Use the sofa cushions to make a bed on the floor." She directed him to a closet in the hallway for a pillow, and after checking on Thomas one last time,

Mac settled into his sleeping bag on the floor. A balmy harbor breeze rippled through the window sheers, and the full moon cast a glow upon the room.

"How's the pain?"

"Okay."

"Want some more pain pills?"

"No, thanks."

"What time do I have to be at work tomorrow?"

"Nine thirty."

"Maybe you should tell me what I'm going to do once I get there—if you're not too tired."

"The first thing you have to do is report to housekeeping in the basement and punch in."

Mac listened to her talk about crazy Sundays and how to stock the cart with towels, clean sheets, toiletries, toilet paper and cleaning supplies. Lulled by her soft voice, he had to force himself to pay attention.

"Are you listening to me?"

"Absolutely. No DNA. Check."

"I said more than that."

"But DNA is the deal-breaker with Ethel."

"She freaks out if she finds any sign of the previous guest—and I mean any sign."

Mac chuckled. "Does she go through the rooms with a black light after you clean?"

"You're better off leaving nothing to chance."

"How much DNA are we talking about?"

"That's for me to know and you to find out."

"Ewww, gross."

"Precisely."

"I'm feeling another anxiety attack coming on."

Her sharp intake of breath made him regret the joke. "Really?"

"I'm fine, but I appreciate your concern."

Maddie threw a sofa pillow that hit him square in the face.

"Oof," Mac said, laughing. "Good shot."

"Don't joke about that. You scared me."

"Whoa! I think she might be starting to care about me."

"Nah, I just don't need the scandal of you kicking it in my house."

"That hurts, Maddie."

"You'll survive."

"Wanna make out?"

"No!"

Mac smiled, imagining the look on her face. "Yes, you do."

"I'm going to sleep now."

"Talk to me some more."

"About what?"

"Anything."

"My life is kind of boring."

"Was it just you and Tiffany?"

"And my mom."

"Where was your dad?"

She paused for a long time. "He went to the mainland one day and never came back."

Mac winced. "You've never seen him again?"

"No. He sent my mother a letter a couple of weeks later saying he couldn't live on an island anymore."

Mac could understand that but kept the thought to himself.

"That was the last we ever heard from him."

"How old were you?"

"Five. Tiff was three. She doesn't remember him at all."

"But you do."

"Vividly. He used to toss me over his head, and I'd scream and laugh."

"You must've missed him terribly."

"We could see the ferry landing from our apartment over the Galley." She referred to a restaurant in town. "For weeks, I watched every person come off every boat. I really thought he'd change his mind."

Mac's heart broke for her. Life could be so unfair. He also had a better idea now of what an uphill climb he faced in getting her to trust him. "I'm sorry."

"It was a long time ago."

Mac didn't know if it was wise to pursue it, but he had so many questions. "It must've been hard on your mom all by herself."

"We were always struggling. She never has been able to handle money, which is how she finally managed to land in jail." Maddie released a nervous-sounding laugh. "Anyway, you don't want to hear about my soap opera life."

"I want to hear it all."

"Even how the other kids tormented me from sixth grade on because I was the first one to develop?"

"If you want to tell me."

Mac waited, hoping she would trust him with her deepest secrets. Then, finally, she began to talk.

CHAPTER 6

"I started getting chest pains when I was ten. I was too afraid to tell anyone because I thought I might be dying or something. I was a B cup by eleven, and the kids at school called me Chesty Chester. My mother bought me a bikini the summer between sixth and seventh grade. That was the first time I became aware of boys and grown men checking out my chest and figure. That was also when my big T-shirt phase started." She paused and released another nervous-sounding laugh. "Jeez, what is it about you? I *never* talk about this stuff."

"You don't have to now if you don't want to."

"I don't mind. It's all ancient history anyway."

But it wasn't. Mac doubted she could hear the hurt that resonated even as she attempted flippancy.

"In middle school, the boys started snapping my bra in the lunch line. It became a contest to see who could get to me the most times in a day. I started carrying my books around in a heavy backpack so they couldn't get to my bra."

"Doesn't that count as assault or something?"

"Reporting them would've only made things worse for me."

"That's so wrong."

"I thought it couldn't get any worse, but I got my period in eighth grade, and within six months I was a D. Suddenly, *every* boy in school wanted to date Maddie Chester and her big boobs."

"Did you go out with any of them?"

"There was this one boy. . . John." Her voice went soft, her tone wistful. "He was really nice to me. For months he walked me home and carried my backpack. He wouldn't let the other boys snap my bra. I thought he was different."

Mac's stomach began to hurt. He so didn't want to hear this. With every tale she related, the mountain before him seemed to get a little steeper and the potential fall that much more sheer. "But he wasn't?"

"Turns out all that time he was pretending to be my friend, he was really hoping to get his hands on my breasts. The first time I let him kiss me, he went right for second base. He was quick, and before I could even react, he had his hands under my bra, mauling me. I'm pretty sure he . . . you know . . . in his pants."

Mac uttered an expletive under his breath. If that guy walked into the room right then, Mac would've beat the hell out of him.

"He was the first to kiss and tell. It was all over school the next day that he'd scored the first feel of Maddie Chester's famous boobs. After that, I faked sick for a week so I wouldn't have to face them."

"But eventually you had to go back."

"Uh huh, and everyone looked at me differently. That was the start of people thinking I was easy."

"It's just so unfair," he said, pained for the defenseless girl who had been betrayed by someone she considered a friend.

"Since then I've never known if a guy was interested in me or in *them*, you know?"

"I can imagine."

"It got worse in high school. The boys were all over me, and the other girls hated me because I was so popular with the guys."

"Sounds like it was lonely for you."

"It was. After awhile, I got sick of being alone all the time and decided to go out with one of them."

"How'd that go?"

"Just like I expected—him constantly trying to cop a feel and me constantly fending him off. After a while, he got pissed. He said he'd treated me well and it was time for me to return the favor."

"What the heck did that mean?"

"He demanded I have sex with him."

"How old were you?"

"Fifteen."

"Jesus," he whispered. "What'd you do?"

"I refused, because by then just being around him made me sick. He got so mad. For a few minutes, I thought he was going to hit me or something."

"Tell me he didn't—"

"No, but it might've been better if he had. Instead, he went to school the next day, told everyone I'd done him and all his friends on the beach the night before, and the Maddie Mattress nickname was born."

Mac wanted to weep. "And none of the other guys spoke up to say it wasn't true? No one?"

"They wouldn't have dared to contradict him."

"Who was he?" Mac's chest contracted with familiar pains, but that was the least of his worries at the moment.

"I'm sure you don't know him. . ."

"*Who was he?*" He made an effort to keep his voice down when he wanted to roar.

"Darren Tuttle."

A sharp pain took Mac's breath away. "He was my brother Evan's friend."

"Yes."

Mac's hand rolled into a fist. "Did he name my brother as one of the guys who was there that night?"

Maddie's silence answered for her.

"*And he didn't deny it?*"

"None of them did."

"I'll kill him."

"Mac, really, it was a long time ago. It doesn't matter now."

"It does matter! Those rumors ruined your life."

"It was my fault for sticking around here after high school. I should've gone somewhere else as soon as I was old enough, but money was always an issue, and I couldn't leave my mother. Believe it or not, she has it in her head that she needs to be here in case my father comes back."

"Nothing about this is your fault, Maddie. Nothing."

"You're supposed to be relaxing, not getting all upset."

Mac was so far beyond upset he wasn't even sure what to call it. "Who is Thomas's father?"

He could almost hear her thinking and deciding.

"Tell me."

After another long pause, she said, "He was a guest at the hotel two winters ago. He was writing a book, and we got to be friends. One thing led to another . . ."

"Was he the first one, you know. . ."

"First and only."

Mac released a long deep breath. How could she say that what Darren Tuttle and his friends did to her hadn't ruined her life? She was twenty-eight the first time she had sex. "What happened with him?"

"He was ten years older than me. He told me he'd had a vasectomy years ago because he didn't want kids. I stupidly fell for that, thinking we had something special."

Mac wanted to cover his ears so he wouldn't have to hear about yet another terrible hurt.

"We were together twice before he texted me to say he had to get back to the mainland to take care of some business, but it'd been nice knowing me. He'd been gone three weeks when I realized I was pregnant."

"That bastard."

"I don't regret it. Thomas is the best thing to ever happen to me. I love him more than anything."

"His father should be helping you. Financially, at least."

"I'd never want him to know. What if he came back and tried to take Thomas from me? I'll never tell him."

So the woman everyone thought of as the town tramp had had sex exactly twice in her life. Mac churned with things he wished he could say and anger he didn't know what to do with. He wanted to find all the men who'd harmed her, starting with her deadbeat father, and pummel them until they hurt the way she had. Even that, however, wouldn't be enough. It would only be half of what they deserved.

"What're you thinking?" she asked tentatively. "You're so quiet."

Mac made an effort to keep the fury out of his voice. That wasn't what she needed from him after sharing secrets he suspected she probably hadn't shared with anyone but her sister. "You're one of the bravest people I've ever known, and I'm honored you told me all this."

"I'm not what they think I am."

Her quiet dignity affected him more than anything else. "I already knew that."

"I didn't want to like you. You're Evan McCarthy's brother and Linda's son. But you're not like them. You're so much better."

"Thank you, honey," he said, his voice hoarse with emotions he'd never felt quite so strongly before. That she had trusted him with her deepest secrets was one of the best gifts he'd ever received. He reached up for her hand and laced his fingers through hers. "I wish I could take a big broom and sweep away all the old hurts."

"You're sweet to want to."

"I really wish I could."

"No one's ever wanted to do anything like that for me before."

"That's too bad. You deserve to be happy."

She squeezed his hand. "I told you all my stuff. Now you have to tell me some of yours."

In an effort to lighten the mood, Mac regaled her with funny stories of growing up with three brothers and a sister that made her laugh, and he swore he made her cry when he told her about the injury that ended his professional baseball aspirations. As she continued to hold his hand, she asked about the women he'd dated, and he told her. After what she'd shared with him, keeping secrets from her—any secrets—just seemed foolish. By the time they ran out of conversation, the first hints of daylight were peeking through the windows, and his arm had fallen asleep hours ago, but still he held her hand.

He'd never felt more energized by a sleepless night.

Maddie couldn't find Thomas. He wasn't in his crib or at Tiffany's. She ran through the yard screaming for help, tears streaming down her face. Someone had taken him from her. The one person she truly loved. She screamed for him again and fought the hands that tried to stop her from running down the street.

"Maddie. Honey, you're dreaming. Wake up."

Mac. All at once, she was fully awake with sickening pain radiating from her knee and arm. He sat on the edge of her bed, brushing the hair off her face.

"Thomas," she said, her voice rough with sleep and fear.

"He's sleeping in his crib."

"Will you make sure? Please?"

"Of course."

While he was gone, Maddie tried to calm her racing heart and shaking hands. *Only a dream. Only a dream.*

"He's fine," Mac reported. "Sound asleep." He returned to sit once again on the side of the bed. "Are you all right?"

"Yeah. Just a crazy dream."

"You seem to have a lot of those."

"Always have. Some are better than others." She recalled the dream about him the previous afternoon. That had been a good one.

He took her hand. "You're shaking."

"It was scary."

"Want to talk about it?"

"No. Thank you."

"Scoot over."

"Excuse me?"

"You heard me." He nudged her with his hip. "Come on."

She moved to the far side of the bed and then gasped when it dipped under his weight. "W-what're you doing?"

"This." He slid his arm under her and carefully brought her into his embrace, making sure to accommodate her injured arm and leg. By the time he had her all arranged, her face was pressed to his chest, and he held her snugly against him. Maddie couldn't breathe from being this close to him, and she had nowhere to rest her sore hand but on his firm belly.

Brushing a kiss over her hair, he said, "Go back to sleep."

Um, yeah. Sure. With her senses overwhelmed by his sporty scent, the feel of his soft chest hair under her cheek, and his hand caressing her back—how did he expect her to *sleep*?

"It's okay, Maddie. Nothing will happen to you or Thomas while I'm here. I promise."

How could he know that was exactly what she needed to hear right then? That nothing he could've said would have meant more to her? Tears leaked from her closed eyes. She was so tired—and not just from the sleepless night. The heavy weight of responsibility resting on her fragile shoulders was enough sometimes to make her buckle under the strain. Now here was this man wanting to make it all better—even if just for a little while—and it was so very tempting to let him. Tomorrow she'd get back to fighting him off. For right now, it felt too good to be held by him to think about fighting. She sank into Mac's embrace and absorbed the comfort he so willingly offered.

Mac didn't dare move. He'd had no idea how overwhelming it would be to hold her like this, to have her soft, fragrant hair brushing against his face, to have her body yield trustingly into his, and yes, to have her breasts pressed to his side . . . If she moved, even the slightest bit, she'd be able to feel what her closeness had done to him. So Mac focused on breathing the way the doctor had taught him—in through the nose, out through the mouth.

"Does your chest hurt?" Her breath fanning his heated skin only added to the problem in his lap.

"No."

"Why are you breathing like that? Does something else hurt?"

Mac chuckled. She was so cute. "Nothing that'll kill me."

After a long pause, she suddenly got it. Gasping, she began to move away from him.

He tightened his hold on her. "Stay. Please. I love holding you like this, but I can't help that having you so close turns me on."

"Oh."

In the waning darkness, he smiled. The innocent way she always said that single word was adorable—as if it was a huge surprise to her that she turned him on. She had no idea what she did to him, but apparently she intended to find out. Her injured hand moved from his belly to his face, her fingers caressing his jaw. Mac swore his heart stopped while he waited to see what she would do next. "Maddie. . ."

"Hmm?"

"What're you doing?"

"Touching you."

Jesus. Kill me now. He'd never been more painfully erect in his life. "Honey, you're going to be tired tomorrow—or I guess I should say today."

"S'okay. I've got someone covering for me at work."

He laughed. "Poor sucker."

"Mmm." Her fingers moved to his mouth, smoothing over his bottom lip in a light caress that once again stopped his heart.

Releasing a tortured groan, he held her tighter while being mindful of her injuries. They didn't seem to be bothering her at the moment.

"You're so handsome," she whispered.

Startled by the unexpected compliment, he cleared his throat. "Is that so?"

"Sure," she said, laughing. "Like you don't know."

"I had no idea until this very minute."

She poked his ribs, making him startle and then laugh again. "You're so full of it."

Brushing a soft kiss over her lips, he studied her face for a long time. "You're the most beautiful woman I've ever known."

"That can't possibly be true."

He stopped her from looking away and forced her to meet his gaze. "It's absolutely true."

Her fingers skimmed over his chest to his belly, which quivered under her tentative touch. Mac inhaled sharply as he reached out to stop her wandering hand. "Sleep." Glancing at his watch, he discovered it was after five. For a long time, he lay there listening to the bleat of a foghorn and squawking seagulls before he finally fell into a deep sleep.

Thomas's crib chatter woke Mac at six thirty. His eyes were gritty from lack of sleep, but when he remembered the night he'd spent with Maddie, he was filled with energy and renewed determination to take care of her and Thomas. He moved slowly to extricate himself from her embrace without waking her. Pressing a kiss to her forehead, he brought the sheet up over her and went to find the baby bouncing in his crib.

Thomas let out a happy squeal when he saw Mac.

"Hey, buddy," Mac whispered. "You're up early." Mac scooped him up and carried him to the changing table where he removed what felt like a twenty-pound diaper. Amazing to think that just yesterday he'd never changed a diaper before, and now he handled the squirming baby like an expert—and didn't mind doing it. That was the odd part. He, Mac McCarthy, commitment-phobe and bachelor extraordinaire, was taking care of a baby and *liking* it.

"You and your mother have done quite a number on me, mister," he told the baby.

Thomas rewarded him with a smile full of new baby teeth and a good dose of drool. What a cutie.

Mac changed him into a clean all-in-one shirt contraption that snapped between his legs and picked him up.

Thomas grabbed a handful of Mac's chest hair and gave a healthy yank, bringing tears to Mac's eyes. "Yikes," he said. "No no. That *hurts*."

Thomas's mischievous smile made Mac laugh. "You're a devil, aren't you? What'd you say we let Mom sleep a while and take a walk?"

When the baby seemed to approve of the plan, Mac put him back in the crib for a few minutes so he could get ready. They snuck out of the apartment a short time later. Mac debated taking the stroller that was parked under the stairs but decided he'd rather carry the baby.

In town, workers swept and washed the sidewalks in front of the various establishments. Shopkeepers carted samples of their wares to the street and rolled back awnings. Mac and Thomas wandered down to the ferry landing where Captain Joe supervised the loading of a fuel truck onto one of the smaller ferries.

"Whoa, dude," Joe said when he saw Mac carrying the baby. "You work fast!"

"Very funny."

Joe toyed with Thomas's pudgy foot, earning a squeal from the baby. "Who've you got there?"

"This is Thomas. My friend Maddie's baby."

"And how long, exactly, has Maddie been your 'friend'?"

"Since I knocked her off her bike about ten minutes after I left you yesterday."

"Awww, and now you've got yourself a little family. Isn't that sweet?"

"It's not like that." But wasn't it? "Exactly."

Joe barked with laughter and tugged cigarettes from his shirt pocket.

"You can't smoke in front of the baby," Mac said.

"Wow, look at you. All paternal and everything. Never thought I'd see the day."

"If you're quite finished, Thomas and I are going to grab some coffee. Want to join us?"

"He's kind of young for coffee, isn't he?"

Mac shot him a withering look.

Joe checked his watch. "Yeah, I've got some time. My first run isn't until eight." He hollered for someone to take over for him and walked with Mac and Thomas up the hill to the South Harbor Diner. When Mac walked in with Thomas in his arms, everything came to a halt in the small restaurant, and every eye in the room landed on him.

"Morning, everyone," Mac said.

Murmured greetings followed as Mac and Joe slid into a booth.

"Jeez, man, you've got the whole town buzzing," Joe said.

"Apparently."

Mac told Joe about what'd happened since yesterday while sharing tiny bites of his corn muffin with Thomas. If the boy's bouncing antics were any indication, he loved the treat. Before long, the muffin was a pulverized mess of crumbs that Mac scrambled to contain. The kid moved fast!

"You know what people say about her, don't you?" Joe asked tentatively after hearing Mac's story.

"It's not true, Joe." He told his friend what Darren Tuttle and the other boys, including Evan, had done to her.

Joe swore under his breath. "God, that's horrible." He leveled a steady look at Mac across the table. "What're you gonna do about it?"

Mac appreciated that his old friend knew him so well. "Haven't decided yet. But I plan to have a chat with my brother. Soon."

"Tuttle owns an auto body shop out on Sunflower Road."

"Good to know."

"He's still as much of a jerk as he was in school."

"Also good to know."

"That's one cute baby," Joe said a bit wistfully.

"He really is."

"You're getting kind of involved here, huh?"

"I think maybe I am." It still amazed Mac to realize all that had happened in the last twenty-four hours. "There's something about her that just gets to me. I can't explain it."

Joe shrugged. "Happens to the best of us."

Mac knew he was referring to his feelings for Janey. After spending time with Maddie, he had a new appreciation for what it would be like to want someone who didn't return the sentiment. That thought struck a chord of fear in Mac. Suddenly, he needed to get back to her. He needed to see her, to reassure himself that what they'd shared during the long night had started them down a path toward something important.

"I need to get Thomas back to his mom," Mac said, tossing some bills on the table. "Give me a ring when you have time to kill."

Joe raised an eyebrow as his lips quirked with amusement. "Sticking around for a while, are you?"

Mac glanced down at Thomas and then back at Joe. "Looks that way."

Tingling breasts woke Maddie. Shifting in the bed, she moaned when her knee and elbow protested the movement. Her injuries hurt more this morning than they had the day before, if that was possible. Ignoring the sharp blast of pain from her knee, she got up too fast and hobbled into Thomas's room. His crib was empty.

Maddie gasped. Where were they? Where had he taken her son? Her heart racing and her throat tightening, she tried not to think about her terrifying dream as she went to the front door and looked down over Tiffany's yard. No sign of them.

"Oh, please," she whispered. "Please come back. Bring my baby back."

You don't really know him at all, the devil on her left shoulder said. *Of course you do*, said the angel on the other shoulder. *You know him better than you ever knew the baby's father.* To which the devil said, *He could be anywhere by now.* Maddie's panic mounted as she watched the day's first ferry clear the breakwater on its way to the mainland. The angel scoffed at the devil. *He'll be right back. You'll see.*

As if she had waved a magic wand, a minute or two later Mac came strolling down Tiffany's driveway holding Thomas. He carried a white bag in his other hand and kept up a steady flow of chatter with the baby. Even though she was furious with him for taking Thomas without her permission, she couldn't help but notice how completely focused he was on her son.

"There's Mommy," he said to Thomas on the way up the stairs.

They came in the door, and she reached for Thomas.

"Hey, whoa," Mac said. "Wait a minute. Sit down, and I'll hand him to you."

"I'll just take him now."

"But your hand—"

"Please give me my son."

Surprised by her sharp tone, he did as she asked. "Uh oh, buddy. I think Mom's mad at us."

"I'm not mad at him." She returned to the sofa bed and painfully managed to arrange Thomas so her shirt was covering her breast and sighed with relief as he latched on for the one feeding she still managed to get in each day. Feeling exposed, she reached for the sheet and tugged it up over them.

Mac dropped the bag he'd been carrying on the kitchen table. "I brought you a muffin and some coffee." He turned to her. "I didn't know how you like it. Are you. . ."

"Feeding him? Yes."

"Oh." He didn't seem to know where to look.

"Don't take him again without telling me."

"I'm sorry. We wanted to let you sleep for a while. You were up late." His eyes finally met hers. He looked proprietary, as if he was gazing at something that belonged to him. Not knowing whether to be flattered or fearful, she looked away.

"I didn't like not knowing where he was."

"I'm sorry," he said again. "I should've left a note."

"You should've told me you were taking him."

"That would've required waking you up, which would've defeated the whole 'let you sleep in' purpose of our mission."

"Have you ever had an argument you didn't win?"

"Hmm, not that I can recall."

Maddie growled in frustration, which startled Thomas, causing him to release her nipple. She resituated him and patted his bum to reassure him. Venturing a glance at Mac, she found him watching her with thinly veiled hunger that zipped through her like an electrical current, settling into a throb between her legs.

As if he knew exactly what he did to her just by looking at her that certain way, he sat on the edge of the bed.

Maddie wished she could run away, but the twenty-pound baby anchored to her breast and the cut on her knee kept her from moving.

Thomas let out a cry to tell her he was ready to move to the other side.

"Could you. . . Turn away?" she asked.

"Do I have to?"

"Yes!"

Reluctantly, or so it seemed, Mac turned his back to her. "That's about the sexiest thing I've ever seen," he said in a strangled tone.

"You can't see anything."

"I have a very vivid imagination. Can I turn back now?"

"If you must."

He not only turned back, he put his hands on either side of her hips and leaned in so his face was close to hers. "Kiss me."

"No," she said, turning away from him.

He took that as an invitation to lean over Thomas to nuzzle her neck.

She jolted. "Mac! Stop!"

"Not until you kiss me."

"I haven't even brushed my teeth," she muttered.

"I don't care." Turning her face, he rubbed his lips over hers. "You make me crazy, Maddie. I've never wanted anyone the way I want you."

"I wish you wouldn't say those things. Whatever you think is happening here, I don't want it."

"I don't believe you," he whispered against her neck, sending a shiver racing through her.

A knock on the door interrupted the intense moment.

"We'll finish this later," he whispered, pressing one last kiss to her lips.

"No, we won't."

"Wanna bet?"

Oh, that cocky smile of his made her so mad! He always got exactly what he wanted, which was just one more reason to resist him. Maddie watched him swing open the door.

"Hey," he said. "Come in."

His friend Libby stepped into the room. "Hi, Maddie. How're you feeling?"

"Like I got knocked off my bike by a big oaf who wasn't watching where he was going," Maddie said with a scowl for Mac.

"Cute," he said, flashing that irresistible grin of his.

Libby giggled at their banter. "I'm glad I was able to help out today."

"What do you mean?" Maddie asked.

"Oh," Mac said. "About that. . . I meant to tell you. . ."

"Tell me what?"

"Libby agreed to hang out with you and Thomas while I'm at the hotel today."

"But I never asked her—"

"I did."

Maddie walked a fine line between wanting to yell at him and not wanting to be rude to Libby, who hadn't done anything more than agree to help her misguided friend.

"That's not necessary," Maddie said. "We'll be fine by ourselves."

"But, honey, your hand—"

"Don't call me that! I'm not your honey! And it's not up to you to arrange a babysitter for me."

"I told you I'm going to help you."

Maddie wanted to scream but kept her voice even when she said, "You have helped me, but this is too much. I can't put Libby out—"

"Oh, it's no problem. I love babies! My kids are teenagers now, and they're off with their friends today at the beach. I'd love to help out with Thomas."

"Don't you have a hotel to run?" Maddie asked, aware that she now sounded ungrateful as well as rude.

"Today's my day off."

"Fabulous." Maddie shot what she hoped was a hateful look at Mac.

He just smiled at her. "Great, then it's all worked out. I can't be late on my first day, so I'm going to head out." Leaning down, he tried to kiss her, but Maddie turned away. "I'll be back to get you for dinner, so be ready by six."

"I'm not going to dinner."

"See you then." He tweaked Thomas's foot and kissed Libby's cheek on the way out the door. "You girls have fun."

"Oh, we will," Libby assured him. "Don't worry about a thing."

They listened as he started his motorcycle and headed down the driveway to the main road.

"Ugh!" Maddie said. "He's the most aggravating person I've ever met!"

Libby raised an eyebrow. "Is that so?"

"He's bossy and pushy and—"

"Totally smitten," Libby said with a smug smile.

"*What?*"

"You heard me. He's got it bad for you."

"He does not."

"I've known him a long time, Maddie. I've never seen him look at any woman the way he looks at you."

Unable to process that tidbit on top of all the other emotions storming around inside her, Maddie shifted Thomas onto her shoulder and used her good hand to burp him.

Libby perched on the end of the bed. "He's one of the best guys I know. You'd be a very lucky girl to end up with him."

"It'll never happen." Why was she even bothering to have this conversation? Like her "relationship" with Mac, it was pointless. "Linda McCarthy will never allow her golden boy to end up with the likes of me."

Libby laughed. "The McCarthy brothers have made a blood sport of defying their mother all their lives. If she doesn't like you, that'll make you even more attractive to him."

"Great, that's just what I need—a guy who wants me only because his mother hates me."

"That's not the only reason he wants you."

"Right. He wants the same thing every other guy wants."

"You'll underestimate him if you think that poorly of him, Maddie. Look at what he's gone to do for you today. Do you think just any guy would do that?"

Maddie hated to admit that Libby had a point, but she wasn't about to convince one of his oldest friends that she didn't believe his intentions were entirely honorable. "You really don't have to stay if you have other stuff to do."

Libby reached for Thomas. "There's nothing I'd rather do."

***

Mac couldn't believe it had finally happened to him, but he suspected he'd probably fallen in love with Maddie at some point in the last twenty-four hours. Since he'd never been in love before, he couldn't say for sure. But he hadn't ever felt anything even close to what happened to him when she looked at him with those caramel eyes that gave away her every emotion, especially those she didn't want him to see.

He'd never given much thought to being a father. He'd just assumed that, like the true love other people went crazy over, it wasn't going to happen for him, and he'd been fine with that. But now he was imagining playing baseball with Thomas and teaching him how to fish and drive a boat and throw a football. How could it have happened so fast? That was the part he didn't get.

After nearly thirty-five entanglement-free years, here he was wrapped in a net so tight it should've been strangling him. Instead, as he steered the bike toward North Harbor, all he felt was exhilaration and determination to do whatever it took to make it work. She said she didn't want it—didn't want *him*—but he'd show her how wrong she was. He *knew* she felt the same way about him. He knew it. Now he just had to find a way to convince her that his intentions were sincere.

A stab of fear nearly knocked him off the bike. What if he couldn't do it? What if she was just too scarred from past hurts to take a chance on him? What if he'd waited all this time to find her only to lose her before he ever had her? That couldn't happen. He wouldn't let it.

Shaking off those unpleasant thoughts, he took a right turn into the hotel parking lot.

On the spacious front porch, decorated with white wicker furniture and pots that exploded with colorful, fragrant blooms, guests enjoyed morning coffee and a pristine view of North Harbor. Entering the hotel was like taking a step back in time: dark paneling on the walls and ceiling, potted palms, Victorian-era furniture and well-worn carpet. Large ceiling fans kept the harbor breeze moving through the lobby, dining room and lounge that made up the spacious first floor.

A sweeping staircase led to the second floor, and from that a small stairway took guests to the third floor. No elevators, no air conditioning and not a television or telephone to be found. Mac's mother, who managed the hotel, believed in providing a place where guests could truly escape the rigors of modern-day life.

Mac bounded downstairs to the housekeeping department. The smell of laundry detergent and the whir of washing machines and dryers greeted him as he made his way to Ethel's office at the end of the long hallway.

She was just as he remembered her—wiry build, wrinkled face, a row of studs lining one ear and dyed red hair that looked like it had been shocked into standing straight up. Mac and his brothers used to speculate endlessly about her sexuality. Grant was convinced she was a lesbian, but Adam swore he once saw her making out with a guy on the town beach. That comment had brought about much moaning, groaning and eye scrubbing.

Ethel lumbered to her feet to greet him with a fierce hug. As always, she reeked of cigarette smoke and cheap perfume. "Aren't you a sight for sore eyes?" she asked in that raspy smoker's voice that Evan imitated so well.

"How are ya, Ethel?"

"Oh, you know, arthritic and constipated. Nothing new."

Mac winced at the information overload. Grant would howl when he heard that one.

"What brings you down to the bowels?"

Interesting choice of words, he thought, suppressing an inappropriate chuckle. "I'm filling in for Maddie Chester today." Over Ethel's shoulder, he spied the time clock. "I need to punch in on her card."

Ethel stared at him as if he'd lost his mind. "You can't be serious."

"Sure am. I knocked her off her bike by accident yesterday. She's banged up pretty bad and can't work. All she's worried about is losing her job, so I told her I'd cover for her until she can get back to it."

"But, you. . . You can't! Your people own this place. What will folks say?"

"What do I care?"

"Your mother will care."

"That's her problem." Mac stepped around Ethel, found Maddie's timecard and punched in. "Now, where am I supposed to be?"

They engaged in a visual standoff, but Mac refused to blink.

Finally, Ethel said, "I'll need to shift some things around."

"Whatever Maddie normally does is fine. No special treatment."

Mac couldn't believe that Ethel actually looked guilty and wondered what that was all about. He joined the other housekeepers, who were filling gigantic baskets in a crowded stockroom. He met Betty, Sylvia, Patty, Sarah, Maude and Daisy, all of whom were wearing yellow dresses and white aprons. Maddie would look some kind of sexy in that getup, he thought before pushing the image aside and focusing on the filling of the baskets. Mac wondered how some of them managed to carry the heavy load up three flights of stairs. He wondered how Maddie did it.

Ethel handed out room assignment sheets to the women and Mac. As he scanned the long list, it suddenly occurred to him that this was not going to be as easy as he'd thought.

"This is Mac," Ethel said begrudgingly. He noted she didn't mention his last name, which was just as well. "He's filling in for Maddie, who'll be out a couple days."

The other women, who ranged from twenty to sixty, gave him the once-over with a mixture of curiosity and blatant interest.

A young blonde sidled up to him. "What's wrong with Maddie?" she whispered as Ethel continued to bark out orders and reminders about Sunday changeover and DNA.

Keeping his voice down, Mac gave her the abbreviated version of the story.

"So you're filling in for her? That's so nice." She lowered her voice even further. "No one's ever nice to Maddie. It makes me really mad. She's the sweetest girl."

"Yes, she is," Mac said, touched by the tiny woman's loyalty to Maddie. It warmed him to know she had at least one friend on the island.

"Daisy!" Ethel barked. "Are you listening to me?"

Daisy quaked in her sneakers. "Yes, ma'am."

"Take room 303 from Mac's list," Ethel said.

"It must be bad," Daisy whispered to him. "Maddie always gets the grossest rooms."

Mac fumed when he heard that. Things were going to change around here after today. "That's not necessary, Ethel," he said. "I've got it."

Daisy glanced up at him with an expression of awe and fear. Apparently, no one dared to cross the mighty Ethel. To hell with that. His parents owned the place. She couldn't intimidate him.

"I want Daisy to do it."

"I'll do it."

Another visual standoff. Again, Mac refused to blink.

"Fine," Ethel said with a dismissive wave of her hand. "Have at it. Get to work, everyone."

Daisy took pity on him and helped him stock his basket. By the time he had everything he needed to clean the ten rooms on his list, he could barely lift the thing. He watched in amazement as Daisy lifted hers, propped it on her shoulder and headed for the stairs.

By the time he reached the third floor, his back was breaking and sweat rolled down his forehead. *How does Maddie do this?* The hallway was stifling, and the lack of air-conditioning promised to make for a long, uncomfortable day. He decided to start with what promised to be the worst room on his list—303. On the ring of keys he'd been given, he found the one he needed, took a deep breath and opened the door to hell.

The smell smacked him in the face, making him gag. Someone had puked all over one of the two beds, bottles and cans littered the floor and the bathroom floor was flooded. "Holy DNA," he muttered as he put a hand over his mouth and nose and rushed in to throw open the windows. As his stomach fought back a retch, his foot skidded on something. He looked down at a discarded condom on the floor. "Oh my God."

Mac turned to find Daisy standing at the door, looking sympathetic. "Maddie always gets these rooms."

"Not anymore."

Daisy glanced over her shoulder as if she was worried that Ethel might appear any second. "I'll help you."

"You don't have to. You've got your own rooms to deal with."

"None of mine come close to this. Maddie's my friend, and you're doing her a favor, so let me help you."

Since Mac had no idea where to even begin, he sent her a grateful smile. "Thanks. I owe you one."

CHAPTER 7

By the time Mac opened the door to his tenth and final room, he could safely say he'd never worked harder in his life. Even with Daisy's help, room 303 had taken two hours and all of Mac's plumbing skills to restore it to pristine condition. Daisy told him that guests who left such messes were permanently banned. Unfortunately, there were plenty of others just like them looking for a place to bust loose for a summer weekend.

When he saw nothing too gross or out of the ordinary in the last room, he breathed a sigh of relief. He'd already had enough contact with foreign DNA to last a lifetime. As he stripped the bed and quickly remade it, he decided something had to be done about the deplorable way Maddie was treated here. No wonder she'd called her employers bastards. They were!

"Having fun, darling?"

Speak of the devil. His mother leaned against the doorframe. "I'm having a blast."

"This is entirely inappropriate, but of course you know that."

"How's it inappropriate for me to help a friend?"

"She's not your friend! You just met her yesterday, for heaven's sake."

"Be careful, Mother. I'm not a child who needs you to define friendship for me."

"I just don't understand this, Mac. Why in the world would you want to lower yourself to" —she waved her hand around— "this. . . just to prove a point to me."

He stopped what he was doing to stare at her, incredulous. "It's got nothing to do with you! God, you're unbelievable! You think everything revolves around you."

"I think no such thing."

"What I want to know is why Maddie gets all the crappiest rooms. Did that direction come right from you? Or does Ethel do that on her own?" He glanced at her in time to catch her guilty expression. "That ends today. Do you hear me?"

"You can't come in here and start barking out orders."

"Do you want my help at the marina?"

She had the good grace to at least squirm a little. "You know I do."

"Then you'll make sure she's treated fairly here from now on, or I swear to God, I won't lift a hammer down the street." He had no intention of making good on that threat, because he planned to help his father no matter what. But he could let her think that he'd walk away if it meant improving Maddie's situation.

"I can't imagine what's gotten into you to talk to me like this."

"I've gotten an eyeful of the way you treat one of your employees today, and I don't care for it."

"She's gotten her hooks into you, hasn't she?"

He released a short bark of laughter as he ran the duster over the tables and dresser. "I wish."

"What does that mean?"

"She doesn't seem all that interested in me."

Linda expelled what sounded like a sigh of relief. "Oh, well, that's good, I suppose."

Mac whirled around to face her. "No, it isn't. I like her. I really *like* her."

"Don't be ridiculous. You could have any woman you want. Just this morning, I talked to Doro Chase. She can't wait to meet you."

"What're you talking about?"

"I told her you're home, and she'd love to meet you. I said I'd set it up."

"That ain't happening. I don't need my mother arranging dates for me."

"You need something because that woman you're shacking up with in town is all wrong for you."

"That woman I'm shacking up with is all *right* for me." Mac enjoyed watching his mother blanch. "In fact, she's more right for me than any woman I've ever met."

"You can't be serious."

Deciding he'd said enough for now, he grabbed the last of the towels from his basket and headed for the bathroom. "We'll see you at dinner." He poked his head out the door and made eye contact with her. "You be nice to her, or I swear you won't see me again for a long, long time."

"Honestly. I don't know what's happened to you."

"Believe me, you don't want to know." He'd fallen in love with a woman his mother had nothing but disdain for. Any doubt he'd had about the love part had disappeared during the long day at the hotel. He loved her. He wanted her. He couldn't wait to see her again. He was going to do anything and everything he could to be with her.

And if his mother didn't like it? Too bad.

Mac limped out of the hotel at three thirty. The long night without sleep, the long day without so much as a ten-minute break and the battle with his mother had left him weary and drained. He wanted to go straight back to Maddie's and sleep until dinner. But first he needed to see his father, so he started the bike and headed for the marina.

The aroma of fried food and diesel fuel blended with sunscreen, dead fish and something being cooked on a grill. A group of boys raced crabs down the ramp into the water, and their shrieks filled the air. Overhead, a flock of seagulls watched the action onboard one of the big powerboats where the day's catch was being cleaned. Just another summer day at McCarthy's.

Big Mac sat at one of the picnic tables outside the restaurant, surrounded by a crowd that hung on his every word as he retold the story of hooking a great white in Long Island Sound—for what had to be the ten thousandth time since it happened twenty years earlier.

"Not that old fish story again," Mac interjected.

His father's face lit up with delight. "Hey! Look who it is! Fellas, meet my oldest boy, Little Mac."

"Just Mac is fine." He shook hands with the other men. "I dropped the little part years ago." To his father, he said, "Got time for a beer?"

"Hmm, fellas, what do you say? Do I have time for a beer with my son?"

"You do own the place," one of them said drolly.

"That I do. Luke!"

Luke appeared from behind the main building. "Yeah?"

"I'm cutting out. You're in charge."

"Right."

"What happened with the shark?" one of the guys asked as Big Mac got up.

"He got away," Mac said.

"Well, thank God for that."

"No shit," Big Mac said with that winning smile of his. "I'll see you fellas around. Gotta spend some time with my boy." He put his arm around Mac and led him to the Tiki Bar at the end of the main dock.

They pulled up stools at Big Mac's latest brainstorm. The outdoor bar had been added two summers ago, and from what Mac had heard, it was turning a nice profit.

"Carol Ann, this here's my boy Mac. He drinks on the house while he's home. Two of my usual."

"Yes, sir, Mr. McCarthy," the pretty young bartender replied.

While she fetched the beers, Mac snorted behind his hand. "She calls you *Mr.* McCarthy?"

"She respects her elders. What can I say?"

Carol Ann put two frosty bottles down in front of them.

"Thank you, sweetheart," Big Mac said without an ounce of guile. Only on Gansett Island could an employer get away with calling a female employee "sweetheart."

"My pleasure," she said with a toothy smile, and Mac could see that it was. Everyone loved his father. You couldn't spend ten minutes in his orbit and not be sucked into his effortless way with people. He was the heart and soul of the place, and Mac couldn't imagine it without him.

Carol Ann moved to the far end of the bar to give them some privacy.

Big Mac tapped his bottle against Mac's and then took a long drink.

"You're really gonna sell this place, Dad?"

"I think it's time," Big Mac said, but Mac heard the sadness in his voice and saw it on his face. "Your mom wants to travel, get off the island some. You hear about people waiting too long to retire, then one of 'em gets sick. . ." Shrugging, he picked at the label on his bottle.

"I can't imagine someone else owning it, running it."

"Believe me, neither can I. But I'm not gonna live forever, you know."

"Don't say that."

Big Mac laughed. "Okay, I won't."

Slipping into contemplative silence, they looked out over the bustling pond, which had thinned out as it always did on Sunday afternoons.

"I love this time of day around here," Big Mac said. "Everyone who's coming is in, everyone who's leaving is gone. Most of the work is done for the day. People want to hang out, pass the bull. Hardly feels like work most days."

Mac knew they came back year after year to see his father, to catch up on the news, to hear the latest stories. He had a way of making each guest feel special, as if he'd been waiting all season just for them to arrive. It occurred to Mac that no one could ever replace him.

They watched Luke guide a latecomer into a spot next to another powerboat. The captain did a nice job of maneuvering the big boat into the tight space. After the boat was tied up, Luke and the captain exchanged a few words. The captain reached for his wallet, pressed a wad of cash into Luke's hand, and nodded at something Luke said to him. Luke pocketed the cash and made his way back up to the main dock.

Mac watched the exchange with growing dismay. "Tell me that money will make it into the till." He glanced over to find his father's face hard and unreadable.

"Eventually, I'm sure."

"But you don't know?"

"I hope."

"Dad! Is he ripping you off?"

"Nah, I pay him plenty. He doesn't need it."

Mac wanted to cause a scene but knew his father wouldn't appreciate it. You could bet that he'd be keeping an eye on Luke while he worked on the renovations.

"You know, son," Big Mac said tentatively, "if you have even the slightest interest in the place, all you have to do is say so. I'd never sell it if you wanted it."

Mac knew it, but hearing the words made it real. "I know that, Dad."

"Absolutely no pressure, though. I wouldn't want you to feel obligated. Island life isn't for everyone. Lord knows you and your brothers split the minute you were old enough."

"It looks a little different to me this time around, for some reason." The words were out of his mouth before Mac could ponder the consequences.

"That so?"

"Yeah."

"Why do you think that is?"

"I'm not sure. Maybe I stayed away too long. Maybe because things in Miami have been beyond insane lately. Or maybe it's because I met someone yesterday who has my head turned all around."

"Ahhh," Big Mac said with a satisfied grin. "Now we're getting to the heart of the matter."

Mac smiled. "Remember me asking you how I'd know when the right one came along? You said, 'You'll know, son. You'll just know.'"

"Sounds like something I'd say."

"Well . . ."

Mac watched the awareness dawn on his father's face. "No kidding?"

Mac shrugged.

His father's eyes went shiny. "It's about time," he said softly. "Wow, just like that?"

"I took one look at her, and that was that."

"And we're talking about Maddie who cleans up the hill?"

"Yeah," Mac said, still awed by the wonder of it all. Two days ago, he was in Miami. Two days ago, he didn't even know she existed. And now his every hope and dream was somehow mixed up in her and her son.

"I don't know her real well, but she seems like a sweetheart of a gal," Big Mac said. "Had some tough breaks, though."

"She sure has. And because of that, she's kind of. . . skittish."

"Can't really blame her. That father of hers. . . No one could believe it when he just walked away from his wife and kids. That's the thing about this place— you can jump on a ferry and run away from it all."

"I don't think she ever recovered from that."

"Who would?"

Mac decided to level with his father. "I'm kind of in uncharted territory here."

"How's that?"

"You're gonna laugh. . ."

His father did just that. "Spill it, boy!"

"It's just that usually when I like someone, they tend to. . ." Mac combed his fingers impatiently through his hair as he searched for the words. "How can I say this without sounding like a total jackass?"

This time Big Mac howled. "They tend to fall at your feet in gratitude that Mac McCarthy has chosen to give them the time of day?"

"That is *not* what I was going to say!"

His father continued to laugh at his own joke. "Am I warm?"

"Sort of," Mac said begrudgingly.

That set his father off again.

"I'm glad you're getting such a kick out of this."

Big Mac wiped the laughter tears from his eyes. "I'm very sorry, but I think it's a riot that you finally find one who makes your head spin and she could take or leave you."

"Well," Mac said, thinking of their passionate kisses, "I wouldn't say *that*, exactly. But she doesn't seem to be jumping for joy that she's attracted my interest."

Big Mac had the good grace to at least try to hide his smirk. "She's probably overwhelmed. A good-looking, self-assured guy like you would scare the pants off a gal who's been treated the way she has by other men."

"None of the stuff they say about her is true, Dad." He thought of his brother Evan and the conversation they needed to have—soon. "None of it."

"That so? Interesting."

"What do I do? If she had her way, she'd send me packing, and I'd never see her again."

Big Mac ran a hand over the white stubble on his jaw. "You gotta keep showing up, prove to her that you're different than all the others who've let her down."

"Make a nuisance out of myself?"

"If that's what it takes."

"I can do that," Mac said, settling into the idea. He'd done a pretty good job of it so far.

"'Course you can. But don't grovel, son. Any woman would be lucky to have you. You remember that."

Mac smiled. He could always count on his father to be on his side. "So would it be okay if, while I'm making a nuisance out of myself with her, I try this place on for size for a while? No promises or anything."

Big Mac squeezed his son's forearm. "That'd be more than okay with me."

"Don't say anything to Mom about what I said about Maddie. She's got something against her, for some reason."

"I won't say a word."

Mac downed the last of his beer. "Mind if I borrow your truck for the night? I'm bringing Maddie and her son over to the house for dinner."

Big Mac withdrew the keys from his shorts pocket. "Have at it."

Mac gave his father the key to the motorcycle. In an impulsive move, he leaned in and kissed his father's cheek. "Love you."

Big Mac hugged him for a long moment.

Mac realized he'd rendered his old man speechless. "Thanks for the beer. See you at dinner."

Mac parked the truck in Maddie's driveway and went up the stairs to the small deck where Libby was stretched out in a lounge chair, reading a book.

"Hey," she said. "Back already?"

"How's it going?"

"It's been great. They're both sacked out at the moment."

"Thank you so much for hanging out today. I really appreciate it."

"I enjoyed it. She's really very lovely. I'm sorry I haven't taken the time before now to get to know her better."

Mac glanced at the door. "She could use a few friends in this town."

Libby stashed her book in her tote bag and got up to give Mac a kiss on the cheek. "She doesn't know it yet, but she's damned lucky to have you in her life."

Hit with an unusual burst of insecurity, Mac rolled his bottom lip between his teeth. "If she had her way, she'd never see me again."

"I don't think it'll take all that much to change her mind. You know what you need to do."

"Yeah." He thought of what his father said about showing up and proving that he'd never let her down. "Thanks again, Lib." He gave her a hug and watched her walk down the driveway toward town where she lived in a suite of rooms at the Beachcomber with her husband and two children.

Taking a deep breath, Mac opened the screen door and stepped inside. Maddie lay on the bed with her uninjured arm hooked over her head and the sheet pulled up to her shoulders. It was the first time, he realized, that he'd seen her so unguarded. Moving carefully so as not to disturb her, he went to the bathroom, quickly showered off the grime from the long day and, wearing just his boxers, crawled into bed next to her, intending to sleep for at least an hour and a half of the two hours they had before they were due at his parents' house.

But then she turned toward him, slipped an arm around his waist and drew him in close to her.

Steeped in her scent and softness, Mac was suddenly wide awake and fully erect. He had no idea if she was awake or having yet another of her vivid dreams. Curious as to what she would do, he put an arm around her and brought her as close to him as he dared.

Her breath skittered across his chest, stirring him even more.

With his heart beating a rapid staccato, he couldn't move or breathe. *This is love.* Finally, he understood. This was what made sane men into fools. He smoothed his hand over her hair and down her back.

She released a contented sigh and burrowed in closer, until her lips were pressed to his bare chest.

Mac had never been happier in his life.

In her dream, Maddie was falling. From where or what she didn't know, but the falling sensation had her flailing for traction. She woke up suddenly to find her face pressed to a hard male chest. His now-familiar scent found its way through the sleepy fog in her brain.

Mac.

Where had he come from? She studied his strong, handsome face, slack with sleep, and wanted to kiss him all over. Had she ever felt that way about any man before? No. Never. He was so big and strong, and he held her just right. She couldn't even think about the pain radiating from her arm and leg when she was so wrapped up in his embrace. But then she remembered all the reasons why this was a bad idea and began to work her way free of him.

His arms tightened around her. "Stay," he muttered, his voice groggy and sexy with sleep.

"I can't."

"Shhh." He kept his eyes closed as he combed his fingers through her hair. God, she loved when he did that. "Stay with me. I need you."

All the fight went out of her when he said those words. No one had ever needed her before. Only Thomas, and as wonderful as that was, it wasn't the same as being needed by Mac McCarthy.

Maddie didn't exactly relax, but she stopped trying to get away from him.

After a long period of silence during which she reveled in the feel of his fingers spooling through her hair, she said, "How was it today?"

"Enlightening."

"What do you mean?"

"I see now why you think they're bastards."

Maddie winced. "Mac, when I said that, I didn't know—"

"S'okay, honey. They treat you like crap, but that's going to change."

"What's going to change?" she asked, nervous about what he'd done.

"You won't get the worst rooms anymore."

"What did you do?"

"Had a little talk with my mother. It's all taken care of."

"You're going to get me fired."

"They wouldn't dare. Don't worry about that."

"Libby mentioned a job today." Maddie hadn't even allowed herself to think about the possibility. . .

"You aren't really going to make me go there for dinner, are you?"

"It'll be fun."

"It'll be torture."

"I'll be right there with you the whole time."

"Promise?"

She couldn't get over the way he looked at her, as if she was everything he'd ever wanted. How was that possible? The warmth she saw in his cool blue eyes made her heart flutter with desire. If this was one of her crazy dreams, she hoped she never woke up.

"I promise." He caressed her face for a long moment before he leaned in to touch a tentative kiss to her lips.

Even knowing she could be making the biggest mistake of her life, Maddie reached for him. Even knowing if he left her the way the others had, she might never recover, she kissed him. Even knowing he had a power over her that she'd never given anyone before him, she caressed his tongue with hers and loved the groan that rumbled through him.

Mac rolled them so he was on top of her and then froze, tearing his lips free of hers. "Oh, man. I'm sorry. I got so carried away I forgot for a second about your cuts."

"It's okay." She sank her fingers into his hair and brought his mouth back to hers. Suddenly, she was starving for more of the way he made her feel. She slid her good leg free of the sheet and hooked it around his much longer leg.

"Maddie," he whispered, his lips hovering just above hers. "God, you make me so crazy." Rocking against her, he drew a gasp from her and recaptured her mouth for the most carnal, sensuous kiss of her life. He used everything in his arsenal—tongue, lips and teeth—to devour her. She clung to him, certain that if she let go she'd be hurtled into space. Just when she thought she couldn't bear the intensity of the desire he'd stirred in her for another second, he softened the kiss and destroyed her with tenderness.

Mac drew back so he could see her face. "What kind of job?"

"Head of housekeeping at the Beachcomber."

"Really? That's awesome, honey!"

She wanted to remind him once again that she wasn't his honey, but as they were lying in a bed together, it didn't seem like the right time to mention it. "The woman who does the job now is retiring after this season. When Libby found out I'd worked at McCarthy's for eight years, she offered me the job. It's full-time, year-round with benefits."

"Wow. What did you say?"

"I told her I had to think about it."

"What's there to think about? It would take care of a lot of your worries."

"She only offered it to me because of you."

"No way. Libby's totally turned that place around. Remember how it was on the brink of bankruptcy ten or so years ago?"

Maddie nodded.

"Libby brought it back to life. In fact, not too many people know this, but the owners made her a partner two years ago."

"Good for her."

Mac linked his fingers through hers, careful as always not to touch her sore palm. "And good for you. If she offered you a job, it's because you're right for it."

"You really think so?"

"Of course I do. I got a good idea of how hard you work today. Wouldn't it be nice to make more money and not have to work that hard?"

"It'd be different, that's for sure."

"So you'll do it?"

"I have friends at McCarthy's. People I've worked with for years."

"Nothing says you couldn't hire them away to work at the Beachcomber."

Maddie smiled. "Then your mother would hate me even more."

"She doesn't hate you." He released her hand and looped a strand of her hair around his finger. "She just doesn't know you very well. Yet."

His lips sank into hers before moving over her face, her nose, her eyelids and then down to her neck.

Maddie shuddered as sensation after sensation zipped through her, settling into a throb of desire between her legs. She wanted him just as much as he wanted her, but still the fear outweighed the desire.

"I could kiss you forever," he whispered, "and never get enough."

"You frighten me," she replied in the same soft tone.

His entire body tensed. The mouth that had been toying so deliciously with her ear went still. He raised his head to meet her eyes. "I do?"

As she stopped him from shifting off her, she realized he thought she meant physically. If only it was that simple. "You make me want things I decided a long time ago weren't in the cards for me."

Awareness dawned on him, and he relaxed a bit. "Maybe life has dealt you a new hand. A better hand. Isn't that possible?"

"I've learned not to gamble. It doesn't work out well for me."

"I wish there was something I could say or do to convince you that you can trust me."

"I wish there was, too."

"You're making me pay for things other people did to you."

"I know that."

"It's not fair."

Unable to resist the urge to touch him, she brushed the hair off his forehead, delighting in the silky feel of it. "I know that, too."

"I'm going to show you." He shifted off her to lie on his back next to her but kept a firm grip on her hand.

Glancing down, she noticed his still-impressive erection and quickly brought her eyes back to his face. She had to acknowledge that unlike most men she'd known in the past, he didn't seem to be driven solely by the whims of his little brain. "Show me what?"

"That I'm different. That you can trust me."

"I don't want you to think I don't appreciate—"

"I have no interest in your appreciation." He turned his head so he could see her. "I want so much more than that from you."

She studied the face she'd grown so fond of so quickly. Already he was more familiar to her than people she'd known all her life. "Why me?"

His mouth quirked at the corners. "Because."

"That's all you've got?"

Shrugging, he said, "If I told you all the reasons, you'd run screaming for your life."

"Try me. Give me one good reason."

Mac rubbed at the stubble on his chin as he gave that some thought. Then he turned those formidable blue eyes on her, and the blood heated in her veins. "Promise you won't run screaming?"

Maddie gestured to the bandage on her leg. "I promise."

He brought their joined hands to his lips and pressed a kiss to her palm. "Being around you makes me breathless and needy and horny as hell, but that's only the start of it. You make me want to be a better man so I'll deserve you and Thomas."

Maddie stared at him. No one had ever said such things to her.

"How was that?" he asked after a long period of silence.

She wished she had words to match what he'd given her, but her brain had turned to mush along with the rest of her. Clearing her throat, she said, "Pretty good."

Mac winced. "Only pretty good? Well, at least you didn't run off screaming." He glanced at his watch and groaned. "We need to get going or we'll be late."

Maddie desperately wanted to convince him to stay right here where everything felt safe and a tad bit magical. She feared their bubble would burst the minute they let others inside. "You must be so tired."

"I'll sleep well tonight unless you decide to talk my ear off again."

Maddie laughed as she play-punched his shoulder. "I can't believe you said that!" She sat up slowly and painfully.

"We should see to those wounds."

"Libby did it earlier after I took a shower. She said the one on my elbow looked like it might be infected."

"I want to see it."

"Later. I need to go get Thomas up, or he'll be awake all night."

Mac bounded off the bed and headed for Thomas's room. "I'll do it. You take it easy."

Maddie sat there for a long time after he left the room, thinking about what he'd said and wishing she had it in her to believe they really had a chance.

CHAPTER 8

She didn't say a word on the ride to North Harbor. With Thomas in his car seat between them, Mac tried to engage her in conversation that went nowhere. Instead, she stared out the passenger-side window, and he wondered if he'd made a huge mistake insisting she join him for dinner at his parents' house. She'd fretted for half an hour over what to wear and had finally settled on a pale pink T-shirt and a denim miniskirt that showed off her long, toned legs. Libby must've painted her toes, because Mac didn't recall seeing the sexy hot pink polish the day before—and he was fairly certain he'd noticed everything about her.

Half a mile from his parents' house, Mac pulled the truck over to the side of the road.

"What're you doing?"

"Do you really not want to go? We can go back to your place, get a pizza from Mario's, rent a movie—"

She startled and amused him when she reached over to squish his lips shut. "After I went through all that to figure out what to wear, we're going to your mother's. Now drive."

Mac smiled at her show of bravado. He had no doubt that she'd much prefer the pizza and movie. "Yes, ma'am."

Her bravado had faded again by the time they pulled up to the big white house. Mac freed Thomas from his car seat and carried him around to the other side of the car to help Maddie. "Take your time," he said, moved by the flash of pain that crossed her face as she slid down from the cab.

She clutched his arm. "Stay close, okay?"

"I will." Before they stepped into the light, he stopped her, tilted her chin up and kissed her. "You're here because I want them to know you're important to me. If anyone makes you feel uncomfortable, we'll leave, okay?"

"I don't want to cause trouble between you and your family."

"You won't."

"If you say so," she said as they stepped through the gate into the light.

"I say so."

Big Mac met them at the door. "Come in, come in."

He greeted Maddie with a kiss to her cheek and tickled the bottom of Thomas's foot, drawing a deep chortle from the baby.

"Looks good on you, son," Big Mac said with a nod to the baby on Mac's hip.

"He's a cool little dude." Mac felt a surge of pride as he showed off the baby. "Always happy."

"I didn't know what you liked to drink, Maddie." Big Mac ushered them into the formal living room Linda reserved for company. Mac and Maddie sat together on the sofa. "So I got three kinds of wine and three kinds of beer." He ticked them off on his fingers.

Mac could tell that Maddie was touched by his father's attentiveness. And while it was odd to be treated as a guest in the house where he grew up, he appreciated the warm welcome his father had given her.

She turned those big caramel eyes on him, and his belly fluttered with awareness. "What're you having?"

"A light beer."

"That sounds good to me, too."

"Two light beers, coming right up," Big Mac said. "Is the baby all set?"

"Yes," she said. "Thank you."

When they were alone, Mac squeezed her hand. "So far so good?"

"Your father is very sweet. I haven't really talked to him before. He's never here when I clean."

"He's the best guy I know."

Janey came bursting through the front door. "Hey! Sorry I'm late." She stopped short when she saw Mac, Maddie and Thomas on the sofa. "Oh well. You're front room company now, big brother?"

"Apparently." Mac rose to kiss his sister. "This is Thomas."

"Wow, what a doll!" Janey extended a finger, and Thomas wrapped his hand around it while studying her with the serious expression he used to size up new people.

"I don't think you know Maddie," Mac said.

"We knew each other years ago in school," Janey said. "Nice to see you."

"You, too. Congratulations on your engagement."

Janey flashed a grin. "Thanks. It's the longest engagement in the history of the world."

"The big day will be here before you know it, brat," Mac said.

"Until then, I have to be satisfied with a monthly booty call," she said with a long-suffering sigh.

Mac cringed. "I don't know *why* you have to say that stuff to me."

"Because it makes you nuts," Janey said, laughing.

Mac glanced at Maddie, who sent him a sympathetic smile. "My *baby* sister," he grumbled as he rejoined her on the sofa. "Horrifying."

Big Mac came back into the room with three bottles of beer and handed two of them to Mac and Maddie. "Hi, honey," he said, kissing Janey. "I suppose you'll want my beer."

She plucked it out of his hand. "But of course."

Big Mac shook his head and glanced at Maddie. "See what I put up with?"

Maddie responded with a girlish giggle, and Mac could tell that his father had already won her over.

Big Mac left the room muttering about a man not being able to get a beer in his own house and returned a minute later with Linda, who he seemed to propel ahead of him into the room.

"There you are," Linda said, swooping in to kiss Mac. "And Maddie, hello, how're you feeling?"

"A little better, Mrs. McCarthy. Thank you for having me."

Linda's smile was brittle, but Mac was certain only her family would know it as less than genuine. "It's my pleasure. This must be Thomas, who I've heard so much about."

As he thrust the baby up and into his mother's arms, Mac hoped she wasn't referring to the speculation around town about the baby's father.

"Oh," Linda sputtered. "My. Well. You're a cute little fella, aren't you?"

Thomas picked that moment to loudly fill his diaper.

Janey howled with laughter.

Maddie gasped, tried to get up quickly and grimaced when her injured limbs refused to cooperate.

Mac eased her back down. "I've got it."

"You don't want to deal with that."

"Believe me, it's the least of what I've dealt with today." He took the baby from his mother and grabbed the diaper bag. "Come on, pal. Let's get you cleaned up." Before he left the room, he noticed his father and sister watching him with nothing but amusement while his mother fumed. Mac was torn between needing to tend to the baby and not wanting to leave Maddie.

"We'll take good care of Maddie," Big Mac said.

"Thanks, Dad." On the way up the stairs, Mac caught Maddie's eye and winked at her. "I'll be quick."

She sent him a grateful smile that warmed him all the way through.

Over the pot roast dinner Mac had requested, Maddie stayed quiet and listened to their banter. Mac clearly adored his father and sister as well as his three brothers. Maddie found it interesting that he tended to give Linda one-word answers but engaged more naturally with his father and sister. He kept Thomas on his lap and managed to eat with one hand in a manner that was more common after months—rather than days—of practice.

Maddie wondered if anyone else noticed that Linda completely ignored her as she managed to work a list of the island's most eligible women into the conversation. Maddie could definitely see Mac with someone like Doro Chase or one of the other prominent women Linda mentioned. At least with Doro he'd be on an equal social footing and wouldn't be fodder for the gossip mill the way he would with her. The idea of him with someone else saddened her, which was ridiculous, really. It wasn't like he belonged to her or anything. What was she even doing here, eating at this table in the house where she was hired help?

Mac's hand landed on her thigh.

Stirred by his touch—as always—she glanced over at him.

"Everything all right?"

"Of course," she managed to say but could tell he didn't believe her.

"Mom," Janey said, "maybe you should can the social register for tonight. Mac's here with a date. He doesn't want to hear about other women."

Mac sent his sister a grateful smile.

"No one told me they were on a date." Linda's frosty eyes skipped over Maddie and landed on her son. "I thought we were just having dinner."

"I believe I was quite clear about that when we spoke earlier," he said, apparently capable of the frosty stare himself.

Maddie's stomach began to hurt.

"What'd you make for dessert, Lin?" Big Mac asked with a warm smile for Maddie.

"Chocolate cake for Mac."

"Thomas is getting tired," Mac said. "We aren't staying for dessert."

Thomas was fine, but Maddie appreciated that somehow Mac sensed she wasn't.

"You can't go yet!" Linda said. "You just got here."

"We need to get the baby home, and Maddie's still recovering from her injuries."

"She looks fine to me."

Mac got up and helped her out of her chair. "She's not fine. I probably shouldn't have dragged her out tonight." To his sister, Mac said, "You'll help Mom clean up?"

"Yep." Janey got up to kiss him good-bye. To Maddie, she said, "If you ever need a babysitter for that cute little guy, call me."

"That's very sweet of you," Maddie said as Janey and her father started clearing the table.

Mac escorted Maddie to the front hall. "I just realized I forgot the diaper bag upstairs. I'll be right back." Still holding Thomas, he dashed up the stairs. As she watched him go, Maddie noticed the bruise on his leg from the bike crash had gotten dark and angry-looking overnight.

"You're fooling yourself," Linda said in an exaggerated whisper.

Startled, Maddie turned to her. "Excuse me?"

"He might be having fun playing house for now, but you'll never get him to stay."

Shocked, Maddie had no idea what to say and was relieved to hear Mac's heavy footsteps on the stairs. She needed to get out of there. Right now. Even though she desperately needed the money, she decided she'd never clean this house again.

"Ready?" Mac said, his hand on the small of her back.

"Thank you for dinner," Maddie said on her way out the door.

Mac gave his mother a kiss on the cheek. "Thanks, Mom."

On the way back to town, Maddie's heart beat fast with shock and dismay. Part of her wanted to take him home and have her wicked way with him just to prove Linda wrong. If she wouldn't be risking her own well-protected heart, she'd do it in a minute. She ventured a glance over at him. His eyes were fixed on the road, his jaw tight with tension.

"That was a mistake," he said.

"It was fine."

"No, it wasn't." He reached over Thomas's seat for her hand. "Don't hold my mother against me. She has no power over me whatsoever, and she hates that."

Maddie didn't know what to say. Sure he was his own man, and his mother couldn't tell him what to do. But Linda could make their lives miserable if she chose to, and Mac was the kind of son who wanted to please his parents, not alienate them. Maddie had no desire to be responsible for a rift between Mac and his mother, which was just another reason not to let things with him get out of hand.

"What're you thinking?" he asked.

"That I'm tired and I hurt." He didn't need to know the pain was mostly on the inside.

He winced. "I'm sorry. We'll get you home and into bed. I shouldn't have dragged you out tonight. Next time I'll listen to you."

There won't be a next time, Maddie thought, filled with sadness. She knew that not pursuing a relationship with him was the right thing for both of them. If only it didn't hurt so much to think about never seeing him again after he moved out.

Mac beat himself up all the way back to town. *What the hell was I thinking? Huge, huge mistake.*

Back at Maddie's, Mac helped her out of the truck and noticed she was moving even slower than she had earlier. *We should've stayed home and had pizza. Damn it!*

As he carried Thomas and walked slowly up the stairs with Maddie, Mac tried to think of how he could undo the damage this night had done to their fledgling relationship. What could he say? What should he do? Unaccustomed to feeling so insecure around a woman, he had no idea what to do.

"I'll give him a quick bath and get him ready for bed," he offered.

"Thank you."

The night before, she would've argued with him. Mac found that he much preferred the arguments to this weary acceptance. He moved quickly to take care of Thomas and brought him and his last bottle of the day to Maddie. Mac wanted to stretch out next to them on the sofa bed and hold her while she fed the baby, but instead, he straightened the apartment and gathered the growing pile of laundry the three of them had generated.

"I'll toss this in at the marina when I go to work tomorrow."

"You don't have to do ours—"

He bit back a burst of temper. "It's no problem." When she didn't fire back, he knew it was bad. Whatever progress they'd made had been undone by a couple of hours with his mother.

She was quiet, docile even. Not at all like the Maddie he'd enjoyed sparring with the last two days. He discovered he didn't like her this way, even if it was easier. He wanted his smart-mouthed Maddie back.

After he got Thomas settled in his crib, he returned to the living room where Maddie had removed her bandages. The wound on her elbow had gotten pink and puffy with infection since Mac last saw it. "We should probably get that looked at."

"Libby gave me some antibiotic ointment to put on it."

Mac reached for the tube. "I'll do it."

She took it from him. "I couldn't bear to have someone else touch it."

Because it hurt or because it was him? Frustrated, he watched her dab the clear ointment gingerly on the angry-looking cut. Then she did the same to her knee and hand.

"Libby said I should leave them uncovered tonight to let the air get to them."

"She knows what she's talking about. She's had a lot of medical training." Mac stood, peeled off his T-shirt and tossed it into the pile of laundry. Turning, he caught Maddie staring at him with a needy, hungry look on her face. He took a step toward her. "Maddie—"

Her expression shifted immediately to that impassive, unreachable thing she did so well. "Would you mind terribly sleeping on the floor tonight? I don't even want the sheet to touch me."

Tension lodged in his chest. "Of course not." He set out the couch cushions and unrolled his sleeping bag. When they were both settled, he reached up to turn off the light. Unlike the night before, there was no conversation. Earlier in the day, he'd been happier and more content than he'd ever been in his life. Now, even though he was as tired as he'd been in ages, Mac lay awake for a long time feeling edgy and desperate—as if he had somehow managed to lose something he'd never really had in the first place.

Over the next three days, they slid into a routine that began with Mac taking Thomas on a morning walk for coffee and breakfast. After Maddie nursed the baby, Mac delivered him to Tiffany's, rushed through Maddie's shifts at the hotel and spent as much time as he could at the marina measuring and outlining the needed repairs. He planned to start on the roof of the main building and had a four-man crew lined up to help him beginning the following Monday. By three o'clock each day, he was back at Maddie's to help out at Tiffany's daycare.

He spent the nights on Maddie's floor, wishing they could somehow get back to where they'd been before he made the mistake of subjecting her to his mother. Wednesday evening, after they finished up at the daycare, Mac suggested they walk over to Mario's for pizza. Since Maddie was finally getting around much better, she agreed.

By now, people in town had grown accustomed to seeing them together, and while they still attracted some stares, Mac had learned to ignore the unwanted attention. He wasn't sure Maddie was able to ignore it, but she hadn't mentioned it to him. In fact, she hadn't said much of anything at all to him in three days. She seemed to be biding her time until she could be rid of him, and with every passing day, Mac's desperation grew more intense.

He'd tried to give her some space to get used to him and the idea that he was interested in her. But like the disastrous dinner at his parents' house, that, too, had backfired on him. The more space he gave her, the more remote she became, until he was certain he would explode if something didn't change—soon.

"Tomorrow's your day off at the hotel, right?" he asked.

"Yes, and the daycare. Tiffany doesn't teach dance on Thursdays. That's when I usually clean your mother's house."

"I have to go to the mainland for some building supplies. I thought maybe you and Thomas would like to come. We could go anywhere you want to while we're over there."

He watched the debate play out on her face—wistfulness, yearning, nervousness and finally, resignation.

"Thanks, but I think I'll just stay here with Thomas. I'm feeling much better. There's really no need for you to take care of us anymore."

Mac had never experienced such pain. Reaching for her good hand, he linked his fingers with hers and watched her take a nervous look around the crowded restaurant. "Come with me. It'll be fun. We can buy Thomas some new big boy clothes and a bike. And a football. He needs a football. I noticed he doesn't have one."

That drew a tentative smile. "He can't even walk yet."

"It won't be long now."

"I don't know," she said with a worried glance at the baby, who sat on Mac's lap like he belonged there.

He squeezed her hand. "Come with me. It'll do you good to get off the island for a day." Knowing most of her expressions by now, Mac could tell she was tempted. He flashed his most charming grin. *"Come on. . ."*

"All right! Fine. We'll go. God, you're relentless!"

Swamped with relief, Mac sat back in the booth but didn't release her hand. "Good." It wasn't a breakthrough, exactly, but it was one more day together. Right about now, he'd take it.

Thanks to his connections with Joe, Mac was able to get his father's truck on the first boat off the island at eight the next morning. Joe invited them to join him in the wheelhouse, but Mac wanted as much time alone with Maddie as he could get, so he declined.

"Whatcha got going on there, pal?" Joe asked with a grin as Mac bought their tickets.

"Hopefully, the most important thing I'll ever do in my life."

Joe's eyes nearly fell out of his head. "No way."

Mac glanced over at Maddie, who was watching the seagulls with Thomas while she waited for Mac to drive the truck on the boat. "Yes way."

Once onboard, they stood on the bow of the ferry where a light spray hit them every time the boat crested a wave. Thomas loved the air and the water and the motion of the ferry. Mac kept a firm grip on him as they stood at the rail.

"This is nice," Maddie said, looking more tranquil than he'd ever seen her as they watched the northern end of the island disappear into the morning fog. He'd known that getting her off the island would be good for her. He hoped it would also be good for *them*.

"When was the last time you were off-island?"

Maddie thought about that. "About a year ago. Before he was born."

"That'd make me nuts! Don't you ever feel confined?"

She shrugged. "I've gotten used to it.

"You know, it's funny, when I lived here as a kid, I couldn't leave if I felt confined. It would be totally different as an adult. I could leave any damned time I wanted to." He laughed at the somewhat major revelation. "That never occurred to me until right this second."

Maddie flashed him a rueful smile. "The confinement used to drive me crazy, especially when I wanted to go to college. I didn't have the money to pay tuition and live there, too, and it wasn't like I could commute."

"I've never thought about that before." Of course he hadn't. He'd gone to college on a full athletic scholarship and never once had to worry about paying for it. "What would you have studied?"

"Maybe oceanography or biology. Something to do with the water. I've always been obsessed by anything involving the ocean."

Fascinated by this new insight, Mac studied her face as she stared out at the water, lost in thought. "There're online courses you could take."

"I was halfway through an online associate's program when I got pregnant." She took Thomas's hand and smiled warmly at the baby, making Mac jealous. "Now I have other priorities."

He wanted her to direct that dazzling smile at him. What he wouldn't give for just one genuine smile, the one that engaged her eyes as well as her full, sexy mouth. "Maybe you can go back and finish someday."

"Maybe."

They docked just after nine in the fishing village of Galilee on Rhode Island's south shore. With Thomas in his car seat and Maddie riding shotgun, Mac drove the truck off the ferry into the crowded port.

"How about some breakfast and then we can do whatever you want?" Mac suggested.

"Sure, that sounds good."

Over eggs and toast at a greasy spoon, he asked where she wanted to go.

She hesitated, but only for a moment. "The mall," she said with a delightfully girlish grin.

Thrilled to see her playful side reemerging after three days of distance, Mac McCarthy—a man who had never once willingly stepped foot in a shopping mall—took his lady to the biggest, brightest, busiest mall in the state of Rhode Island.

Maddie loved the excitement and elegance of The Providence Place Mall. A ruthless bargain shopper, she haunted the sale racks in all the children's clothing stores and got some nice deals on summer clothes for Thomas. Worried, as always, about her finances, she bought nothing for herself.

Pushing Thomas in the stroller they'd brought from the island, Mac followed her around with unwavering patience. He never rushed her or showed an ounce of displeasure, but she knew he had to be hating every minute of this. Mindful that he had things he needed to get done that day, she glanced up at him. "I'm all set if you want to go."

His brows narrowed over those steel blue eyes. "We just got here. You haven't looked at anything for yourself."

"I don't need anything."

"Thomas and I are going for a walk. We'll meet you back here in an hour."

"What will you do with all that time?"

"Pick up a few things Janey asked me to get."

Maddie nibbled on her thumbnail as she studied him. "Are you sure?"

He leaned in and kissed her cheek. "Go. Have fun. Spend some money. That's what credit cards are for."

Laughing, she didn't even mind the kiss that zipped through her like a live wire. "You're a bad influence."

"Thank you. Now go."

An hour to herself in a mall! Flitting from store to store, she bought a few new tops and some jeans. She gave herself one hour off from worrying about money and stocked up on underwear, bras and socks. Outside Victoria's Secret, she stared longingly at an ivory silk nightgown in the window that would look ridiculous on her. Still, it was fun to look and to imagine. . .

When she met Mac at the designated spot, she discovered that he, too, had put the hour to good use. The basket under Thomas's stroller was full to over-flowing with bags. She saw a baseball bat sticking out the top of one of them. When she raised a questioning eyebrow, he replied with a shrug and adorably sheepish grin. Mixed in with the others, a pink-striped bag caught her attention. "You bought something for Janey at Victoria's Secret?"

"It's not for Janey," he said with a secretive smile.

Maddie's knees weakened. What had he done? She had no idea, but she was not about to ask him. She'd learned not to encourage his outrageous behavior.

"Ready to go?" he asked, sliding an arm around her shoulders.

"Yes." As they walked to the parking garage, Maddie glanced up at him. "Thank you."

He kissed the top of her head. "My pleasure, honey."

Mac took the long way back to the ferry, driving them through Newport to stop at the carousel at First Beach. Thomas loved the merry-go-round, and Mac sprang for five rides before Maddie reminded him of the time. They had a ferry to catch.

"You're totally spoiling him," Maddie said as they set out across the Newport Bridge to the lumber supply place. And me, she wanted to add but didn't.

"So?"

"I'd hate to get him used to it. This time next week, he'll be back to his boring life, wondering where his sugar daddy has gone." The instant the words were out of her mouth, Maddie regretted them. To refer to Mac as Thomas's daddy, even as a joke, was so wrong and unfair. She could see that Mac was becoming attached to her son and vice versa.

"I'm not going anywhere," he said, but his hand tightened on the wheel.

"You're going back to Miami."

"Not anytime soon."

Maddie didn't want to be relieved, but the more time she spent with him, the more she wished she could keep him forever. She'd never known a man so thoughtful and caring and sincere. Add that he was sexy as hell and he become one heck of an irresistible package. During their lovely day together, she'd begun to feel like a fool for resisting him. Maybe she should give in and have a rip-roaring affair with him. The whole town thought she already was, so why not go for it? At least then, after he went home to Miami, she'd have the memories to sustain her. But what would sustain her heart if she gave even a portion of it to him?

Too late, the devil on her left shoulder said. *You already have.*

CHAPTER 9

Tucked into his stroller, Thomas slept on the ferry ride back to Gansett. Sleepy herself after the nicest day she'd had in years, Maddie let her head drop to Mac's shoulder. He put his arm around her and settled her against his chest. Maddie was letting her eyes drift shut when they connected with a familiar face on the other side of the ferry.

He smiled at her.

Maddie gasped.

"What, honey?" Mac asked.

"Oh my God," she whispered. "Thomas's father." Automatically, she brought the stroller closer to her.

As the tall, dark-haired man approached them, Maddie straightened, and her heart began to hammer in her chest. She noticed he had more gray in his hair than the last time she'd seen him, but otherwise he hadn't changed.

Mac tightened his arm around her.

"I thought that was you, Maddie. How are you?"

Momentarily paralyzed, she couldn't form a rational thought. "I'm. . . ah . . . I'm good."

He glanced at Mac, and Maddie remembered her manners. "Tom Wilkinson, this is, um—"

Mac extended his right hand. "Mac McCarthy, Maddie's husband." He gestured to the stroller. "Our son Garrett. Nice to meet you."

Twisting her head, Maddie stared at Mac, but he just gave her a bland look that said, "Roll with it."

"You're married," Tom said with the charming smile that had convinced her to part with her virginity—not that he ever figured that out. "Well, that's disappointing."

"Excuse me?" Maddie asked in a strangled tone.

"I was on my way to see you."

"Oh."

"Yeah, my bad," he said with what seemed like genuine regret. "I guess I waited too long."

"Maddie's not the kind of girl you let get away," Mac said.

Maddie's breath got caught in her throat when Tom leaned over to peek in at Thomas.

"Beautiful baby."

"Thanks," Mac said. "We like him."

Good answer, Maddie thought, grateful that he could speak, since she was incapable at the moment. Her heart beat so fast she wondered if it would explode in her chest.

"You're a lucky man," Tom said to Mac.

"Believe me, I know."

"It's good to see you, Maddie."

She cleared her throat and stuck her shaking hands between her knees. "Yes, you, too."

"Good luck to you both."

"Same to you."

Tom walked away, and Maddie sagged with relief. She'd imagined this moment a million times, expecting him to take one look at his son and just *know*.

But he hadn't. Because Mac had been so quick to say just the right thing, Tom had never even entertained the possibility.

Mac held her tight against him. "Breathe, baby," he whispered in her ear, raising goose bumps on her suddenly sensitive skin. "It's all over. Take a deep breath."

Maddie did as he said, and it helped to slow her galloping heart.

"You gave him his father's name."

"I wanted him to have something. . ."

"I understand."

She glanced at him, the contact with his beautiful eyes filling her with an overwhelming awareness of him, of what he seemed to feel for her, of what she was beginning to feel for him. "I've been saying this a lot lately, but thank you. What you did—"

He tilted her chin and laid a soft, wet kiss on her lips. "Was also my pleasure."

After Mac got Thomas settled in his crib to finish his nap, he turned to Maddie, who had followed him into the bedroom. "Go out with me tonight."

She rolled her bottom lip between her teeth. "Like on a date?"

He took a step toward her. "Uh huh. A real date."

"We were out all day, and I can't leave Thomas."

Another step. "My sister will watch him. She'll love it." To hell with giving her space. He wanted her in his arms. Right now. Mac took a final step to close the distance between them and rested his hands on her hips, drawing her in close to him. "I want to take you out. Buy you a nice dinner. Woo you."

Maddie's face flushed. "You've already done so much. . ."

"I haven't done nearly enough." He leaned in, brushed his lips over hers, and reveled in her sharp intake of breath. Encouraged, he went back for more. As he kissed her, his hands traveled down her back to her bottom. When her arms encircled his neck, Mac lifted her and groaned into her mouth as her legs curled around his hips. Worried about disturbing the baby, he walked them to the hallway where he pressed her against the wall and kissed her as if he'd been starving for her, which, of course, he had.

Her fingers fisted in his hair, keeping his mouth anchored to hers. Wiggling tight against him, she made his legs go weak and stars dance in his eyes.

Mac kissed her until he had no choice but to come up for air. He buried his face in her fragrant hair and breathed in the scent he would recognize anywhere as hers. "Now that we've gotten the good-night kiss out of the way, what do you say? Will you go out with me?"

She smiled. "Are you sure Janey won't mind?"

"I'm positive."

"Then yes, I'd like to go out with you."

"Have I told you lately," he said, skimming kisses over her neck and face, "how much I like being married to you?"

That earned him the genuine, lusty laugh he'd grown to adore, and it was all he could do not to say the words right then and there. *I love you. I love you so much I ache with it.*

She caressed his face. "What are you thinking? Right now?"

Caught off guard, Mac had no idea what to say. "I can't tell you."

"Why?"

He kissed her lightly, fighting for control of his desire and emotions. "Because it would scare you."

"Oh come on. Just tell me."

"I'll make you a deal: if you still want to know what I was thinking after our date, I'll tell you."

"You'll tell me the truth?"

"Always." He kissed her again before he reluctantly lowered her to her feet. "I have to go drop the wood and stuff at the marina and get my dad's truck back to him. Will you be okay for a little while?"

"I'm fine. You don't need to hover over us like a mother hen anymore."

Kissing her nose and then her lips one last time, he said, "I love hovering over you. I'll be back to pick you up in an hour."

"And you'll call Janey?"

"Already taken care of."

"Awfully sure of yourself, weren't you?"

"I was hopeful. That's all." Framing her face, he kissed her once more. "I'll be back."

Mac unloaded the lumber from the back of the truck into a pile in the parking lot. Sweating under the late afternoon sun, he pulled off his T-shirt and reached for another sheet of plywood. He was just about finished when a willowy blonde approached him from the direction of the Tiki Bar, wineglass in hand. She sported a dark tan and wore a white tube top over hot pink shorts.

"You must be Mac," she purred in a voice that sounded like pure sex. "I've heard a lot about you."

Mac used his forearm to wipe the sweat from his forehead. "I'm afraid you have me at a disadvantage."

She released a sultry laugh. "Where are my manners? I'm Doro Chase."

He remembered the name from dinner the other night—the dinner he wanted to forget. "Ah, yes, you're a friend of my mother's. Good to meet you."

Her gaze traveled up and down his torso in obvious approval. "The pleasure is *all* mine."

God, she was so *ridiculous*! Had he ever seriously gone for this type? Well, yeah, but that was then, and this was now. He thought of the sweet, unassuming woman who waited for him in town, and all he wanted was to get back to her as fast as he could.

"Your mother says you'll be here a while," Doro said.

"That's right."

"We should get together sometime."

"I'm going to be really busy." As he put his shirt back on, he swore he saw disappointment in her blue eyes. He gestured to the sagging roof on the main building. "Lot of work to get done."

Her lip rolled into that foolish pout women did so well, but it had no effect on him. "You can't work *all* the time."

"You're absolutely right." Glancing at his watch, he said, "In fact, I have somewhere I need to be. You have a good night now."

As he got in the truck and drove away, Mac checked the rearview mirror to find her still standing where he'd left her, probably trying to figure out how she'd managed to let a live one slip away. He suspected that didn't happen very often to good old Doro.

At the top of the hill, Mac pulled into his parents' driveway where his motorcycle waited for him. He parked the truck and went into the garage to grab a helmet. Blowing the dust off, he strapped it to the back of the bike and gave the house a quick look. He'd love to say hello to his father but didn't want to run into his mother and have to answer fifty questions. As he weighed the pros and cons, she appeared at the door. Mac suppressed a groan.

"Hello, stranger."

"Hi, Mom. I was just dropping off the truck."

"I see that."

"Is Dad around?"

"In the shower." She opened the screen door and stepped onto the porch. "Want to come in? Have a beer?"

"Got to be somewhere."

"Of course you do."

"Look, Mom—"

"I don't know what kind of power that woman has over the men in this town, but it's apparently quite formidable."

Fighting to control his temper, Mac looked up to the heavens in search of patience. "You have no idea what you're talking about, and once again I'll remind you to be very careful."

"Or what?"

"Or I'll take her and her son and go back to Miami tomorrow. I'm far too old to be justifying myself to my mother."

"Oh, Mac. You could do so much better!"

He released a bitter laugh. "Like your good friend Doro Chase?"

"For one."

"I just had the pleasure, and she reminds me of a hundred other women I've known. Nothing about her interests me."

"And you know that after what? Five minutes?"

"Actually, it only took thirty seconds."

Before Linda could reply to that, Big Mac stepped onto the porch. "Hey, buddy. How was the mainland?"

Mac smiled, relieved to see his father. "It was a great day. I got everything I need to hit it hard on Monday."

"Sounds good. I appreciate that."

"Happy to help." Mac walked up the sidewalk to hand his father the keys to the truck.

"Yours are in the bike."

"Thanks. I'll see you guys tomorrow."

Big Mac slid his arm around his wife. "You have a good night, son."

"You, too."

Linda said nothing as Mac started the bike and drove off with a wave and a smile.

Still babying her injured hand, Maddie got Thomas fed, bathed and into his pajamas before she put him in his crib with some toys while she took a quick shower. Not that she was hoping anything would happen or anything, but she shaved her legs. Just in case. Oh, who was she kidding? She wanted something to happen!

When Mac pretended to be her husband and Thomas's father, he'd won over the last reluctant corner of her heart. She was sunk. How could she resist a guy who was not only capable of that kind of quick thinking but who also had a protective streak a mile wide? That didn't mean she wasn't still worried about a lot of things. But tonight she wasn't going to think about any of them. Tonight she was going to enjoy the first real date she'd had in years with a wonderful, sexy man who seemed to be wild about her.

Glancing down at the evil-looking scab and bruises on her leg, Maddie grimaced. Just what she needed on a night she was hoping for a little romance. She dried her hair until it fell thick and shiny to her shoulders. After smoothing fragrant lotion onto her entire body, she applied the barest bit of makeup and put on some of the new underwear she'd bought earlier. It was nice for once to wear a feminine bra, even if it didn't offer the same level of support. Tonight she didn't care. She cut the tags off a new white eyelet top cut lower than she normally wore and slid into a black miniskirt that came to mid-thigh. In the back of her closet, she found a pair of black high-heeled sandals.

She felt ready. She felt sexy. She felt nervous as hell. Placing a towel over her shoulder to protect her shirt, she lifted Thomas out of his crib and took him into the living room for a snuggle. If anything could calm her nerves, he could.

"We saw your father today, buddy."

His face scrunched into his adorably serious expression. Sometimes Maddie thought he could understand her every word. She couldn't wait to have a real conversation with him.

"I know you might think it's wrong that I didn't tell him about you, but he kept some important information from me, too. I don't think he's the kind of man we want in your life if he lies so easily, you know?"

Thomas reached for her hair and gave it a gentle tug.

"Does Mommy look pretty? I want to look pretty tonight. Let me ask you something—what do you think of Mac? Tell me the truth."

The baby let loose a gurgle and flashed a gummy smile full of new teeth.

"Figures. You guys all stick together." Maddie raised the baby so he could balance on his chubby legs. "He is pretty awesome, though, don't you think? He likes you a lot, too."

Thomas bounced up and down on his rubbery legs as a blob of drool ran down his chin.

Maddie blotted his face. "His sister Janey is coming over to play with you for a little while before bed. Will you be good for her so Mommy can have some fun tonight?"

More gurgling.

"Thanks, pal. I appreciate it."

When she heard Mac's motorcycle in the driveway, her heart skipped into overdrive. "Here he comes," she whispered.

Thomas let out an excited squeal, and Maddie was sure he recognized the sound of the bike by now. Her son was getting attached to their new friend, which pleased and scared her at the same time.

Mac came bounding up the stairs as if he couldn't wait to get to them. "Hey," he said as he came in the door. "Y'all ready for bed, big guy?" He leaned in to kiss the bouncing baby's wet cheek and then glanced at Maddie. His eyes widened. "Wow. You look gorgeous."

"Thanks," she said, her face heating.

He seemed to have trouble taking his eyes off her. "I just need to grab a quick shower. Janey will be here soon."

"I'm ready when you are." It was all so domestic, Maddie thought, as she watched him disappear into the bathroom. Her at home with the baby until Daddy gets home from work. A nice fantasy, that was for sure, and one she'd never pictured for herself until a sexy, thoughtful, decent guy knocked her off her bike. She wondered if that "accident" would turn out to be the best thing to ever happen to her.

"What do you think?" she asked Thomas.

"Does he talk back to you?" Janey asked from outside the screen door.

Maddie laughed and waved her in. "Not yet, but soon, I hope."

"Hey, little man," Janey said, reaching for the baby.

Thomas went to her but kept a wary eye on his mother.

"Look what I found on the way over." Janey produced a soft lamb and held him up for Thomas to see.

He studied the toy in his usual serious way.

Then Janey took hold of a loop attached to the lamb, and the baby smiled at the "Mary Had a Little Lamb" tune.

"That's adorable, Janey," Maddie said. "Where did you get it?"

"My friend owns Abby's Attic."

"Oh, I love that store!"

Mac emerged from the bathroom wearing a towel around his waist. "Forgot clothes," he said with a sheepish grin. "Hey, Janey."

His sister shielded her eyes. "Eww, put something on, will you?" To Maddie, she said, "See what I grew up with? It was like living in a freaking locker room."

Maddie's gaze roamed over Mac's muscular physique. "Mmm," she said, licking her lips. "Must've been a terrible hardship."

Gripping a handful of clean clothes, Mac flashed her that irrepressible grin and went back into the bathroom to get dressed.

"Damn," Janey said, laughing. "You two have a bad case of it, huh?"

"So it seems." Maddie sighed. "I'm probably cruising for disaster, but I can't seem to help myself."

"He's the best, Maddie. And I'm not just saying that because he's my big brother."

"So you wouldn't mind if we, you know. . ."

"I might've, before I got to know you, but now it seems you're just what he needs."

Touched, Maddie looked at Mac's sister with new appreciation. "Too bad your mother doesn't think so."

"Don't let her get to you. We just ignore her when she gets unreasonable."

Maddie smiled. For the second time that week, she felt like she might be making a new girlfriend, and both of them were thanks to Mac.

"Are you ladies talking about me?" Mac asked when he emerged from the bathroom wearing a navy blue polo shirt and khaki cargo shorts.

"Get over yourself," his sister said. "We have much better things to talk about than you."

Mac stuck his tongue out at her and reached for the baby. "I need a minute with my little buddy before we go." He swung him around in circles that had the baby squealing with delight.

"Don't get him all fired up for Janey," Maddie said. "While they're playing, let me show you where everything is."

"Sounds good."

As they were leaving a few minutes later, Thomas began to cry.

Mac put his arm around Maddie on the way down the stairs. "He'll be fine."

"What if he isn't? What if he gives her a hard time all night?"

"We'll call and check in a little while. If it's not going well, we'll come home."

Maddie looked up at him. "You wouldn't mind?"

"Of course not." He kissed her softly. "Whatever it takes to make sure you have a good time." He reached for the denim jacket he'd told her to bring and draped it around her shoulders. "You'll need that." Taking her hand, he led her to the bike and reached for the helmet.

"We're going on *that*?"

"Is that okay?"

Maddie eyed it with trepidation, thinking of her healing wounds.

"You'll be perfectly safe. I promise."

"I'm wearing a skirt."

"It's dark. No one will see a thing—except for maybe me, and that's more than fine with me."

Smiling at his irreverence, she said, "I've never been on a motorcycle."

"Then you're in for a treat." He helped her into the helmet. "You'll love it."

"I'm glad I bothered to do my hair," she said dryly.

"It'll bounce right back." Tipping his head, he pressed a kiss to her neck. "You look amazing, and you smell even better." He adjusted the strap under her chin and helped her onto the bike. Sliding on in front of her, he said, "Hold on as tight as you can."

Maddie laughed and wrapped her arms around him. "I can see right through you, McCarthy."

"Tighter," he said with a chuckle.

As she flattened her hands against his taut abs, she discovered he didn't have an extra ounce on him. With her legs snug against his hips and her hands flat against his belly, Maddie wanted to purr with contentment.

He started the bike and headed down the driveway.

Going by Tiffany's deck, Maddie noticed the glow of a cigarette, which lit her sister's face and illuminated her disapproval. Maddie turned away, refusing to let anyone ruin this night for her.

CHAPTER 10

They took the long way around the south side of the island on their way to Dominic's, an Italian restaurant located off the main drag. Maddie loved being on the motorcycle and was impressed by the skillful way Mac operated it. They leaned into turns as if they'd been riding together for years, and when they finally parked, Maddie took off the helmet and shook out her hair.

"Well?" he asked. "What'd you think?"

"I loved it."

"I did, too."

She looked at him, perplexed. "You do it all the time."

"Not with you pressed against me. That was the best ride ever."

She couldn't believe the stuff he said to her!

Before they went any further, he called Janey and confirmed that Thomas was doing just fine.

"That's a relief," Maddie said. "Thanks for checking."

"No problem. This used to be one of my favorite restaurants. Is it okay with you?"

"I've heard it's expensive."

"I don't care about that."

"You're not even working right now. How can you not care?"

"Honey, I'm a partner in the business. I get paid whether I work or not."

"That must be nice."

"It doesn't suck."

Maddie laughed, and he put his arm around her shoulders to lead her inside. "Does my hair look okay?"

"You're gorgeous. Every guy in there will be envious of me."

Could he be any more outrageous? "Right."

Inside, they were led to a table in the middle of the big busy dining room. Mac held her chair for her and then sat to her left rather than across the table. It pleased her that he wanted to sit so close to her, but Maddie felt the eyes of everyone in the room focused on her as heat crept up her neck to settle in her face.

"What's wrong?" Mac asked.

"Everyone is looking at us."

"They're wondering how I managed to get such a beautiful woman to have dinner with me."

Maddie shot him a withering look. "Sure they are." She took a drink from her glass of ice water. "Want to know what they're really thinking?"

He reached for her hand and linked his fingers with hers, sending a clear message to anyone who was watching. "I couldn't care less."

And just like that, he diffused her anxiety. Why did she care? "It must be nice to go through life not giving a thought to what anyone thinks of you."

"I've had it a bit easier on that front than you have."

When the waiter returned to the table, Mac perused the wine list and ordered a bottle of red. "Is there something else you'd rather have?" he asked Maddie.

"No, wine is fine. Thank you."

"Very good," the waiter said. "I'll be right back to take your order."

Maddie scanned the menu and didn't see a single entree for less than thirty dollars.

"What looks good to you, hon?" Mac asked.

"I'm not really that hungry. I'll probably just go with soup."

"Oh, come on. You can do better than that."

"Really, that's all I want."

He put down his menu and leaned in close to her. "What's the matter, Maddie?"

Her face once again heated with embarrassment. That had happened more since she'd known him than in her whole life before him. "The prices are ridiculous," she whispered.

"Maddie, honey, please. Have whatever you want."

"I could live for two weeks on what this one meal will cost."

"Would you rather go somewhere else?" He brought her hand to his lips. "I want you to have a good time tonight. I don't care where we go."

"I'm sorry. You're trying to do something nice, and I'm ruining it."

"You're being practical, and I'm being frivolous."

"I can't help it. I haven't had much of a chance to be frivolous."

"Would you mind letting me spoil you a bit? Just for tonight? Pick something fabulous that makes your mouth water just reading about it—and don't look at the cost."

"I don't know if I can do that."

"Then I'll do it for you." He flipped open the menu. "You've told me you love shrimp. How about the scampi?"

She wrinkled her nose. "Too garlicky."

"What if I have it, too? Then we'll both stink when we make out later."

Maddie laughed even as his words filled her with edgy anticipation. "What are my other options?"

"Seafood fra diavolo."

"What's in that?"

Mac read the description of the spicy pasta dish that included clams, mussels, scallops and shrimp.

"That does sound good. Is it under fifty dollars?"

When he raised a dark eyebrow, he went from sexy straight to rakish. "We're not looking at that, remember?"

He had a way of making everything fun, even her freak-outs about money. "I don't know how you do it," she said with a sigh.

"Do what?"

"Talk me down off the ledge without breaking a sweat."

"I just want you to be happy. I don't care what I have to do to make that happen."

"You really don't, do you?"

Without taking his eyes off hers, he shook his head. "Whatever you want. Whenever you want it."

"I still can't believe you feel that way about me. I'm finding it hard to get used to."

"Well, you need to get used to it. It's here to stay."

"How can you possibly know that after just a few days?"

"I told you. I knew after a few minutes."

Their waiter returned with the wine Mac had ordered and went through the ritual of uncorking it and giving him a sample. Maddie watched him as he tasted it, nodded his approval to the waiter, and ordered dinner for both of them. Clearly, he'd done this a few times.

"The food here is unreal," Mac said when their calamari appetizer was delivered.

"It should be for what it costs," she muttered.

Mac laughed and fed her a ring of fried squid. "So I was thinking. . ."

Maddie eyed him warily. "About?"

"Tom."

"What about him?"

"You said Thomas's father was a writer. You didn't say he was Tom Wilkinson, the bestselling author."

"Did I forget to mention that?"

"You know you did. But what I don't get is why you'd let him get away with what he did when he could make life so much easier for you and Thomas."

"Because I'd never want to risk him trying to take Thomas away from me. What if he decided he couldn't live without his son? How would I fight back when he has the kind of resources he does?"

"I don't know too much about being an author, but I can't imagine he'd want people to know that he lied to you about having a vasectomy and then left you alone and pregnant with a text message to say good-bye. If I heard that, I wouldn't buy any more of his books, that's for sure."

Did he have any idea how adorable he was when he got so indignant on her behalf?

"What?" he huffed. "What's so funny?"

"You are."

"I'm serious, Maddie! It's ridiculous that you're worried about money when he could be supporting his son in high style."

"We don't need high style. We're managing just fine."

"It's not right."

"Maybe not, but I'd never risk losing Thomas. Besides, now he thinks I'm a happily married mother. I won't hear from him again."

Mac toyed with the stem on his wineglass. "How did it feel?" His eyes met hers. "To see him again?"

"All I could think about on the ferry was that he'd take one look at Thomas and know he was his son." This time she reached for his hand and enjoyed the surprised expression that lit up his face. "But because of what you did, I'll never have to worry about that again."

"You think he bought it?"

She squeezed his hand. "I know he did. You may not realize this, but you saved me from one of my biggest worries today. I used to be afraid all the time that he'd show up at my door someday, and the jig would be up. But because I met you—because you knocked me off my bike and insisted on inserting yourself into my life—"

"Hey! You like having me around!"

Maddie bit back a laugh. "Because of all that and because you were so quick today, you made it so I don't have to worry about that anymore. And I appreciate it. More than you could ever know. If I hadn't been with you, he would've shown up at my door, and who knows what might've happened?"

"I don't want you to have to worry about anything or be afraid." He glanced down at their joined hands and then back up at her. "So you didn't feel, you know, attracted to him?"

Smiling at his concern, she said, "Not one bit. I seem to be rather attracted to someone else at the moment." She loved the befuddled look that crossed his face.

"What's his name?" he asked, attempting a stern tone that failed miserably.

"You don't know him."

"Oh, man!" He clutched his chest, pretending she'd stabbed him. "She giveth and she taketh away!"

Watching him—playful, sexy, generous, solid—Maddie realized that despite all her best efforts to resist him, she'd fallen as hard for him as he seemed to have fallen for her. Now she had to decide if she was willing to risk everything to see where he could take her.

Mac and Maddie held hands as they left the restaurant. Sated after the meal, the wine, the conversation, he wanted to rush her home so they could be together. It was too soon. He knew that, yet he also now knew that she wanted him as much as he wanted her.

Unlike any woman he'd ever known, she made him breathless and anxious and edgy and nervous. He couldn't wait to get her back on the bike, to have her wrapped around him, to have her legs tight against his hips and her breasts flat against his back. Good thing she hadn't seen what having her close to him like that had done to him earlier. She'd never trust him to keep the bike on the road.

"Look at the stars," she marveled.

"That's one thing I miss in Miami. Too much city light."

She continued to gaze upward at a sky littered with stars. "Sometimes I really love it here."

Because he couldn't bear to wait another second, he caressed her face and pressed a chaste kiss to her sweet lips. Her arms came up to encircle his neck, and her tongue traced the outline of his mouth. Mac stopped breathing as she teased her way into his mouth. He groaned from the effort of holding back the need to plunder.

"You're killing me," he whispered.

"Good."

"I won't be any good to you dead."

She laughed against his lips and killed him some more with dainty sweeps of her tongue that sent electrical currents rippling straight through him.

He slid a hand down her back, cupped her bottom and brought her in tight against his throbbing erection.

She gasped. "Mac."

"What, honey? Tell me."

"I want you."

"It's too soon." He wanted to shoot himself for being so honorable. At times like this, that really sucked. "You need time—"

She put her fingers over his lips. "I need you."

"Are you sure?"

Nodding, she rubbed herself against him, and he nearly lost it.

"Maddie," he gasped.

She tossed her head back and laughed.

He took advantage of the opportunity to sink his teeth into her exposed neck.

She shuddered. "Can we go home now?"

"I was going to take you dancing."

"I don't want to dance."

"What do you want to do?"

"You."

His heart tripped into overdrive. "Maddie. . ."

She took a step back from him. "God, that sounded so slutty. I don't know what I was thinking—"

He brought her right back. "No, honey. It sounded so sexy that I'm about to lose my mind. I want you to say whatever you want to me. I'll never think you're anything but beautiful and funny and smart and so freaking sexy you make me crazier than I've been since I was a horny teenager."

She looked up at him with bottomless eyes full of what looked an awful lot like love. God, he hoped so. "Take me home, Mac. Please?"

With shaking hands, he helped her into the helmet and got her settled on the back of the bike. Before he got on, he walked around it a couple of times.

"What are you doing?"

"Trying to cool off so I can drive."

Maddie giggled and never took her eyes off him as he took another lap around the bike.

Finally, he got on in front of her.

"All better?"

"Not hardly, but good enough to get us home. I hope."

Maddie slid her arms around him, caressing his chest and belly before heading south.

He caught her wandering hands with one of his. "No more of that until we get home," he said through gritted teeth.

"You're no fun."

"I'll show you fun. Just let me get us home without crashing."

Whereas before dinner, he'd taken the long way so she'd get a chance to enjoy the bike ride, on the way home, he took the shortest possible route. Having her pressed against him, even more tightly than before, was pure torture. When they arrived at her place, he was relieved to see the lights off in Tiffany's house and only one lamp glowing in Maddie's apartment. How quickly, he wondered, could he get rid of his sister without being rude?

"Don't be obvious," Maddie whispered on the way up the stairs.

He stopped and drew her into another torrid kiss. "That's just to tide me over," he said when he came up for air many minutes later.

Maddie wiped a self-conscious hand over her kiss-swollen lips and preceded him into the apartment.

"Hey," Janey said from the sofa. "You're back early."

"Maddie wasn't feeling well," Mac said. "Her injuries are acting up again."

"Oh, give it a rest, Mac." Janey rolled her eyes. "You want to fool around, and you want me out of here. Don't worry, I'm going."

"That's not true—" Maddie said at the same time Mac began to protest.

"You two are so funny," Janey said, laughing.

"Let me walk you home," Mac said.

"Not necessary. I walk around town by myself all the time."

"I don't want you doing it tonight."

"Tough." She gathered up her purse and the book she'd brought. Going up on tiptoes, she planted a kiss on Mac's cheek. "You're not the boss of me, big brother." She patted his face. "Take care of your lady. I'll take care of myself."

"Call me when you get home. Let it ring once."

Janey laughed at him. "All right, *Mom*, if you insist."

"I do."

"Thanks so much, Janey," Maddie said. "I really appreciate you watching Thomas."

"Anytime—and I mean that. He's adorable. I loved hanging out with him."

"Thanks, brat," Mac said as he held the door for her. He watched her go down the stairs to the driveway before he swung the inside door closed and turned to Maddie.

"You're crazy, you know that?" she said.

"Crazy about you, and I got rid of her in three minutes. That has to be a record where Janey is concerned."

"So much for not being obvious." Maddie got up from the sofa. "I'll be right back." On the way by, she made sure to rub up against him.

He was never going to survive her.

After she disappeared into the bathroom, he got busy pulling out the sofa bed. "We're getting a bigger place and a real bed," he muttered. "Immediately." Going to his pile on the floor, he dug out the gift he'd bought her at the mall and left it on the bed. When she came out a few minutes later, he took his turn in the bathroom, giving her the chance to discover the bag on the bed.

Janey took her time walking home. The mild evening had brought out the crowds, and Main Street was busy and loud. Since it was still early, she decided to stop at the Beachcomber for a beer before going home. No doubt she'd find someone she knew at her favorite bar. Unlike her brothers, she'd never been confined by island life and couldn't imagine living anywhere else. But she missed David so much that she wondered how she'd ever survive another year apart.

They were so close to having everything they'd ever dreamed of. All their plans were in place for a wedding next summer, after which he'd move home to Gansett to take over the practice of the retiring Doc Robach. Janey had graduated from the University of Connecticut with a degree in animal science. She'd had the grades for veterinary school, but David had convinced her that only one of them should go to medical school, or they'd be repaying student loans for the rest of their lives. She knew he was right. Island practices wouldn't generate the kind of income they'd need to live and pay off massive loans, too. Sometimes, however, she wished they both could've pursued their dreams.

Janey's parents had offered to pay for her to go to veterinary school, but she and David had decided they didn't want to be that deeply indebted to them. Her parents had vehemently disagreed with that decision and hadn't hesitated to tell her so. But it was her life—and David's—and they were going to do things their way. Her parents had been a little chilly to David since then, and Janey hoped they'd get over it before the wedding.

She and David had been a team for so long, since their sophomore year of high school, that Janey couldn't imagine her life without him. She just wished they saw more of each other. Once a month or so, she spent a weekend with him in Boston, and he came to the island whenever he could get at least forty-eight hours free. Unfortunately, that hadn't happened very often during his residency. He was either working or sleeping. Often when they were together, he slept through much of it. That was the main reason why they'd decided she should stay on the island with her family and friends, rather than move to Boston to live with him. He worked so much that she'd spend more time alone there than she did on Gansett.

This time next year, all the sacrifice would pay off. Somehow, she just had to get by until then. Seeing Mac and Maddie, so suddenly and stupidly in love, had made Janey wistful and lonely. Taking the steps to the Beachcomber two at a time, she was glad she'd decided to stay out for a while. Before she walked into the bar, she called Mac's phone and let it ring once as requested so he wouldn't come hunt her down.

At the far side of the bar, Joe Cantrell nursed a beer and flirted with the bartender.

Thrilled to see him, Janey snuck up behind him and covered his eyes with her hands.

"Who goes there?" he said.

"Guess."

"Hmmm, smells like Mac McCarthy's bratty little sister to me."

"I've never been able to fool you!" Janey planted a kiss on Joe's cheek and smiled when he flushed with embarrassment. He was such a mush and one of her all-time favorite people. "What does Mac McCarthy's little sister smell like anyway?"

"Sunshine and wildflowers," he said, startling her.

Janey swallowed hard. "Is that so?"

Realizing she no longer had Joe's attention, the bartender stalked off to wait on other customers without taking Janey's order.

"Yep," Joe said. "What're you doing out running the streets so late? Isn't it past your curfew?"

Janey rolled her eyes at him. "I just babysat for Mac's girlfriend, Maddie, so they could go out."

"That seems to be getting serious. I've seen him out with the baby every morning this week."

"He's crazy about them both."

Joe chuckled. "Hard to believe."

"No kidding, but he seems really happy. I love seeing him all befuddled by a woman. It's high time." Taking a handful of pretzels from the bowl on the bar, she popped one into her mouth. "What're you doing here? This isn't one of your usual island nights."

He quirked an eyebrow at her. "Got my schedule memorized?"

She took a drink from his bottle of beer. "It's not exactly rocket science: Friday and Saturday nights from Memorial Day to Columbus Day. Since today is Thursday, it's a reasonable question."

"If you must know, busybody, the wife of one of my guys is in labor, so I'm taking the first run in the morning."

"Ah, I see." Janey noticed him fixating on her engagement ring. Casually, she shifted on the barstool and dropped her left hand to her lap. He'd never said or done anything inappropriate. He'd never treated her as anything other than his best friend's little sister. But there was something—something Janey couldn't allow herself to examine too closely. Truth be told, she was afraid of what she might find just below the surface of her easy friendship with the handsome ferry-boat captain.

He signaled the bartender and ordered a beer for her, pushing forward a ten from his stack of money on the bar.

Janey raised her bottle in toast to Joe. "Thanks."

"My pleasure."

"It's good to see you."

"Janey, it's *always* good to see you."

CHAPTER 11

Maddie emerged from the bathroom and immediately spotted the bag Mac had left on the bed. After he closed the bathroom door, she approached the pink-striped bag as if it was full of explosives. Inside, she found the gorgeous ivory nightgown she'd admired in the Victoria's Secret window. Maddie blinked back tears as silk slipped through her fingers. He must've seen her looking at it and bought it after she moved on.

Glancing at the closed bathroom door, she realized she had just a few minutes to change. She took the bag into the bedroom where Thomas slept and quickly stripped off her clothes and slipped into the nightgown. With only the light from the hallway, she could see that her breasts filled the top to overflowing, and nothing she did lessened the effect of too much breast and not enough nightgown. Fighting back tears of frustration, she told herself that he'd wanted to do something nice for her, to make their first time together extra special. If she made a fuss about the top being too small, she would ruin it.

Mac came up behind her, kissed her shoulder and slid his arms around her.

Maddie startled. She'd been so consumed with worry that she hadn't heard the bathroom door open.

"Stop worrying about how they look," he whispered, his breath warm against her sensitized skin. He had removed his shirt but still wore his shorts. "Every inch of you is perfect to me."

"Thank you," she managed to say, amazed once again by how well he read her in such a short amount of time together. "For the nightgown. I've never had anything so beautiful."

"Neither have I."

Maddie closed her eyes and relaxed into his embrace.

"Are you going to let me see how it looks? I've had all these fantasies. . ."

Gripping his hand, she led him out of the bedroom and into the softly lit living room. Before she could chicken out, she turned, raised her chin and met his eyes. In them she saw heat and desire and love. So much love. Because of that, she didn't flinch when his eyes took a slow journey from her face to her chest and below before returning to her face.

"The fantasies have nothing on the reality," he said after a long moment during which neither of them took a breath. He brought her in close to him and ran his hands up and down her silk-covered back. "I've never wanted anyone or anything the way I want you, Madeline." His big hands spanned her waist, heating her skin through the silk.

"I don't want to disappoint you. I haven't done this very often."

"Baby, you couldn't possibly disappoint me." He dropped soft, open-mouthed kisses on her collarbone, shoulder and neck. "Remember earlier when you asked what I was thinking and I said I'd tell you after our date?"

Caught up in a flood of sensation, Maddie couldn't seem to form words. "Mmmm."

"I want to tell you now."

He raised his face from her neck and looked her in the eye.

Maddie reached up to comb her fingers through his thick dark hair.

A tremble rippled through him.

"What do you want to tell me, Mac?"

"When you asked me what I was thinking. . . My exact thought at the second you asked was that I love you so much I ache with it."

Tears sprang to her eyes. She was a regular waterworks tonight. "Mac. . ."

"I've never said that to anyone before. I had no idea what it meant to be in love until I knocked you off your bike and you knocked me off my feet."

As a fat tear rolled down her cheek, she drew him into a deep, sensual kiss. "Mac, I—"

He stopped her with a kiss. "Don't say anything. Not now. Let me show you."

At that moment, Maddie would've followed him anywhere he chose to take her. She belonged to him, body and soul.

Urging her down to the bed, he dropped his shorts and joined her. They faced each other, touching, kissing, laughing softly when nose bumped nose.

"I wish I wasn't all bruised and scabby for this."

"I love those scabs. Without them, we wouldn't have found each other."

Maddie laughed, drowning in the heady scent of his cologne. "That's crazy logic."

"I'm so glad I stepped off that curb and collided with you. I still hate that you got hurt so badly, but when I think about how you could've ridden right by me. . . That I might've never known you or Thomas. . . That we could've come so close to each other but never had this. . ." His caressing hand found her belly.

Maddie arched into him, wanting him so desperately but not wanting to seem too eager. In the back of her mind, always, were the whispers, the innuendo, the rumors. She tentatively caressed his chest, running her palm over his protruding nipple before coasting down to his taut belly.

Mac gasped and shifted so he was on top of her. He buried one hand in her hair and devoured her mouth with deep sweeping strokes of his tongue that left her weak and trembling. Kissing his way down the front of her, he visited her ear and neck before moving to her chest. Maddie tensed. *Here it comes, the part where he'll want to touch me there.*

With his hands braced on her ribs and using only his tongue, he teased her nipples until the silk was damp and clinging to her fevered skin. He drew her left nipple into his warm mouth, but still he didn't touch her with anything other than his mouth. Just when Maddie was certain that he would fill his hands with her breasts, he moved down, kissing her stomach, her hip bones and then her center.

"Mac. . . please. . ." She arched her hips, hoping to leave no doubt that she wanted him. Right now.

"I need you to say the words, remember?"

How could she forget? "Make love to me, Mac. Please make love to me."

He moved to her ankles and ran his hands over her legs, raising the nightgown as he went. Any minute now she'd be naked and laid out before him. He'd see what she wanted no one to see. But he only raised the gown to her hips and settled between her legs. When she realized what he intended to do, she tried to sit up, but his arm across her middle held her in place.

"Wait, Mac. Don't."

"Shh," he said, his breath fanning the hair that covered her. "It's okay. Let me love you." His broad shoulders forced her legs farther apart. "Relax, honey. I promise you'll like it."

Maddie wasn't so sure but made an effort to relax the muscles in her thighs. However, when his fingers slid through the dampness between her legs, she tensed again.

"It's okay," he said. "I love you. I want to love you."

When his tongue found the center of her desire at the same moment his fingers slid into her, Maddie's heart surged, her skin heated and tingled, and even as she tried to remain still, her hips lifted in response to his deep caresses.

"That's it, baby. Just let go. I want all of you. I want to kiss you everywhere."

A sob erupted from Maddie's throat as she buried a hand in his hair and lifted her hips in time with his questing tongue and fingers. When he rolled her pulsing flesh between his lips and sucked hard on her, she went totally still and came with a cry of completion and desperate desire. He stayed with her through every wave and then started all over again, driving her up and then leaving her hanging.

She moaned and reached for him.

"Wait a sec, hon." He sat on the side of the bed to roll on a condom. When he was ready, he lowered himself over her and devastated her with slow, deep kisses, as if he had all the patience in the world. The erection pulsing against her leg told a different story. Maddie let her hands roam over his back and down to his tight backside.

He jerked, his face tense as he fought for control.

"Now, Mac. Right now."

"It's been awhile for you, honey. I don't want to hurt you."

Even though he was longer and fuller than Tom, Maddie knew it wouldn't hurt the way it had before. "You won't." Guiding him with her hand, she stroked him gently.

He released a hiss and bit down on his lip. "If you do that, this'll be over before it starts."

Maddie raised her hips to guide him. Now he would probably want the nightgown off, but when she started to remove it, he stopped her.

"Leave it," he said through gritted teeth as he entered her with a powerful thrust that took her breath away.

"Oh," she said. "Oh, *God*."

He froze. "Does it hurt?"

"No, no. Don't stop. Just don't stop."

Mac chuckled at her enthusiastic response and gave her what she wanted.

Her legs hugged his hips as her hands gripped his backside.

With his fingers between them, he once again found the core of her desire and stroked her to another shattering climax. This time, he went with her, surging into her over and over again before his arms seemed to collapse. Breathing hard, he rested on top of her without crushing her, even as he continued to throb inside her.

Maddie combed her fingers through his hair, soothing him with soft kisses to his damp forehead.

"That was amazing," he finally said.

"Beyond amazing." With the nightgown bunched between them, Maddie finally understood what he had done—he'd taken her breasts out of the equation, allowing her to focus only on the pleasure, only on him. Never in her wildest dreams or fantasies had she ever expected to find a man who not only loved her, but who understood her the way he did.

"I love you, too, Mac," she whispered. "So much I ache with it."

He released a long deep breath that sounded a lot like relief. "You've made me so happy."

Somehow he'd managed to conquer her every fear, every worry, every doubt. In six days' time, he'd done what no one else before him ever had. He'd loved her, protected her, fought for her and cared for her. She tightened her arms around him, intending to never let him go.

"We might have one small problem."

"Oh? What's that?"

"I only have four condoms. Well, three now."

"Why didn't you get more today?"

"You wouldn't have found that a tad presumptuous?"

She couldn't deny that he had her there. "What'll we do? Neither of us can buy them in this town. It'll be all over the island before we're even out of the store."

"Don't worry, honey. I'll think of something."

"You do that." She tugged on his hair to bring him close enough to kiss. "And get the big box while you're at it. The biggest box they have. Maybe two of them."

Mac laughed as he finally withdrew from her. "You got it."

"And you'll take care of this tomorrow?"

"First thing," he said, still chuckling.

"Good because we'll need some for tomorrow night."

"I knew it," he said with a deep, dramatic sigh. "You're really going to kill me, aren't you?"

She could tell she astounded him when she pushed him onto his back. Her lips hovering above his, she said, "Or die trying."

Mac held her tight against him as she slept. After what they'd shared, he should have been exhausted, depleted, drained. Instead, he was exhilarated and making plans that he couldn't wait to share with her.

They would be married as soon as possible. He'd adopt Thomas and give him his name. Thomas McCarthy had a nice ring to it. Next, he would build them a house—a great big house with a huge bedroom, a brand new bed and a view of the water. He'd take over his father's business and make a life right here on the island with his new family. They'd even find a way to send Maddie to college. Maybe if she spent two days a week on the mainland, she could chip away at a degree over the next few years. He wanted her to have everything she'd missed out on before now. After waiting forever for her, he'd do anything he could to ensure her unending happiness.

She stirred, murmured in her sleep, and pressed her lips to his chest.

Mac smoothed a hand over her hair.

"What're you doing awake?" she muttered.

"Thinking about you."

"What about me?"

"About the life we're going to have together."

"Tell me about it." She caressed his chest, focusing on his nipple, which reawakened another part of him. "I want to know all about it."

He went through the whole plan, from marriage to college.

Maddie propped herself up so her chin rested on his chest. She stayed like that for a long time, studying him with those caramel eyes that made him melt.

"What? You don't like the plan?"

"I love the plan."

"Then what's wrong?"

"I just keep waiting for the other shoe to drop. No one can be this perfect."

"Maybe I'm just perfect for you. Did that ever occur to you?"

"Oh, many times." She shifted so she was on top of him and began to pepper his chest with soft kisses that made his blood boil. No one had ever fired him up the way she did. Her tongue circled his nipple, and he sucked in a sharp deep breath. "Babe, don't forget. We're out of condoms."

"I know." She moved to give his other nipple the same attention.

By now, Mac was hard as stone and pulsating against her belly.

Maddie shocked him when she sat up, reached for the hem of the silk night-gown and lifted it over her head, exposing her breasts to him for the first time. Nothing she could've done would have told him more about how much she'd come to love and trust him.

"You're so beautiful," he said, his voice hoarse. "Like a fantasy come to life."

"Touch me, Mac."

His hands coasted over her ribs to cup her breasts. "I know you hate them, but I think they're magnificent."

Maddie laughed. "I thought you were an ass-and-leg man."

"*All* men are breast men."

She rolled her eyes. "Tell me something I don't know."

Mac drew a nipple deep into his mouth and swirled his tongue back and forth.

"Mmm, that's good."

He held back the overwhelming urge to squeeze and lick and bite, not wanting her to think he was fixated on the part of her she hated most. That was fine, because she seemed to have other plans anyway.

Wiggling out of his grip, she dragged her breasts over his chest and kissed her way to his belly. Under the sheet, her soft hand found him hard and ready, as if he hadn't already had her four times. "Maddie," he gasped.

"Hmm?" This she said against the head of his penis, the vibration nearly undoing him.

"God," he uttered.

Her soft laughter was accompanied by sweeping strokes of her tongue.

"Honey, wait. . ."

"Relax, Mac. I want to kiss you everywhere."

"You can't use my own words against me."

She glanced up at him, a wicked glint in her eyes. "Oh no? Watch me."

He loved her like this—confident and trusting, loving him enough to expose herself to him, to take him into her mouth and give him something special. She probably hadn't done this before, but her enthusiasm more than made up for her lack of experience. It didn't take long for her to drive him to the point of no return. With his hand buried in her hair, he tried to stop her.

"Maddie," he panted, "stop. Baby, come on." But rather than stop, she stroked him faster and took him deeper. By the time she drew a long, intense orgasm from him, he was sweating, breathing hard and his heart raced. Just opening his eyes took all the energy that remained in his body. When he did, he found her watching him with a very satisfied look on her face.

"Welcome back. I thought I'd finally killed you."

"Damn close," he said, reaching for her.

She snuggled into his embrace. "Was it okay?" she asked in a small voice that tugged at him.

"So much better than okay there isn't even a word for it."

"I've never done that before. I always wondered what it would be like."

"And?"

"I really, *really* liked it."

"Maybe I have died and gone to heaven after all."

She giggled, but then she got very quiet. "Thanks, Mac."

"What are you thanking *me* for? After that, *I* should be thanking *you*."

She tilted her head so she could see him. "For not going all nuts over the girls the way most guys would have."

"I wish you didn't dislike them so much." He flashed a salacious grin. "I think I could come to be *very* good friends with them."

Smiling, she caressed the stubble on his jaw. "I don't dislike them. I hate them."

"I don't want you to take this the wrong way, because I mean it when I tell you you're perfect in every way to me."

"But?"

"If you want to have them reduced, I'd happily pay for it, but only because it would make you happy."

"I couldn't let you do that. You've already done so much for me."

"You don't have to decide right now. The offer is on the table, now or later when you and Thomas are on my insurance. Whenever. I wouldn't change a single thing about you, but it's not about what I want."

"I really, really love you," she whispered.

"And I really, really love you. There's nothing I wouldn't do for you—or Thomas."

As if he had heard his name, the baby chose that moment to let them know he was awake. Mac kissed her one last time and pulled the covers up over her, hating to end what had been the best night of his life. "My time with him."

"If you bring him to me and I nurse him, he might go back to sleep for a while—and then we could, too."

"As much as I love my mornings out with him, that sounds too good to pass up."

He retrieved Thomas from his crib, changed the twenty-pound morning diaper, planted some noisy raspberries on his belly that made him laugh like crazy, and then carried him to his mother. For the first time, he got to watch as Maddie guided the baby to her breast.

"God, that's amazing," he said, awestruck by the way the baby's little mouth latched on and went to work. He'd never seen anything quite like it.

Maddie stroked the baby's downy soft hair and smiled at Mac. She looked like a warrior queen, proud and strong, and he loved her so fiercely. "Can I ask you something about that?"

"Sure."

"How come, before, when I, ah, did that, nothing happened?"

Maddie laughed at his exquisite discomfort. "Because the milk doesn't really come in—at least for me—until he wants it. Some people leak like crazy, but I never did. And now that I only feed him once a day, there's not as much."

"I see." He slipped back into bed and shifted her so he could hold them both. "Thomas needs a sister. Maybe a brother, too. Possibly even a couple of them."

Maddie laughed quietly. "Let's not get ahead of ourselves."

"But you want more, don't you?"

"Let's have one more and see how that goes."

"I guess I could live with that." He ran his hand over her belly. "I want to see you round and pregnant with my baby."

She groaned. "I was big as a house with Thomas, pregnant from head to toe."

"I can't wait to see that."

"My back hurt like crazy for months."

"I'd rub it every day."

She rolled her head back on his shoulder so she could look up at him. "You're sure you really want to saddle yourself with all this? A woman you've known a week, a baby who isn't yours—"

"I want him to be mine. I mean, look at him." Mac ran a finger over the baby's milk-dampened cheek. "He's so perfect. I want to see him walk and run and swim and talk back to us. I can't wait for all of that."

"What if it turns out to be too much for you? A few months down the road, what if you start to feel confined or unhappy—"

Placing two fingers gently over her lips, he said, "All I can tell you is I'm almost thirty-five years old, and I've never felt anything even close to what I feel when I'm with you. Both of you."

Maddie's eyes glistened with tears. "I don't know what I did to get so lucky."

"You crashed into me on that big old bike of yours."

"I'm fairly certain we've determined 'the accident' was your fault."

Brushing his lips over her forehead, he continued to watch intently as she moved Thomas to the other side. "That 'accident' might turn out to be the best thing to ever happen to me."

"That's funny," she said, "because last night I had the very same thought."

Mac awakened ninety minutes later to someone banging on the door. Groaning, he willed whomever it was to go away and leave them alone.

Maddie stirred next to him, and wanting her to sleep a while longer, he quickly got up, pulled on a pair of shorts, and went to the door.

"Mom," he said, shocked to see her.

"Mac."

"What're you doing here?" he whispered as he stepped onto the porch and closed the door behind him.

He watched her take a quick survey of his bare chest and whisker-roughened jaw. "I've come to get you."

He ran his fingers through his hair, hoping to bring some order to it. "Get me? What're you talking about?"

"This is entirely unseemly." She gestured to the apartment. "The whole town is talking about you sleeping with her. I won't have it."

Mac laughed, which seemed to infuriate her. "Is that so? You do realize I'm almost thirty-five, right?"

"I don't care how old you are, Malcolm John McCarthy Junior, let me just tell you—"

This was bad if she was bringing out the big Malcolm gun. She was the only one who ever called him that awful name. "No, Mom, let *me* tell *you*. I love her, I'm going to marry her and adopt her son, so you'd better get onboard or get out of the way. Your choice."

Her blue eyes almost popped out of her skull. "*Marry her*? You're going to *marry her*? Have you lost your mind?"

"I've lost my heart—finally—and you can either be part of it or not. That, too, is up to you."

"This is the most ridiculous thing I've ever heard—"

Mac held up his hand to stop her. "This conversation is over. I'm going back inside now, and you need to be on your way. In fact, I'd appreciate if you found someone else to cover for Maddie this weekend at the hotel. We need to spend some time together. We've got a lot of plans to make."

"I don't know what's gotten into you—"

"Love, Mom. That's what's gotten into me, and it's the best thing to ever happen to me. Maybe we'll stop by this weekend to see you and Dad. If we do, I'd advise you to be nice to my future wife and son. Have a good day."

Leaving her staring at him with her mouth hanging open, Mac stepped inside the apartment and closed the door. His heart racing fast from the burst of adrenaline, he stood there for a second until he heard her car drive off, sending gravel flying in her wake.

"That was pleasant," Maddie said.

He glanced over to find her sitting up with the sheet wrapped tight around her. The image of the wall going back up wasn't lost on him. He slid back into bed and reached for her. Thomas was still asleep on the other side of her.

She resisted Mac's efforts to embrace her.

"Don't. Please don't pull away from me again because of her. I can't deal with that."

"I can't deal with coming between you and your mother."

"She'll come around. It's nothing against you—"

Maddie released an sharp laugh. "Sure it isn't."

"She has this idea of who I belong with—"

"And it's certainly not the town tramp."

"Maddie, honey, please. Don't hold her against me." He coaxed her into his arms and tugged at the sheet until he reached the warm, soft skin he craved. "I love you," he whispered, as he kissed his way down the front of her. "That's all that matters." Capturing a pebbled nipple between his teeth, he finally felt her resistance begin to give way to desire. Relief coursed through him. "Did you hear me tell her to find someone to cover for you this weekend?"

"Mmmm," she said, tightening her grip on his hair.

He ran his tongue in circles around her nipple. "Know what this means?"

"What?" she asked, breathless.

"Three whole days together. No work, no obligations."

"We still have the daycare this afternoon."

"That's nothing. What should we do with the rest of the day?"

"I can't think of a thing," she said with a suggestive smile that reminded him of something else he needed to take care of—immediately.

He kissed her cheek and then her lips. "Hold that thought. I'll be back."

Hoping Maddie would go back to sleep for a while, Mac went outside to call Joe. "Hey, buddy, where are you?"

"Just got into Point Judith, why?"

Mac swore under his breath. "I need a favor. Are you coming back to the island today?"

"'Fraid not. I've got Homeland Security coming to do an inspection next week that I'm totally not ready for. I'll be in the office the rest of the day but back over tomorrow. Why? What do you need?"

"It's kind of embarrassing, and now it's even *more* embarrassing because I'm going to have to get my sister to do it for me."

"Please tell me you're not talking about—"

"Don't say it. Please do not say it."

Joe howled with laughter. "What are you? Fifteen?"

"It's an issue for Maddie, not me. She doesn't want it all over the island, and you know it will be if I get them."

That seemed to stifle some of Joe's laughter. "Well, do be sure to let me know what Janey has to say about this."

"I'm sure you'll find it entertaining."

"No doubt." Joe cleared his throat. "So, um. . . I saw her last night."

"Where?"

"At the Beachcomber. After she babysat for you guys."

"That brat! She was supposed to go right home."

"I know this is a newsflash to you, Mac, but she is a full-grown adult."

"She's my baby sister."

"Who you're sending to buy condoms for you today." Joe once again dissolved into laughter. "Not such a baby anymore, huh?"

"Shut up," Mac growled. "I hope you behaved yourself with her."

"The word 'condom' never came up. Not that I would've minded. . ."

"You're very funny."

"I just don't get. . ." Joe stopped himself.

"What?"

"Nothing. It doesn't matter."

"Tell me. Come on, Joe."

"Why do you think that guy who supposedly can't wait to marry her never shows his face on the island?"

"He's finishing medical training. You know how that can be."

"All I know is if she were mine, wild horses wouldn't keep me away."

Mac winced. "You ever think about just telling her that?"

Joe released a bitter laugh. "Right. Like I can compete with Dr. David and all their history. That'd be a suicide mission."

"Maybe if she knew, it'd make a difference."

"It wouldn't, and she's never going to know, you got me, Mac? Don't say a word to her. I mean that."

"I never would, but you should. What've you got to lose?"

"Her friendship, and that would be truly unbearable."

"I'm sorry it's so hopeless," Mac said with a sigh. "I have a whole new appreciation for how hard this must be on you."

"It is what it is. Hey, I gotta split, but do let me know how the rubber run goes, huh?"

"Go to hell." As Joe laughed at his own joke, Mac slapped the phone closed. His stomach clutched with nerves when he realized that Janey really was his only other option. His father would do it for him, but he couldn't ask him. Even at almost thirty-five, he just couldn't. Swallowing hard, Mac flipped open the phone and called Janey.

"Hey, brat, what're you doing?" Mac considered telling her about their mother's visit that morning but decided against it. He wanted to forget the whole unfortunate encounter.

"Heading into work, why?"

"I need another favor."

"You want to go out *again* tonight?"

"Not exactly."

"Then what?"

"I need you to, um, well. . . If you could go to Gold's," Mac said, referring to the island drug store, "and just, you know. . ."

"*What*, Mac? Spit it out, will ya?"

"I need you to buy condoms for me. A lot of them."

Dead silence.

"Janey?"

"You gotta be kidding me."

"I can't do it! It'll be all over the island in ten minutes, and Maddie can't deal with that."

"Get Joe to do it."

"He's off-island until tomorrow."

"So *abstain* for one night!"

"Janey, *please*. I'm desperate here."

"You can't ask me to do this. It's too embarrassing."

"How do you think I feel about asking my baby sister to do this for me?" He let out what he knew was a pathetic wail. *"Janey. . . I need you."*

"Don't do that. Don't you dare play the need card."

"Pretty please."

She let out a swear that shocked him to his core. "Fine," she said through gritted teeth. "But you'll owe me forever, do you hear me? There's no statute of limitations on what you'll owe me."

"I understand."

"I don't think you do. For the rest of your natural life, anytime I say, 'Jump', you say, 'How high, Janey? How high can I jump for you?' Anytime I snap my fingers, you come running. Any. Time. Am I clear?"

"Crystal."

"I'll need at least a hundred dollars."

"What the hell for?"

"Buffer items, you buffoon. I can't just go in there and buy a gross of condoms and walk out."

"So you're going to soak me for a year's supply of nail polish and tampons?"

"That's the very *least* of what you owe me."

"Fine. I'll bring it to the vet clinic."

"Pay me later. I can't look at you right now. Meet me at noon behind the Beachcomber, and do not look at me. Just take the bag, give me the money and walk away."

"I love you, Janey. Have I mentioned that lately?"

"Screw you."

Holding back a laugh, he said, "Get the extra large ones, okay?"

"I hate you."

Mac returned to Maddie's and found her and Thomas still sleeping. He checked his watch and decided this would be a good time to take care of something else he'd been putting off. Taking his keys off the table, he tiptoed out of the apartment. In the driveway, he rolled the motorcycle to the street before he kick-started it. Driving along the south coast, he noticed dense fog—an island staple in June—clinging to the horizon as the sun fought to break through. Mac pulled into the parking lot at the South Point Light and killed the engine. He pulled his cell phone out of his pocket and called his brother Evan, who was on speed dial along with Grant, Adam and Janey.

"Hey, man," Evan said.

"Did I wake you up? You sound rough."

"Nah, late night, but I'm on the way to the studio now. What's up with you?"

"This and that. How're you? How's the recording going?" After years of struggle and toil, a small Nashville label had recently signed Evan.

"It's the most fun I've ever had in my life."

"That's awesome. Been a long time coming."

"You know it. So Janey emailed me that you're on the island. What brought that on?"

"Did you hear about Dad selling the marina?"

"No way!"

"Yep. I'm doing some repairs for him and toying with the idea of relocating and maybe keeping the place in the family."

"Seriously? You won't go nuts stuck on that island?"

"A few things have changed lately."

"What could've possibly changed to make that place look good to you?"

"I met someone—someone you know, in fact."

"Who?"

"Maddie Chester."

"Oh. Really? Wow."

"I hear you've got some history with her."

"Mac, wait. You don't understand—"

It took everything Mac had to keep from yelling at his brother. "You're damned right I don't understand," he managed to say calmly, even though he churned inside. This whole thing made him sick.

"It was Darren. He started it and told us to go along with him or else."

"Or else what?"

"He was like a god in high school. No one wanted to piss him off. When he told us to do stuff, we did it."

"How could you be part of something like this, Ev? After everything Dad was always hammering into our heads about how to treat women?"

"Believe me, it's eaten at me over the years. I never felt good about it."

"What you guys did to her ruined her life. Do you realize that? It *ruined* her."

"It was high school. How could it ruin her life?"

"Because she's never shaken it! The whole island thinks she's a tramp, and until last night, she'd had sex *twice* in her life!"

"God," Evan said softly. "I had no idea. . ."

"You're going to fix it."

"What do you mean?"

"Here's what I want you to do."

Mac's next stop was Darren Tuttle's body shop. The place looked well kept, and judging by the cars lined up out front, it was busy. At the front desk, Mac asked for Tuttle.

"Who should I tell him is calling?" the dowdy-looking receptionist asked.

"An old friend."

She got up and went through the door to the work area, returning a few minutes later with Darren, who was greasy, dirty and thirty pounds overweight. His hairline had receded into unattractive baldness. The "god" who'd once been able to intimidate a legion of boys into going along with his every plan had clearly fallen a few notches in the twelve years since graduation. From the quirk in his lips, Mac could tell that Darren recognized him.

"What do you want?"

"A word outside." Without waiting for Darren to reply, Mac turned and went out the door.

"I heard you were back in town," Darren said as he followed Mac outside.

Mac kept his back to the other man, planning to give him the benefit of the doubt.

Darren snickered. "You and Maddie Mattress, huh? Have you ever *seen* knockers quite like those?"

Screw the benefit of the doubt. Mac spun around and plowed his fist in Darren's doughy face.

Knocked to the dirt, Darren flopped like a fish out of water. Blood poured from his nose. "What the *hell?*" he sputtered. "What's your *problem?*"

Mac reached down with one hand and hauled Darren to his feet. Speaking right into his fat, red face, Mac said, "What you did to her—that's my problem."

Darren tried to wriggle free. "I don't know what you're talking about."

"Yes, you do." Mac tightened his hold. "You know exactly what I'm talking about."

Darren wiped at the blood on his face and winced when he connected with his bloody nose. "I'll have you arrested."

"No, you won't." Mac released him abruptly, and Darren stumbled backward. "Do you have any idea what you did to her? What your stupid-ass-she-rejected-me-so-I'll-make-her-pay crap did to her life?"

"*I* rejected *her.*"

"Rewriting history now?" Mac raised an eyebrow. "She didn't want you, so you trashed her all over town."

"That's not what happened."

"My brother Evan confirmed her account. Right now he's contacting everyone else who was involved." The bead of sweat that appeared on Tuttle's brow pleased Mac. "You married, Darren?"

"Yeah," he muttered, sending a nervous glance at the office where the receptionist watched them anxiously through the window.

"That your wife in there?"

"So what if it is?"

"What version of this story you want her to hear? Mine or yours?"

"Are you threatening me?"

"You bet I am. Here's what you're going to do."

CHAPTER 12

Mac returned to Maddie's bearing a handful of wildflowers he'd picked by the side of the road.

She was on the floor with Thomas, who was engaged in a battle with the baby gym propped over him. When she saw the flowers, her eyes went soft with emotion. "They're beautiful," she said, getting up to find a vase. "What's the occasion?"

Mac came up behind her, nuzzled her neck and planted a kiss on her warm skin. "To say thank you for the best night of my life."

"Oh."

"What?" he asked. "It wasn't good for you, too?"

"You know it was."

"But?"

She turned to him, her face unreadable. "I can't stop thinking about the things your mother said."

Mac wanted to scream with frustration, but he showed her none of that. "Forget it. She can't get to us unless we let her, and I have no plans to let her."

Maddie linked her hands behind his neck and brought him down for a kiss. Running her tongue back and forth over his lips, she had him fired up and ready in two seconds flat.

He groaned. "That's more like it."

"Did you take care of our problem?"

"All set."

Pressing against his straining erection, she said, "Who's doing it? Joe?"

Mac was having trouble thinking, let alone talking. "He's off-island."

"Then who?"

"It might be better if you didn't know."

Her face slackened with shock. "Tell me you did *not* ask your sister."

"It was either that or wait for Joe to get back tomorrow." He cupped her bottom to pull her in tighter against him. "I didn't think that would work for us."

"I'll never be able to look at her again."

"Sure you will." Remembering the meeting with Janey, he checked his watch.

Maddie gasped. "What happened to your hand?" She ran her fingers softly over purple, swollen knuckles. "Did you *hit* someone?"

"Of course not. I banged it."

She raised a skeptical eyebrow. "On what?"

"I ran up the stairs earlier and connected with the rail. It was stupid." He kissed her nose. "Don't worry about it."

Hands on hips, she said, "I want to know who you hit and why."

Taken aback, Mac studied her. "Is this the kind of wife you're going to be?"

"Yep. Who'd you hit? It wasn't your mother, was it?"

Mac laughed and then squirmed under the heat of her glare. "It was a misunderstanding."

"Over me."

"Nothing like that."

"You're lying, Mac. I'm not a child who needs you to protect me."

"Maybe I need to protect you." He rested his hands on her shoulders and tried to massage away the tension. "Please don't make me tell you about it. It's over and done with."

Maddie studied him for a long moment. Then she went to the freezer, retrieved an ice pack and wrapped it around his hand. She looked up at him with those potent eyes. "Don't keep things from me, and do *not* lie to me. Ever."

"Okay."

"Those are deal-breakers for me, Mac. I mean it."

He swallowed hard. "I understand." Caressing her cheek, he leaned in to kiss her. "I need to go meet Janey. After that, you want to go to the beach for a while?"

"I don't do the beach."

"You live on an island. How can you not do the beach?"

She shot him her now-familiar withering look. "I'm not big on giving out cheap thrills."

"I'll be there to scare the mean boys away."

"They'll still be gawking."

"So let 'em gawk. They can't touch you if you don't let them—and you know I mean that entirely figuratively."

"And you'll be just fine with the gawking?"

"I'll ignore it."

"Well," she said, "I suppose you can't punch anyone else today with your hand all bruised and battered."

He flashed his most charming grin. "I've still got a mean left hook."

Janey was waiting for him when he arrived at the back steps to the Beachcomber.

As Mac approached, her eyes narrowed. *Uh oh.*

She swung the bag and smacked him right upside the head.

"Hey! That hurt!"

"Mrs. Gold herself was working the register. You know what she said to me?" Without taking a breath, Janey launched into Mrs. Gold's nasally New York accent. "'My oh my, *Janey*, Doctor David must be coming for a *good* long visit this weekend.'"

Mac knew it wasn't a good idea, but he laughed anyway.

She pelted him again with the bag. "It's not funny! I have to live in this town!"

He attempted to wipe the smile off his face and withdrew a wad of twenties from his pocket.

Janey snatched the money and thrust the bag at him. "It's going to take *years* of therapy to recover from this."

"You're the best, Janey." Mac gave her a noisy smooch on the cheek.

She pushed him away. "I hate you more than anything."

He poked her ribs. "Do not."

"I'm off to get a brain scrub to erase this unsavory incident from my memory."

"Come by Maddie's this weekend. Let's hang out."

"No way I'm coming near the two of you until the supply is exhausted."

Mac grinned. "We'll be giving thanks to Janey McCarthy *every time*."

Hands over ears, she shrieked and stalked off.

Mac laughed all the way home.

Even though Maddie wore a conservative one-piece bathing suit, sure enough every guy on the beach checked her out. Mac told himself it didn't matter, but he was lying. He wondered if he'd ever behaved so stupidly around a full-figured woman. Probably. A nearby group of young men were particularly enthralled, and Mac glared at them.

"Lucky man," he heard one of them say with a snicker.

It took every ounce of self-control Mac possessed to keep from going over there to smack the smirk off the guy's face.

"Told you," Maddie said.

"What?"

"That you wouldn't like it."

"They're idiots."

"Men will be men. They can't help themselves." She reached for her T-shirt to cover up.

"Don't," Mac said, resting his hand on her arm. "Don't let them bother us."

"Easy for you to say. They're not gawking at you."

Mac's cell phone rang, and he dug it out of his backpack. He didn't recognize the Gansett number but took the call anyway.

"Hi, Mac," a breathy female voice said. "I hope it's okay that your mother gave me your number."

"I'm sorry, who is this?" he asked, even though he had a sneaking suspicion.

She giggled. "Doro. We met the other night at McCarthy's? Your mother said—"

"Whatever she told you, it was bad information. I'm seeing someone."

"I heard about that. Maddie, right? I don't know her, but then again we don't exactly run in the same circles."

"Lucky for her."

"Excuse me?"

"Listen, Doro. I'm not interested. Sorry if that hurts your feelings, but please don't call me again." Regretting taking the call, he closed the phone before she could reply and stashed it in his bag.

"She doesn't give up, does she?"

"Who? Doro?"

Maddie rolled her eyes at him. "Your mother."

He shrugged, knowing he needed to act fast—again—to minimize the damage with Maddie. "That's her problem, not ours." He scooped up Thomas and reached out to Maddie. "Come on, let's go swimming."

She hesitated for only a second before she took his hand.

At the water's edge, she eyed the waves with trepidation. "He's never been in the water before. I don't know if he'll like it."

"We'll take it nice and slow." As they waded into the surf, Mac dipped the baby's feet into the cool water. Thomas bicycled his legs and let out a happy squeal that made them laugh. "Just like the bathtub, buddy, only bigger." After half an hour of wave jumping, Mac stretched out on the wet sand at the water's edge and dug a small hole for Thomas to sit in. The waves rushed to the beach, making a pool out of the hole. Thomas splashed and shrieked as Mac drizzled wet sand on his chubby legs.

Mac looked up at Maddie, who was taking pictures of them. "I think it's safe to say he likes the beach."

"We'll be washing sand out of his crevices for a month."

Mac laughed and plopped an even bigger pile of wet sand on Thomas. They played until Thomas began to yawn and rub at his eyes with sandy hands. "Whoa, dude," Mac said, grabbing the baby's hands. "Don't do that."

Thomas let out a lusty wail of distress.

Mac took him back in the water to rinse off as much of the sand as he could. Removing Thomas's tiny bathing suit, he cleaned him up and carried him back to Maddie for a diaper.

"You've become an old pro."

"He makes everything fun."

Maddie smiled at him. "So do you."

Mac slid a hand around her neck and brought her in for a tender kiss. "That's nice of you to say." He reached for the baby and lowered himself into a beach chair.

Maddie prepared a bottle. "Want me to feed him?"

"Nope."

Once the bottle was finished, Mac burped him and snuggled him in close. The baby's sweet breath fanned against his neck. "Is he out?"

"Like a light. You can put him down if you want to."

They'd brought an umbrella and set up a spot for Thomas to nap.

"That's okay. I like holding him." He tugged a beach towel up over the baby to protect him from the sun.

"What would your friends in Florida say if they could see you right now?"

"They'd never believe it."

"What will you do about your business there?"

"They'll buy me out and find someone to replace me."

"Will they be mad that you're not coming back?"

"Maybe. The three of us have busted our butts to build up a thriving business."

"It'll be a blow to them to lose you."

Mac sighed. The same thought had been weighing on him since he'd decided to stay. "They've been texting me with all kinds of questions and problems. We've got a lot going on right now. We always do."

"Did you have a girlfriend there?"

Mac glanced at her, not sure where this was heading. "Sort of."

Maddie laughed. "How can you 'sort of' have a girlfriend?"

"I dated my assistant for a while—and yes, I know that's a terrible cliché—but we didn't see much of each other outside of work, which irritated her. But that was over before I came home."

"What's her name?"

"Rosanne."

"Is she beautiful?"

"You're beautiful."

"Nice try. What does she look like?"

"Short with buck teeth and a wart on her nose. Nothing at all to look at."

Maddie dissolved into laughter. "You're so full of it. She probably looks like a super model."

Mac linked his fingers with hers. "She can't hold a candle to you. The second I saw you, every other woman faded to the background. You're the only one who matters now—the only one who's ever mattered."

"Mac. . . You're so sweet." She brought their joined hands to her lips. "Now tell me, what does she really look like?"

He laughed at her persistence. "Well, she has six toes on her left foot."

"*Mac!*"

After they finished the shift at the daycare, Mac told Maddie he had an errand to run and would be back shortly. He sat on the sofa to tie his running shoes.

"So you're literally going to run?" Maddie asked.

"Yep."

She eyed the bag from Gold's on the counter. "Do you think maybe you could hurry up?"

Mac stood and wrapped his arms tight around her. "I'll be so fast you won't even know I'm gone."

She ran the tip of her tongue over his neck. "I'll get Thomas fed and put down while you're gone."

Mac shuddered. "Hold that thought."

"Hurry."

He had never moved faster as he jogged over to pick up the black SUV he'd spotted for sale earlier in the day. After completing the transaction, he enjoyed the smooth ride and the easy way it handled. Mac went next to the grocery store and bought a rotisserie chicken and salad for dinner and was back at Maddie's forty-five minutes after he left. He walked in to soft music and candlelight. The blinds were drawn, and the bed had been pulled out.

She came out of the bathroom wearing the nightgown. Crossing her arms, she leaned against the wall and looked at him with hungry eyes. "What took so long?"

Stemming the urge to drool, Mac stashed the grocery bags in the refrigerator. "I need a shower," he said.

Maddie put her hand on his chest and directed him to the bed. "No, you don't."

"But I'm all sweaty—" With her hands in his hair, she dragged him down to her and kissed the life out of him.

The back of his knees connected with the bed, and he tumbled backward, bringing her with him.

"Did this seem like a *really* long day to you?" she asked between torrid kisses.

"Mmm, the longest day ever." He tried to roll them over, but she stopped him.

"Can we do it like this?" she asked, her cheeks flaming with color.

"Baby, we can do it any way you want, as long as we do it very, very soon."

She bit her bottom lip and smiled down at him, causing his heart to skip a beat.

He reached up to bury his fingers in her hair and brought her back to him. "Have you done it this way before?"

She shook her head.

"You'll like it."

"Will you?"

Mac laughed. "Absolutely." He ran his hands over the silky gown, gathering it up as he went. "Can we lose this or do you want to leave it on?"

"It can go."

"Are you sure?"

"Yes! Hurry!"

Moving quickly, they got rid of the rest of their clothes and broke open one of the new boxes of condoms.

"Let me," Maddie said, taking the foil package from him.

Mac exhaled a long deep breath and counted backward from one hundred as she used her teeth to tear open the package, keeping her eyes fixed on his as she rolled it slowly over him.

"You're so hard," she whispered, shifting her eyes from his face to his groin. "Doesn't that hurt?"

"No," he said with a groan. "But if you don't move a little faster, we'll miss the best part."

When he was finally sheathed, Maddie straddled him, and Mac decided he'd truly died and gone to heaven as she slowly took him in and began to ride him with tremendous enthusiasm—as if she'd been waiting forever to give this a whirl. Her heavy breasts swayed in time with the movements of her hips. With his arms around her, Mac brought her with him when he sat up against the back of the sofa, putting him at face-level with her breasts. He filled his hands and then his mouth.

Maddie threw her head back, lost in sensation.

Since he was watching her so closely, he saw the change come over her as she reached the first peak and then came back down to discover he wasn't finished with her. "Do it again," he whispered.

"I can't," she said, spent.

"Yes, you can." He leaned her back against his raised knees and used his hips to lift her up and down.

She gasped as he went deeper than before.

"Hurt?" he asked.

Apparently unable to speak, she shook her head.

Mac took advantage of her preoccupation to skim his hands over her toned legs and belly, causing her to quiver under his touch. As he stepped up the rhythm of his hips, his fingers focused on the pulsating bundle of nerves between her legs, drawing a long, keening moan from her. Once again, her thighs tightened around him, and her body stiffened with fulfillment.

Mac kept a tight hold on her hips as he went with her, his face buried between her breasts.

Sagging into him, Maddie wrapped her arms around him and held on tight as he continued to pulse inside her.

He combed his fingers through her hair. "Like it?"

"Oh yeah," she said breathlessly.

Mac's soft laugh was interrupted when she raised her head to kiss him.

"How soon until we can do it again?"

"I've turned you into a regular sex fiend."

She bit his neck. "How soon?"

Mac flinched as a zap of pure lust raced through him. He smoothed his hands down her back to cup her soft buttocks. "How does right now sound?"

"Perfect," she said with a sigh of contentment.

"Where did you go before?" she asked after they ate a picnic dinner in bed.

Mac yawned and ran a hand through his hair. "I bought Thomas a car."

Maddie sat right up. "*What?*"

Laughing, he guided her back down. "We needed a way to get the three of us around, so I bought a truck."

"I can't believe you just went out and bought a truck."

"Why not? We needed it." Mac reached up to turn off the light. "This was a nice day."

"This was a *great* day."

"We'll have many more just like it."

"You're starting to make me believe it's really going to happen."

Mac turned on his side and caressed her face. "Believe it. You and Thomas have given me so much—things I didn't even know were missing."

"And you've given us things I knew were missing but never dreamed of having."

"I love you," he whispered. "I want everything with you."

"If I'm dreaming, don't tell me, okay? I don't want to wake up."

Smiling, he snuggled her in close to him. "Go to sleep and dream about how good it's going to be." He whispered to her about plans and dreams and houses and kids until he was certain she had fallen asleep. Only then did he close his eyes and drift off.

He woke the next morning alone. "Maddie?"

She emerged from the bathroom dressed in a floral skirt and matching top.

He pushed himself up on an elbow. "What're you doing?"

"Going to church. Thomas and I go every Sunday at nine. We only missed last week because I was a bloody mess."

"Oh."

"Do you want to come?"

"I'm not very religious."

"That's fine. We'll be home in an hour. Why don't you go back to sleep for a while?"

"I can't sleep without you."

She bent over to kiss him. "Don't pout. It's not pretty on you."

He pulled her down with him and kissed her more intently.

"Mac!"

"You're sexy in your church clothes."

"Let me go! I'll be late."

"You're really going to leave me for a whole hour?" he asked, releasing her.

"You'll survive."

"I might not."

"Then come with us."

"I haven't been in twenty years. You'd be risking your life taking me into a church—the lightning bolt and all that."

Rolling her eyes at him, she went into the bedroom and returned with Thomas, who wore a tiny red polo shirt with khaki shorts and sandals. "Don't be ridiculous. There's no lightning in our church."

"You're going to leave me, too, buddy?" Mac said to Thomas. "This is our time together."

Thomas kicked his feet and reached for Mac.

"Traitor," Maddie muttered, giving the baby to Mac so she could finish getting ready.

By the time she came out of the bathroom again, Mac was dressed. "Give me five minutes."

Maddie stared at him.

"What?"

"You're really going to come?"

"Since it's either that or live without you for an hour, yeah, I'm coming."

She shook her head. "You're too much."

On his way past her, he hooked an arm around her and brought her in close to him. "If you ever wonder how much I love you, remember this day."

"It's only eight thirty, and I already know I'll never forget this day."

CHAPTER 13

On the way to North Harbor Monday morning with Maddie behind him on the bike, Mac relived the best weekend of his life. After church on Sunday, he'd unearthed an infant lifejacket from his father's garage and took Thomas and Maddie on ride around the Salt Pond in his father's vintage Chris Craft. Thomas had loved being on the water.

They'd met his parents for a drink at the Tiki Bar afterward, during which his mother seemed to make an attempt to be friendly to Maddie but gave Mac the cold shoulder. He figured she'd come around in time and decided not to waste any time worrying about it. Linda even took a turn holding Thomas, who reduced Big Mac to mush with his sweet disposition. For the most part, it had been a successful visit, and Mac was more hopeful about taking a harmonious step into matrimony.

Married.

God, a couple of weeks ago the word would've given him hives. Now here he was with the woman he loved on the back of his bike and a baby he wanted to do everything for. Amazing what a difference the right woman made. Pulling up to the hotel, Mac parked and cut the engine. He helped her off the bike and removed the helmet.

"I want you to take it easy today. That elbow still looks bad. Don't bang it on anything."

"I won't, don't worry."

"I'll be right down the hill." He pointed to the marina. "You can look out the window and see me on the roof."

She reached up to caress his face. "Be careful up there. I've become quite fond of this body, and I want it all in one piece." Her hand moved from his face to his chest and began to slide south.

He stopped her at his belly. "Don't start anything," he growled. "I already hate that I have to let you go for six whole hours."

"You're pouting again."

"Come see me at lunchtime?"

"If I can get away."

Mac gave her a lingering kiss. "Try hard."

She clung to him. "Gotta go," she whispered.

"Okay."

Except neither of them let go.

He kissed her forehead and then her lips. "Go. I'll pick you up at quarter to three."

"You won't be done working by then. I can get a ride home."

"I'll be here, and don't you dare let me see you on the back of anyone else's motorcycle."

Maddie giggled. "No worries." She slung her tote bag over her shoulder and gave him a sultry look. "Yours is the only motor I want between my legs."

Mac groaned at the suggestive comment and rested against the bike to watch her fine rear end stretch against tight denim shorts as she walked up the hill. He whistled softly.

"Cut it out," she said over her shoulder, but he saw her smile.

"Madeline."

She had reached the top of the hill, but turned back, feigning exasperation. "What?"

"You forgot something."

"I did?"

He raised an eyebrow.

Her face flushed with color. "Love you."

Smiling, he said, "Now I can go to work." He slung his left leg over the bike, fired it up, and turned toward the marina, feeling her eyes on him all the way down the hill.

At a picnic table outside the marina restaurant, Mac found his father entertaining a baby from one of the boats while holding court with Ned and several other locals. Each of them had a tall cup of coffee, and they were sharing a platter of sugar donuts.

"Hey!" Big Mac shouted. "There he is! The man who's going to keep this place from falling down around me."

"Formidable task," Ned muttered.

"You said it," Mac replied. "Any of my guys here yet?"

"Haven't see 'em," Big Mac said. He nudged his old friend Sam Pressley, the retired Gansett police chief, to make room for Mac.

"Let me get some coffee," Mac said. He returned a few minutes later and joined the men at the table.

Ned reached for another donut.

"You're going to eat your way to diabetes," Big Mac said to his friend as he kissed the baby and handed her back to her mother.

Ned licked the sugar off his fingers. "Helluva way to get there." He wiped his face on his sleeve and turned to Mac. "I hear you're all shacked up with that gal from the hotel."

"Jeez," Mac said. "Cut right to the chase, why don't ya?"

"What gives?" Ned said.

Big Mac snickered but didn't bail out his son.

The others leaned in, waiting for the scoop.

"Let's see: I love her, we're getting married, I'm staying here, probably going to take over this dump and see if I can save it from bankruptcy, I bought a new truck, I'm looking for some property to build a house on, and, oh yeah, I'm going to adopt her son. Good enough?"

The other men, including his father, stared at him, mouths hanging open.

"All that in a week?" Ned finally said.

"Yep." Mac drank his coffee and enjoyed a donut while the others processed the news.

"If you want property," Sam said, "you've come to the right place."

"How's that?" Mac asked.

"Talk to Ned. He can fix you up."

Mac glanced at Ned, who squirmed in his seat.

Big Mac let out a lusty laugh. "Looks like you're about to be thrust outta the closet, old buddy."

Mac had no idea what they were talking about.

"Ned owns half this island, boy," Cliff Sutter said. "You want property for less than a mil, you go to him."

"I might even cut you a deal," Ned said gruffly.

Mac stared at him. "You drive a cab and dress like a hobo, and you own half this island?"

Big Mac and the others howled with laughter.

"What the hell's wrong with the way I dress?" Ned huffed. "And I'll have ya know that I drive a cab because I *like* to. Owning property doesn't keep me all that busy, and sitting around the house watching soaps ain't exactly my style."

"I'll be damned," Mac said. "You think you know a guy. . ."

As the construction workers Mac had hired arrived, they were welcomed into the circle. Mac hoped this would become his new routine as he settled into working at McCarthy's: waking up with Maddie, taking a walk with Thomas and then coffee with his dad and the boys before beginning work for the day. That he could find such contentment and sense of purpose on an island that once made him feel so confined still amazed him. Now he just had to find a way to tell his partners in Miami that he wasn't coming back.

***

Maddie was greeted with hugs from coworkers full of questions about Mac. She filled them in as quickly as she could before Ethel started spewing orders at them.

"Mac is sooooo cute," Daisy whispered to Maddie.

"I never get tired of looking at him."

"And that he filled in here for you like that. . ." Daisy rested a hand on her chest and seemed to swoon a bit.

"He wants to marry me and adopt Thomas," Maddie whispered, dying to tell someone who'd be happy for her. Tiffany didn't qualify.

"Oh my God," Daisy squealed.

"Ladies, are you listening to me?" Ethel barked.

"Yes, ma'am," they said together, choking back giggles.

When Ethel went back to giving orders, Maddie told Daisy about the job offer at the Beachcomber. "I'd want to take you with me."

"You mean it?"

"Of course, I do."

"Oh, Maddie, I'm so happy for you. No one deserves all this more than you do."

Maddie squeezed her friend's arm. "Thanks."

Later that morning as his workers began removing the existing roof on the main building, Mac crawled around in the eaves and made an interesting discovery. Much of the building's frame had been recently replaced. "What the heck?" he muttered. "Why wouldn't Dad have mentioned that?" It definitely made his job easier but presented a baffling mystery. Who would take the time and considerable effort—not to mention the expense—to prop up the sagging building? Certainly not Big Mac, who seemed to do nothing more than land boats, play with kids, and pass the bull with his buddies these days. Mac took a closer look at the quality craftsmanship, which had probably kept the building from falling down around them. "Very interesting."

Climbing down the ladder from the attic, he couldn't figure out who could've done the work. Out of curiosity, he ducked into his father's office, which was located upstairs from the restaurant. On the desk were disorderly piles of paper, an open check register, discarded paper cups and general chaos.

Mac groaned.

"It's quite a mess," a voice behind him said.

Mac turned. "Luke. I didn't hear you come in."

Luke focused on the desk. "I can't remember the last time I saw him in here."

"That so?"

"He loves being out on the docks, hanging with people, coming up with new ideas to grow the business. It's this part he tends to forget about."

Mac heard the affection for his father in Luke's voice. "The bills getting paid?"

"Doubt it."

Right in that moment, Mac got it. It made perfect sense. Everyone loved Big Mac. Why not the quiet young man who'd worked for him for twenty summers? "You've been making repairs, haven't you? That's what you're spending the money on."

"What money?"

"The money I've seen you pocketing."

"And of course you thought I was stealing from him," Luke said, sounding bitter.

"I saw the new beams and couldn't figure out who would've done that. Since he never mentioned it, I figured he didn't know."

"The place is a wreck, and I'd tell him, 'Mac, we need to make some repairs around here.' He'd say, 'Oh, come on, Luke. We can get one more year out of it, can't we?' We've had that same conversation every May for four years."

Mac smiled. "I can picture it."

"Since all he wants to do is hang out with his buddies, I started working nights to prop up the roof before it collapsed and killed someone. I was relieved to hear he was finally going to let you replace it. One more good blow and we would've been screwed."

"You did a really good job."

"Thanks. Let me know what I can do to help with the rest of it."

"I appreciate that." After Luke went back to work, Mac stared at the mess on the desk, wondering how he'd manage to get the repairs done and reorganize the business at the same time. "Looks like I got here just in time."

Mac worked long days that week, spending hours in the hot sun on the roof and taking home stacks of paper from the office every night to sort through. He quickly discovered the business was in arrears to just about every major supplier and talked to his father about writing some checks.

"Go right ahead," Big Mac said. "You got the same name I do. Sign away."

"Is there money in the account?"

"Plenty."

"Is there a bank statement lying around somewhere so I can confirm that?"

Big Mac gestured to the office. "In there somewhere."

"Fabulous."

Early each morning, he continued to take Thomas out for a walk, and on Tuesday they began work on a special project. Sitting in the South Harbor Diner, he propped the drooling baby up on the table so they faced each other. "Okay, buddy," Mac said, "let me hear you say Ma-ma. Ma-ma. You can do it."

"Mmmmm," Thomas said, chewing on his fingers.

"Close, but not quite." Mac tugged the fingers out of his mouth. "Ma-ma. Ma-ma."

More drool. "Mmmmm."

Mac was so focused on the baby that he didn't see another man approach the table.

"He's awfully cute."

Mac glanced up and fought back a gasp.

"Mind if I join you?" Tom Wilkinson asked.

Mac lifted Thomas off the table and rested him on his shoulder, facing away from Tom. "Sure."

Tom slid into the booth across from Mac and accepted a cup of coffee from the waitress.

"I didn't think you'd be hanging around," Mac said.

"I wasn't going to, but something about this island calls to me. The writing really flows here."

Mac once again found himself fighting for self-control when all he wanted to do was tell this guy what he really thought of him. "I've read some of your books," he said, trying to stay on safe ground.

"That so?"

"Uh huh." Mac wouldn't give him the satisfaction of hearing he'd enjoyed them.

"May I be honest with you, Mac?"

"If you must."

"It took about thirty minutes on the island to find out you and Maddie aren't really married."

Mac's heart began to beat faster. "We will be soon."

As if Mac hadn't spoken, Tom continued. "And to learn you only met her a week or so ago."

Mac tightened his hold on Thomas. "What's it to you?"

Tom sat back in the booth and stretched out an arm along the top. "Writers are notoriously bad at math, but even I can add nine plus nine to determine that's probably my son you're holding there."

Mac swallowed a surge of panic. "He's Maddie's son."

"No question about that. I guess the only remaining question is who's his daddy? A DNA test should straighten that right out, wouldn't you say?"

Mac refused to blink. "What do you want?"

Now Tom leaned forward, arms resting on the table. "Assurances that she's not coming after me for money."

"Has she yet?"

"That doesn't mean she won't."

"She has no interest in you or your money. I can guarantee that."

"What about him?" Tom nodded to the baby. "When he's old enough to know who is father is?"

"He'll have a father, and he'll want for nothing."

"Are you willing to put that in writing?"

"If you're willing to sign away your rights to him."

"I'll have my lawyer draw up the documents."

With one arm tight around Thomas, Mac reached for his wallet and laid it flat on the table to withdraw a business card. "Send the papers to my Miami office. They'll get them to me."

"And I won't hear from any of you again?"

"If you hadn't come here, you never would've heard from us in the first place. You have nothing we need."

After a long pause, Tom said, "Is he a good baby?"

"The best."

"I don't suppose. . ."

"Don't even ask."

Tom shrugged as if he couldn't care less, and apparently he couldn't, which was just fine with Mac.

"Can I ask you one thing?" Mac said.

"Sure."

"What kind of guy tells a woman he's had a vasectomy when he hasn't?"

"The kind who's allergic to latex but loves sex."

Mac stared at him, incredulous. Maddie was lucky that Thomas was the only thing she'd gotten from this guy. "We're done here," Mac said, anxious to be rid of him.

Tom took the hint and stood up. "I'll be in touch."

Mac just nodded and watched him walk away, praying he'd leave the island before Maddie ran into him again. Mac kissed Thomas's forehead. "Let's hope you got more of your mama in you than that scumbag, buddy."

"Mam."

Mac stared at him, breathless. "Ma-ma?"

"Mammmmmmm."

Mac grinned at the baby. "We're getting closer."

"Looks like it's going to rain," Mac said Thursday morning. "Let's take the truck. You can drive."

"I can't drive your new truck!"

"It's *our* new truck, and yes, you can. You do have a driver's license, don't you?"

She nodded. "But I haven't driven in ages, and the truck is so new and perfect."

Mac laughed at her distress. "It's yours to use whenever you need it. In fact . . ." He rummaged around in his backpack and produced a set of keys. "Your own keys. I meant to give them to you before now."

Maddie eyed the keys with trepidation as she reached out to take them. "All right," she said with a sigh, "but don't say I didn't warn you."

"Before we go, Thomas and I have something we want to show you." Mac picked up the baby from his mat on the floor. "You ready, buddy?"

"Ayeyayyayay."

"I'll take that as a yes." Mac pointed to Maddie. "Who's that? What's her name?"

Thomas looked from one of them to the other.

In Thomas's ear, he whispered, "Mama." They'd had a breakthrough that morning. Mac prayed the baby would do it again.

"Mama," Thomas said, clear as day.

Maddie gasped. "Oh my God!" Tears sprang to her eyes. "Did he just say . . . *Oh my God*!"

"Mama," Thomas said again.

Maddie burst into tears and reached for the baby, hugging him close to her. "I can't believe it! Where did that come from?"

"We've been practicing," Mac said, overwhelmed by her reaction.

"I just can't believe it."

Thomas ran a chubby hand over the tears on her face. "Mama."

"Yes, baby." She hugged him tight. "I'm your mama. Who's that crazy guy?" She pointed to Mac.

"Dada."

Mac's mouth fell open. "I swear I didn't teach him that."

She laughed through her tears. "He seems to have come to that conclusion all on his own." Maddie reached for Mac to bring him into their hug. "That was the best surprise ever. Thank you."

"It was all Thomas."

"With a little help from his dada."

After they dropped Thomas off with Tiffany, Maddie drove painfully slow and made a full and complete stop at every intersection on the way to North Harbor.

"At this rate, we should get there by next Tuesday," Mac muttered.

"Be quiet. I'm concentrating." When they finally arrived, Maddie released a long sigh of relief. "That was stressful."

"You'll get used to it."

"Whatever you say."

He kissed her and sent her on her way to the hotel.

As she worked her way through her list of rooms, Maddie thought about the job offer from the Beachcomber and how it would make her life—and Thomas's—much easier. She was on her last room when Daisy came rushing in, clutching the *Gansett Gazette*.

"You're all over the paper, Maddie!"

A ripple of fear settled in Maddie's belly. "What do you mean?"

"Look." Daisy thrust the paper at her.

Maddie did a quick scan, gasping as she read one of the letters to the editor. "Oh my God. No. *No!*"

"You didn't know?" Daisy asked, looking stricken.

"I have to go." Leaving the room unfinished, Maddie rushed past her friend and headed for the stairs. On the hotel's expansive front lawn, she fought back tears as she lowered herself into one of the Adirondack chairs and read the letters.

To the Editor,

I'm writing this letter to clear up a misunderstanding dating back to high school. Maddie Chester did nothing to earn the nickname we gave her, and it was wrong of us to say what we did about her.

Darren Tuttle

Gansett Island

"Oh my God," Maddie whispered as tears poured down her face. "How could he do this to me? I told him that stuff in confidence!"

To the Editor,

It is with great shame that I write a letter that should've been written years ago. As a high school student concerned with the approval of my peers, I went along with something that I knew was wrong. It has haunted me ever since. Maddie Chester was branded with a nickname she didn't deserve. She was never anything but a lovely girl with a sweet personality who didn't deserve the way we treated her. The nickname she was given in high school was unfair and untrue. I regret the role I played in perpetuating rumors that have plagued her ever since. I sincerely apologize.

Evan McCarthy
Nashville, Tennessee

Maddie read letters from the four other men who'd participated in Darren's scheme. While none was as eloquent as Evan McCarthy's, each said roughly the same thing. By the time she finished reading them all, her hands were shaking and her cheeks were wet with tears.

She glanced at the marina and saw Mac at work on the roof. Oh, the things she'd like to say to him right now! Too bad she planned never to speak to him again.

CHAPTER 14

Ned broke the bad news to Mac—it took forever to get anything built on the island, especially a house.

"We've got three guys in the building business, and they're all running about two years behind," Ned said.

"Damn," Mac said. "I guess that doesn't bode well for getting someone to help me build a house anytime soon." No way could he and Maddie survive in that tiny apartment for two years, and it would take at least that long to build a house on his own.

"I've been thinking 'bout that," Ned said. "I've got a few properties in inventory that might work for ya, if you'd like to take a look. Nice houses, good views, lots of property." Ned shrugged. "Might be quicker than building yer own."

"You got time to show me these places today?"

"I got nothing but time, boy."

Mac let his guys know he was leaving for a while and followed Ned to the cab. Over the next two hours, they looked at five different properties, and as they drove around, a new idea began to germinate.

"Let me ask you something, Ned."

"Yep."

"This building glut—you think there's room for a fourth guy in the mix?"

"Hell yeah. It's not just new stuff. Ya can't even get renovations done in less than a year."

"One of the things that's worried me about sticking around here full-time is what I'd do in the off-season."

"Now ya know."

Mac laughed, and as simply as that, McCarthy Construction was born.

The fifth house they looked at called to Mac on first sight. An angular contemporary situated on six acres, the house faced a grassy meadow and the ocean beyond. Set back far enough from the coast to be out of danger during hurricane season, the house was mostly glass and deck.

"It was built in 1990, but it's been fully renovated," Ned said. "New hardwood floors, granite countertops, thermal windows. Kitchen and bathrooms all redone."

Mac gazed at the cathedral ceiling in the living room, the stone fireplace and the breathtaking views from every room and could picture himself living there with Maddie and Thomas. Excitement coursed through him. He couldn't wait to show it to her.

"It's perfect. Just what I wanted."

"And ya don't have to build it yerself."

"Even better." Mac ran a hand over sand-colored granite in the kitchen. "How's a place like this even available?"

"Major real estate glut on the island since the economy went bust. A lot of these houses are second homes for rich folk in Connecticut and New York. When the market imploded, they had to sell fast. I snapped up some great deals, and I've been sitting on 'em, waiting for the market to recover. I'll give ya this one for what I paid for it." He rattled off a price that astounded Mac.

"It's worth easily twice that."

"I don't need the money, and yer family to me," Ned said gruffly. "Ya know I ain't got no kids of my own. You and yers are mine, so don't insult me by haggling 'bout it."

Touched, Mac shook the other man's hand. "Thank you."

"I hope you and yer little family will be happy here."

Mac took another long look around. "I know we will be."

Ned dropped him at the top of the road that led to the marina. Filled with anticipation, Mac whistled as he walked toward the main building.

Big Mac stepped away from the Whiffle ball game he was playing with kids from the boats.

Mac stopped to wait for his father. "Wait 'til you see the house I found. It's fantastic."

"Son, Maddie was here. She's real upset.

That stopped Mac cold. "What happened?"

"She saw today's paper."

Mac gasped. "*It was already in?*"

"Yeah."

"*Shit!* I thought I had at least another week to talk to her about it."

Big Mac's normally amiable expression hardened. "Were you planning to tell me about what my son was involved in?"

"I figured it was up to Evan to tell you."

"One of you could've given me—and your mother—a head's up. She's beside herself."

"All that mattered to me was restoring Maddie's reputation."

Big Mac held up the keys to the SUV. "She said to give you these because she won't need them anymore."

Fear crept up his spine as Mac took the keys from his father. "Where is she?"

"She took off about twenty minutes ago."

"Where was she going?"

"Didn't say."

Mac strode toward the truck.

His father trailed behind him. "Son, wait." With his hand on Mac's arm, Big Mac stopped him. "Don't go off half-cocked. Take a breath."

"I need to find her, Dad. I've got to fix this."

"You might want to give her some time to figure out that your heart was in the right place."

"Everything will be fine. I just need to see her and explain."

Big Mac patted his face. "Call me later? Let me know you're all right?"

Mac nodded, got into the truck and raced into town. Wondering if she might refuse to see him, he broke into a cold sweat. "She has to. We have to work this out." The alternative was simply unimaginable.

He pulled into Tiffany's driveway and generated a cloud of dust on his way back to Maddie's. Pounding up the stairs, he stopped short at the sight of his backpack and running shoes sitting on the deck. "She can't be serious."

After a deep breath to slow his racing heart, he knocked softly on the door. "Maddie. Honey, open the door. I need to talk to you." He tried the door and was astounded to find it locked. "Baby, come on. Let me explain."

"She isn't going to talk to you—now or ever—so you should probably get your stuff and go," Tiffany said from the bottom of the stairs.

Mac spun around. "This is none of your business, Tiffany."

"Who do you think mops up the mess every time she gets crapped on by a guy?"

"I didn't crap on her."

Tiffany shrugged with indifference that infuriated him. "Seems to me if you knew her at all, you'd get that being the center of attention in this town is the *last* thing she'd ever want."

"Even if it means restoring her reputation?"

"You're so clueless. You think you can come in here, wave your magic McCarthy wand and make everything all better. I hate to break it to you, ace, but it doesn't work that way for the rest of us."

"This is between me and Maddie. I'll wait to talk to her about it."

"She's not here."

"Where is she?"

"Even if I knew, you'd be the last person I'd tell."

He sat on the top step. "Then I'll wait for her. She has to come home eventually."

"Suit yourself, but it won't do any good. Once Maddie sees a guy's true colors, she doesn't give second chances."

"Good to know."

Tiffany turned, crossed the yard and disappeared into her house.

Mac sat there for a long time before he heard the unmistakable sound of a baby crying inside the apartment. He jumped up and went to the door. "Maddie, I know you're in there. I just want to talk to you. We can work this out."

Thomas's cries broke Mac's heart. He leaned his head against the door. "Maddie."

"Go away, Mac," she said through the open window. "I have nothing to say to you." Her voice was rough, as if she, too, had been crying.

"I'm not going anywhere until we talk."

After a long silence, the door finally opened. Mac was taken aback by her tear-ravaged face and saddened to know he was the cause. He reached for the screen door.

"Stay out there."

Thomas brightened at the sight of Mac and reached out to him.

Through the screen, Mac pressed his hand to the baby's. "Hey, buddy."

"The other day I told you that lying to me and keeping things from me were deal-breakers. You did both. What do we need to talk about?"

"I was going to tell you about the letters. I had no idea they'd run this week, or I would've told you."

"You could've told me the other day when I asked you who you'd hit. It was Darren, wasn't it?"

Mac looked down at the deck.

"Still not willing to be truthful with me, Mac?"

"Yes, it was Darren! He made a crude comment about you, and I belted him. Does it make me a jerk that I didn't want you to know what he said about you?"

"I'm not a wilting rose who can't take life's harsh realities. By now, I'm an expert."

"And that's exactly why I didn't tell you. I don't want anyone to ever hurt you again."

"Instead, you did. You took something I told you in the strictest of confidence and made sure the whole town was once again talking about me."

"Maddie, they needed to know you aren't the person they think you are. How could I hear something like that—something my own brother was involved in—and not try to make it right for you?"

"Did you really do it for me? Or was it for you? To make it easier to marry the town slut?"

As if she'd physically hit him, Mac stepped back, staggered by the accusation. "Baby, this was all about making things better for *you*. I never once considered how it would affect me."

Tears rolled down her cheeks. "I *trusted* you, Mac. I told you things I never tell anyone. I can't believe you'd do something like this and not even warn me."

"I was going to. I swear to God."

"You had ample opportunity. I can't be in this kind of relationship. I'm sorry. I appreciate all you did to help us when I was hurt, but it's over."

Mac had never been more desperate. "No, it's not. I love you. You love me. We can work this out."

"We have *nothing* if I can't trust you."

"You can trust me. There's nothing I wouldn't do for you. You have to know that. What about all our plans? How can you walk away from what we have together? Just today, I found us the perfect house. It's so beautiful, Maddie, and I can see you there. I can see Thomas there. Are you really going to throw away everything we have over this?"

With her free hand, she swiped at the tears wetting her cheeks. "I'm sorry, Mac." She started to close the inside door, but he moved quickly to open the screen.

"Wait. Please." He reached out to run a hand over her soft hair. "What am I supposed to do without you? Without Thomas?"

A sob shook her entire body.

"I love you so much. Both of you. I'm sorry you were hurt by what I did. I just wanted everyone to know the Maddie I know. The Maddie who's sweet and innocent and so beautiful she makes me ache. I wanted the people who hurt you to take responsibility for what they did to you."

Maddie stepped back from him. "Did it ever occur to you that there are people on the island who didn't know? Who'd never heard the rumors? Like the women I work with who'll be full of questions now?"

"I didn't think of that."

"You didn't think at all—that's the problem."

"I couldn't let those guys go on with their lives without owning up to what they did to you. I was only thinking of you."

"If only you'd thought to discuss it with me instead of going off on a rogue mission that had more to do with your ego than with my reputation."

"That's just not true, Maddie. I did it because I love you, and I wanted you to be able to live here in peace without rumors plaguing you. Half your life was long enough to live like that."

"The other day when I told you that lying and keeping things from me were deal-breakers, you'd already done this, hadn't you?"

Mac winced. "Yes."

"And you didn't think that would be the ideal time to tell me?"

"We had a whole weekend free to be together, and I didn't want to spoil it by bringing that into it."

"Instead, you spoiled everything. I really want you to go now."

"Maddie. . ."

With her face set in an unreadable expression, she held the door expectantly.

"I'll go, but this isn't over."

"Please get your stuff and just go."

"Dada," Thomas said, reaching for Mac.

Mac's eyes filled with tears. "Don't do this, Maddie," he whispered. "I can't live without you."

She tightened her grip on the door and waited for him to move as new tears spilled down her cheeks.

The moment he stepped onto the porch, the door closed and the lock clicked into place.

Mac sat for a long time on Maddie's top step listening to her and Thomas inside going through the rituals of dinner, bath and bedtime. Even though she spoke softly to the baby, Mac could hear the tears in her voice. And Thomas seemed fussier than usual, crying for long periods as Maddie tried to calm him.

Mac buried his head in his hands. He couldn't believe how badly he'd screwed up the only relationship that had ever really mattered to him.

The sun set, daylight faded to twilight, and still he sat there.

"Mac."

He looked up to find Janey at the bottom of the stairs. "What're you doing here?"

"Dad called me. He was worried when he didn't hear from you."

"I'm okay."

Janey came up a few steps. "Why are you out here?"

"She's upset about the letters in the paper, but we'll work it out."

"Why don't you come home with me tonight?"

He shook his head. "I need to be here."

"You should give her some space, Mac. Maybe with a little time she'll come to see that you were just trying to help her."

"I don't know why she can't see that now!"

"Because she was caught off guard. We all were."

"I never meant for that to happen. I thought the letters would run next week and I'd have time to tell her—and Mom and Dad."

"You can't sit out here all night. Get your stuff and come with me."

Mac worried that if he left, he might never get the chance to come back.

"Come on." Janey took his arm and helped him up. "You'll feel better after you get some sleep."

Mac couldn't imagine sleeping without Maddie. In one week's time, she'd become so essential to him. The thought that he might've lost her forever filled him with the kind of anguish he'd seldom experienced in his life.

"It's okay," Janey said. "Everything will be okay."

Mac let her lead him down the stairs to the driveway. He looked back at Maddie's place just as she turned off the last light. Imagining her crawling into bed upset and alone was more than he could bear.

"I can't lose her, Janey. I just can't."

His sister kept a firm grip on his hand and carried his backpack as they walked to her house at the other end of town. "We'll figure it out in the morning."

Through the screen, Maddie heard Janey come to get Mac. While she was relieved that he had finally gone, she was also filled with overwhelming sadness. After what they'd shared, losing him was going to ruin her like none of her previous disappointments ever could have.

Reaching out to lay her fingers on the pillow that had become his, Maddie choked back another sob. She brought the pillow closer and rested her face on it, drowning in his familiar scent and wetting the pillow with new tears.

"I know you meant well," she whispered. "I know that. But how could you not tell me? How could you keep a secret like this from me? How could you convince me to take this huge chance on you and then disappoint me this way?"

Her gut-wrenching sobs must've woken Thomas, because he let out a wail from his crib.

Wiping her face, Maddie got up to go to him. "What's the matter, baby?" Tuning into her distress, he'd cried more tonight than he had in months. She leaned into the crib to pick him up.

Thomas clung to her, crying his little heart out.

"I know, baby. I know. But we'll be okay. We were okay before he came along, and we'll be okay after." Even as she said the words, they rang hollow to her, and apparently to Thomas, as well. He cried until his tiny body was worn out and shuddering. "I'm so sorry, Thomas. I wanted it to work out as much as you did, but I can't be with someone who thinks it's okay to keep important things from me. I just can't."

Like she had when he was a newborn, Maddie walked the baby from one end of the small apartment to the other until he finally fell into a fitful sleep. Then she broke one of her own rules by bringing him into bed with her so she wouldn't have to sleep alone.

Mac lay awake all night on Janey's sofa. When daylight began to filter into the room, he got up, took a shower and got dressed for work. The simplest of tasks seemed to take all his energy, and the pit of emptiness inside him grew larger with every passing moment. As a quiet rain fell on the island, Mac walked along Water Street, past several bicycle rental outfits before he found one that was open.

"Morning," the young man in charge said. "Help you with something?"

"I'm looking to buy a bike—as close to new as you've got."

"Sure thing." He pulled out several before Mac found one that seemed to be in almost perfect condition. Painted a deep royal blue, the mountain bike had multiple gears and hand brakes. He'd wanted to buy her a new one, but this was the best he could do at the moment—and it was a major upgrade from what she'd had.

"I'll take a helmet, too, if you can spare one."

"No problem."

Ten minutes later, Mac rode the bike into Maddie's yard where his truck was still parked in the driveway. As he sat on the stairs and waited for her and Thomas to emerge from the apartment, the light rain became a downpour. Right on schedule, the door opened, and Maddie stepped out with Thomas in her arms, both of them wearing yellow raincoats. The baby let out a happy squeal at the sight of Mac.

"What are you doing here?" Maddie asked, her face set in the closed, guarded expression he remembered from their first days together. After experiencing her open, loving side, the regression pained him.

"It occurred to me that I never replaced your bike." He gestured to the new one parked at the bottom of the stairs.

"Oh."

He knew her well enough to suspect she was wrestling with whether or not she should accept it.

"I got you a helmet, too, in case some other guy knocks you off your bike."

She finally looked right at him, and the impact of those caramel eyes meeting his almost knocked him over. "That was probably a once-in-a-lifetime event."

He kept his gaze trained on her. "It was for me." Rain wet his hair and face, but, afraid to break the spell, he didn't dare move to brush it away.

"Thank you for the bike."

"You're welcome."

In the midst of an awkward silence, Mac scrambled to think of something—anything—he could say that would keep her talking to him. "You'll be soaked by the time you get to North Harbor."

"I'll be fine."

"Let me drive you. I'm going to the same place. We can toss the bike in the back so you can get home later."

"A little rain won't hurt me."

"It'll hurt me to think about you riding your bike in the rain. What if you fall again?"

"Fine," she said, exasperated. "But it's just a ride."

"Okay."

She came down the stairs.

Thomas lunged for Mac.

"Could I hold him? Just for a minute?"

Reluctantly, Maddie transferred the baby to Mac's waiting arms.

He hugged Thomas in close to him. "Hi, buddy," he said, breathing in his sweet scent. "I missed you this morning."

Thomas took a handful of Mac's hair and tugged. "Dadadadadada."

Mac winced, and not from the pain of having his hair pulled. His eyes flooded, and he was grateful for the rain on his face. "You have a good day with Aunt Tiffany, pal." Mac kissed the baby's pudgy cheek and handed him back to his mother.

Thomas wailed in protest as Maddie walked him across the yard to her sister's house.

Mac put the bike in the back of the truck and got in to wait for her. With the window down, he could hear her arguing with Tiffany, who probably didn't approve of her sister taking a ride from him.

A few minutes later, Maddie slid into the passenger seat and slammed the door. Her face was flushed and her breathing choppy.

"Everything okay?" he asked.

"Yes." She didn't say another word on the short ride to North Harbor.

At the hotel, Mac got out to retrieve the bike. When she joined him, he kept a firm grip on the handlebars. "You know where I am if you change your mind."

"Yes," she said without looking at him.

"I love you. Only you. I always will."

Her brief nod was the only indication she gave that she heard him.

Mac held on to the bike, knowing the moment he let go she'd walk away and never look back.

"I need to go to work."

He reluctantly released his hold on the bike and watched her wheel it up the hill, his heart breaking. "Maddie!" The single word burst from his chest in a desperate cry.

Her shoulders stiffened, but she put her head down and kept going.

CHAPTER 15

Maddie had considered leaving the island—taking Thomas and the things they couldn't live without and just going. Unfortunately, she didn't have quite enough money saved to make it happen. So she'd had no choice but to face whatever might be waiting for her outside the safe confines of her apartment.

Rattled by the encounter with Mac, Maddie somehow managed to get through the long day at the hotel. Her coworkers were clearly curious about the letters in the paper, but no one asked. At the end of the day, when they were gathered in the supply room folding clean towels and sheets, she decided she had to say something.

"So, um, I know you all saw the paper yesterday."

The other women stopped what they were doing and turned to her.

Maddie's face heated with embarrassment, but she forced herself to say the words. "I had a bit of trouble with some of the local boys in high school. One of them was mad I wouldn't sleep with him, so he made up a story and got his friends to go along with it. I was given a horrible nickname that has stuck to me ever since."

Daisy gasped. "I'm so sorry, Maddie."

"These," she said, gesturing to her breasts, "apparently come with expectations, and if you don't live up to them. . ." Maddie shrugged.

"How did it end up in the paper, honey?" Sylvia asked.

"I told Mac about it, and he flipped out, especially since his brother was involved."

"So he made them write the letters?" Patty asked.

Ethel stormed into the room. "What's going on here?"

"Leave us alone, Ethel," Betty snapped back.

The others watched nervously as the two women stared each other down.

Seeming to realize she'd interrupted an intense moment, Ethel spun around and left.

Sarah closed the door behind her.

"Mac forced them to write the letters?" Patty asked again.

Maddie nodded. "Unfortunately, he failed to mention anything about it to me, so we're over."

"No!" Daisy wailed. "You love him! You're going to marry him!"

Maddie fought back tears. "I can't marry someone who'd keep something like that from me. I just can't, Daisy."

The others got busy again with the sheets and towels.

"You guys don't agree?" Maddie asked.

"It's just that he came here and filled in for you," Patty said. "That was so sweet."

"And remember how nice he was to us?" Sylvia added. "Bringing us coffee and that one day he got pizza for everyone?"

"I know he's a good guy," Maddie said. "That's not what this is about."

"Honey, he wanted to fix it for you," Betty said. "Granted he went about it all wrong, but he can't help that. He's a man. His intentions were good."

"You guys think I'm crazy to break up with him over this." She'd expected her friends to share her outrage.

No one replied, which spoke volumes.

"I told him that keeping things from me was a deal-breaker, and still he didn't tell me about the letters or that he'd punched Darren, even after I asked him what happened to his hand."

"You have to stand up for what's important to you," Sylvia said.

"Absolutely," Daisy said.

If that was true, why was Maddie suddenly worried that she'd made a huge mistake?

On the way home, she stopped at the post office to buy stamps.

"Hi there, Maddie," Mrs. Jergenson said with a friendly smile.

Maddie stared at the woman behind the counter. She'd been in there a hundred times over the years and never once had the woman who ran the local post office addressed her by name.

"How are you today?"

"Fine," Maddie stammered. "Thanks." She bought her stamps and went to the drug store. Since she didn't yet have a basket on the new bike, she bought only a few essentials.

"Afternoon, Maddie," Mrs. Gold said. "Nice to see the sun after all that rain this morning."

Again, Maddie was rendered speechless.

When she received the same treatment at the grocery store, Maddie had to acknowledge that her life on the island seemed to have changed overnight. The rumors people had believed for years had been dispelled. Her reputation had been restored. And she had Mac to thank for that.

Over the next two weeks, Mac threw himself into work. He spent twelve to fourteen hours a day at McCarthy's, either making repairs or reorganizing the business's finances. The company had plenty of money to pay for upgrades, and his father seemed more than happy to turn everything over to Mac.

Too bad he was miserable. He wasn't sure he'd be able to stay on the island permanently after what had happened with Maddie. Living without her and Thomas, especially knowing they were so close but out of reach, was just too damned painful. Except for fleeting glances as she came and went from the hotel,

Mac hadn't seen her since the day he drove her to work. He continued to hope she'd come around, but he hadn't heard from her and had begun to accept that he wasn't going to. Janey had convinced him to give Maddie some time and space, but the longer he went without seeing her, the worse he felt.

He'd been consulting almost daily with his partners in Miami on a wide variety of ongoing projects. A few weeks ago, he'd been certain he would stay on the island and had planned to tell his partners he wasn't coming back. Now he wasn't sure, so he hadn't said anything to them about his long-term plans. The more he hedged, however, the more persistent Roseanne became about pinning him down on a return date.

In light of that, he shouldn't have been surprised when she showed up one day at McCarthy's just as he was starting work on the gift shop roof. He watched Ned's cab pull into the lot. Roseanne emerged and took a good look around the marina.

Mac suppressed a groan and wished there was somewhere to hide. But she spotted him on the roof and let out a happy shriek. Teetering on spike heels, she came rushing toward him as every guy on the dock stopped what he was doing to stare at her. Wanting to reach her before she got to the pier and broke her neck on those heels, Mac descended quickly from the roof.

They met in the parking lot where Roseanne launched herself into his arms. Mac had no choice but to catch her.

Gripping a handful of his hair, she wrapped her legs around his hips and planted a huge kiss on him.

He heard the whistles and catcalls, but all Mac could think about while she kissed him senseless was getting rid of her as fast as he could.

"Maddie," Daisy whispered. "Mrs. McCarthy wants to see you in the office."

"Did she say why?"

Wide-eyed, Daisy shook her head. "Good luck," Daisy called after her as Maddie took the stairs from the third floor to Mrs. McCarthy's lobby office.

Outside the door, Maddie steeled herself and knocked briskly. "You wanted to see me?"

Linda looked up from a spreadsheet on the desk. "Maddie, hi." She waved her in. "Close the door."

Maddie took the seat Linda offered.

"Can I get you anything? Some coffee or tea?"

Surprised by the friendly reception, Maddie said, "Um, no. Thank you."

"I heard an interesting rumor when I was in town the other day."

Not more rumors! "Oh?"

"Is it true that the Beachcomber is trying to lure you away from us?"

"Libby made me an offer, but I haven't given her an answer."

Linda folded her hands on the desktop. "Ethel is retiring at the end of the summer. I'd like you to replace her. As a management position, it's full-time, year-round, with benefits and two weeks' paid vacation." She rattled off a salary that shocked Maddie. It was even more than Libby had offered.

"Why me? You have other people on the housekeeping staff who've been here longer."

"Sylvia and Betty wouldn't want the hassle at this point in their lives, and the others aren't qualified. Besides, you're the one I want."

"Why?" Maddie asked, shocked by this sudden shift in Linda's attitude toward her.

"For one thing, I owe you an apology. I'm appalled by what my son Evan was involved in and by what those boys did to you. I can't deny that I've treated you unfairly because I believed what people said about you. I'm ashamed to admit that." Linda paused and then looked at Maddie. "I'm not asking you to forgive me, but I do hope you'll consider the job."

"I'll think about it."

Linda nodded. "Good."

Maddie got up to leave.

"Maddie."

She turned back.

"I've never seen Mac so low. He's working himself to death trying to keep his mind off what happened with you."

Maddie's stomach churned. "I thought you didn't approve of our relationship."

"I was wrong about that, too. He's heartbroken, and I can't bear to see him this way. I was probably as angry at him about those letters as you were, so I understand where you're coming from."

"But?"

"He loves you—and your son. He truly does. Is there any way you can find it in your heart to forgive him?"

Maddie's heart fluttered painfully. For weeks, she'd agonized over the situation. While she still didn't appreciate that he'd kept something so important from her, she had to acknowledge the letters had changed her life.

"Does he know you're offering me a new job?"

Linda shook her head. "No one knows about that but you and me." She paused before she added, "But if you want to discuss it with him, he's at the marina."

"You think he'd be happy to see me?"

"He'd be thrilled."

For the first time since she walked away from him, Maddie felt a glimmer of hope. Without taking another second to consider the implications, she darted from Mrs. McCarthy's office and out the hotel's front door. She was halfway down the hill when a curvy, dark-haired woman launched herself into Mac's arms and kissed him passionately.

Frozen in place, Maddie watched them long enough to see Mac return the woman's kiss.

Maddie turned away, trudged up the hill and went back to work.

"What are you doing here?" Mac asked as he extricated himself from Roseanne's embrace and lowered her to rickety heels.

"I missed you *so* much. I couldn't wait another day to see you." She combed her fingers through his hair. "You look much better. Nice tan."

"I've been working outside for a change."

"This is such a. . . cute. . . place. Very eclectic."

Mac laughed to himself, imagining her reaction if she knew how much the cute little business was worth. "I wish I'd known you were coming. I'm really busy."

Her face fell. "You're not happy to see me."

"It's not that."

"Then what?"

Mac glanced at the hotel and then at Roseanne, trying to find the words.

"You've got someone else."

He sighed and ran a hand though his hair. "It's complicated."

"Actually, it's quite simple—do you have someone else or don't you?"

"I do." Even though he wasn't with Maddie anymore, his heart belonged to her, and he couldn't lead Roseanne on.

"Well, that didn't take long. Are you planning to tell Connor and Tony you're not coming back?"

"I haven't decided what I'm doing yet. They'll be the first to know."

"And were you going to tell me?"

"I told you before I left—"

"That we were taking a break. You never said we were over."

"I thought you understood—"

"Will you ask that old man who brought me to take me back to the ferry?"

"I'll take you."

She folded her arms and looked away. "I'd rather go with him."

"Roseanne. . ."

"Will you ask him or shall I?"

When had his life gotten so damned complicated? Mac went over to where his father, Ned and Luke leaned against pilings, watching the show. "Ned, Roseanne can't stay. Would you mind giving her a ride into town?"

"Boy, ya sure can pick 'em." Ned chortled.

"Will you take her?" Mac asked through gritted teeth.

"With pleasure."

"I'm sorry," Mac said to Roseanne as he helped her into the cab.

She whipped a packet of envelopes out of her oversize purse and shoved it at him. "Here's your mail. Have a nice life."

As Ned's car left the parking lot, Big Mac put a hand on Mac's shoulder. "Are you all right, son?"

"Yeah." Mac hated that she'd come so far to be disappointed, but he took comfort in knowing he'd been perfectly clear about where things stood between them before he left Miami.

"Why don't you come home for dinner tonight?"

Since he had nothing better to do, Mac agreed.

Mac picked at the plate of shrimp scampi, remembering Maddie refusing to order it at Dominic's because it had too much garlic. They'd had so little time together, but they'd created memories that might have to sustain him for a lifetime. That thought destroyed what was left of his appetite.

"Not hungry, Mac?"

"I'm sorry, Mom." Mac wiped his mouth and put down his fork. "It's really good."

Studying him, she took a sip of wine. "Anything exciting happen today?"

Big Mac chuckled. "Other than Roseanne showing up and shocking the heck out of him?"

Linda froze. "She was here? On the island?"

"Yep," Big Mac said.

"When?"

"Around two or so, wasn't it, son?"

Mac shrugged. "I guess."

"Oh, God," Linda whispered.

"What, hon?" Big Mac asked, his brows knitted with concern.

"Maddie."

"What about her?" Mac asked, suddenly on full alert.

"She went to the marina to see you. Right around then. You didn't talk to her?"

"I never saw her." Mac groaned, remembering Roseanne's enthusiastic greeting. He pushed back from the table. "Why was she coming?"

"I think she might be ready to talk to you. About what happened."

"Oh no," Big Mac said, stricken. "Roseanne was quite *happy* to see him."

"I've got to go," Mac said. "I'm sorry, Mom. Thanks for dinner."

Linda tipped her face to receive his kiss. "Go, honey. Find her."

Mac cursed his crappy luck. What were the odds of Maddie finally deciding to come talk to him just as Roseanne wrapped herself around him? Banging his fist on the steering wheel, he let out a string of swears.

He pulled into Tiffany's driveway for the first time in weeks, his heart racing with hope and fear. What would he do if she wouldn't let him explain?

Maddie was sitting at the top of the stairs. Startled by his sudden appearance, she stood up to go inside.

"Wait!" Mac leapt from the truck and ran up the stairs. "Listen to me! She means nothing to me! She never did."

"I know what I saw."

"You saw her jump on me and kiss me. I had no idea she was coming. I didn't want her there, and I certainly didn't want to kiss her." Mac took hold of Maddie's arm to keep her from walking away. "The only one I want to kiss is *you*, and you *know* that. I told her I'm involved with someone else and sent her back to Miami on the first boat."

Maddie's beautiful eyes widened with surprise. "You said that even though we broke up?"

"That hasn't changed how I feel about you. Nothing could." He skimmed his fingers over her arm, gratified when she shivered. "I miss you. I miss everything about you."

Her eyes fluttered closed.

He caressed her cheek, reveling in the soft skin he'd yearned for, and rested his forehead against hers. "You're the only one I want, Maddie," he whispered. "The only one I'll ever want. I'm sorry I hurt you. I never meant for that to happen."

She leaned into him. "I know that now."

"Marry me, Maddie. I can't live without you and Thomas."

"Mac. . ."

"Just say yes."

She studied him just long enough for Mac to realize his whole life had led to her and this moment.

"Yes."

Shocked, he stared at her. "Really?"

"I have conditions."

"Whatever you want."

"You don't want to hear them?"

"Later." Even though he was dying to kiss her, he only held her, drowning in the scent of summer flowers and the feel of silky hair. Overwhelmed with relief, he swallowed the huge lump in his throat. "There's something I need to show you. Can you and Thomas come with me? Is he asleep?"

"Not yet. He's still chattering in his crib."

"So will you come?"

"Okay."

Mac loaded them into the truck and headed to the south end of the island, past Dominic's and the Hydrangea House Bed & Breakfast, taking a right onto Sweet Meadow Farm Road.

Sitting between them in his backward-facing car seat, Thomas gripped Mac's finger so tightly that Mac wondered if the baby was afraid to let go.

"Where are we going?" Maddie asked.

"You'll see." The paved road changed to gravel about halfway down. *I'll need to get a plow for the truck before it snows*, Mac thought. He took the final turn, and the house came into view. "What do you think?"

"Oh, it's beautiful! Whose is it?"

"Ours."

She gasped. "It is not! Don't make jokes like that, Mac!"

"Who's joking?" He laughed at her as he parked. "Come check it out." Before he got out, he reached under the seat for an envelope that he stashed in his back pocket.

Maddie got Thomas out of his car seat and met Mac in front of the truck.

As he wrapped his hand around hers, he felt a tremble go through her.

"What do you think?"

"You can't be serious. This isn't a house. It's a mansion!"

"It's got everything I wanted—lots of land, a good view and room for our family to grow." He appreciated the dazzling glow the sunset had cast upon the property. "All that matters now is if it has everything *you* want."

She looked at him as if he had three heads.

"What?"

"Are you seriously asking me that? Does it have two bedrooms?"

"Um, five actually."

"Then I'm sold."

"You haven't even seen the inside yet."

Tears spilled down her cheeks. "We're really going to live here?"

Mac put his arm around her and kissed her forehead. "We really are."

"It's a palace," she whispered. "I just never imagined. . ." She looked up at him. "You can afford something like this?"

"My father's friend Ned gave me a sweet deal."

"Still, it has to be a fortune."

"I can handle it, honey. My business in Miami does really well. They'll have to buy me out, and I have a condo to sell there."

"I can't imagine having that kind of money."

"Well, you do now."

She shook her head. "It's yours."

"Everything I have is *ours*. Everything." He tipped her chin up and kissed her while Thomas squirmed between them. "You got that?"

"It'll take some getting used to."

"We've got nothing but time. Want to see the inside?"

She nodded, her eyes sparkling now with excitement, and Mac had never loved her more.

When he took her inside and gave her the tour, there were more tears.

"I was thinking," he said, directing her to the deck that overlooked the ocean, "that the yard would be the perfect place to tie the knot. What do you say?"

"Oh yes! Absolutely."

"I want to do it as soon as we can, okay?"

"About that. . ." She glanced up at him, her expression wary. "My mother is due home in a couple of weeks. I'd like to wait for her, if that's all right with you."

"Of course it is. Whatever you want."

"Will you always be such an accommodating husband?"

"Maybe not *always*, but it'll always matter to me that you're happy."

She bent to put Thomas down on the carpet and linked her arms around Mac's neck. "I feel like I'm dreaming," she said, drawing him into a kiss. "I missed you so much."

"Me, too. I thought I'd go crazy without you." Mac wanted to lose himself in the kiss, but he held back. "Hold that thought for a second, will you?"

Moaning in protest, Maddie released him.

"So, um, there's something I have to tell you, and you might get mad at me for not telling you sooner, but I had a really good reason—"

"What've you done now?"

Mac withdrew the envelope from his back pocket and handed it to her.

"What's this?"

"Open it."

Giving him that wary look she did so well, she withdrew the papers from the envelope and scanned them.

He was about to explain when she gasped, and her hand flew up to cover her mouth.

"Before you freak out, will you listen to me?"

She couldn't seem to speak, so she nodded.

"A couple of days after we ran into him on the ferry, he found me in the diner when I was there with Thomas. He said he'd asked around and knew we weren't married and that we hadn't been together long. He'd figured out that Thomas was probably his."

"Oh God," she whispered. The stricken look on her face broke his heart and confirmed he'd done the right thing by not telling her when it happened. "Oh my God!"

Mac rested his hands on her shoulders. "All he cared about was that we'd come after him for money."

"I've never wanted his money!"

"And I told him that, but he wanted assurances. I said we'd sign something releasing him from financial obligation if he'd sign away his rights to Thomas so I can adopt him."

She wrenched free of Mac's hold and began to pace the big, empty room.

From the floor, Thomas watched them with that big-eyed solemn expression of his.

"This happened weeks ago! When were you going to tell me?"

"As soon as I had the signed papers from him, which Roseanne delivered to me with my mail. I was going to bring them to you tonight."

"Why didn't you tell me the day it happened? We're right back to you keeping things from me!"

Mac forced himself to stay calm. "If I'd told you that he knew about Thomas, you wouldn't have been able to breathe or sleep or eat for the two weeks it took him to get these papers to me."

"Is this how it's going to be?" She threw up her hands. "You're going to take care of everything and leave me out of it?"

"Stuff like this? Absolutely."

"That's not how I want to live, Mac. That's not the kind of marriage I want."

"This is *me*, Maddie. *It's who I am.* I see something that'll make you sick with worry, and I make it go away. I love you too much to watch you suffer like that, and you would've suffered over this." He went to her, slid an arm around her waist and brought her in close to him. "You would've suffered."

She expelled a deep, shuddering breath as all the fight went out of her. "Yes. I would have."

"Now you don't have to. He signed his way right out of our lives." Mac pressed his lips to her forehead. "Are you mad?"

"No," she said softly. "I'm sad."

"Because of what I did?"

She shook her head. "Because his father cares so little about him that he'd sign him away without ever even knowing him."

Mac stepped back from her, picked up Thomas from the floor and hugged them both. "His father cares so much about him that there's nothing he wouldn't do for him. His father will love him and care for him and give him his name and protect him every day of his life."

Maddie looked up at him with her heart in those caramel eyes.

He brushed a gentle kiss over her lips. "His father will love him and his mother forever." He kissed her again. "Now about those conditions you mentioned. . ."

"Will Thomas's father try very hard to not keep things from his mother?"

"He'll do his best, as long as he's allowed to occasionally surprise her."

She raised that eyebrow of hers. "And these will be *good* surprises?"

"The very best surprises he can think of."

"In that case, my friend, you've got yourself a family."

"I guess it's official, then."

"Our engagement?"

"That, too." Mac leaned in to kiss her once more. "Knocking you off your bike was the best thing I ever did."

She smiled. "I couldn't agree more."

Turn the page for a preview of Joe and Janey's story, "Fool for Love," available now!

FOOL FOR LOVE

THE MCCARTHYS OF GANSETT ISLAND, BOOK 2

CHAPTER 1

The phone call Joe Cantrell had waited half his life to receive came in around nine on an otherwise average Tuesday evening. He'd put in a twelve-hour day on the ferries, done four round-trips to the island, and had just sat down to eat when his cell phone rang. Since he'd been in a foul mood all day, tortured by images of Janey in Boston with her fiancé, he'd almost ignored the call. Thank God he grabbed it on the last ring before voicemail picked up.

"Joe."

One word set his heart to racing. He'd know that voice anywhere. "Janey? Why are you calling me when you're visiting David?" He kept his tone light, but just saying the guy's name made Joe sick. He couldn't stand the way David went weeks, sometimes months, without so much as a visit to his fiancée. Sometimes Joe wished he didn't have front-row access to who came and went from the island. Some things he was better off not knowing.

He'd seen her earlier in the day, skipping onto the ferry on her way to surprise her doctor-in-training for their anniversary. Thirteen years together. Lucky thirteen, she'd joked. Joe had found nothing funny about it.

"I need. . ."

Was she *crying*? "Janey, honey. What do you need?"

"You."

Joe almost swallowed his tongue. How long had he fantasized about hearing those very words from her? Forever, or so it seemed. "What's wrong?"

"My car broke down on 95, just south of Foxboro."

Why was she south of Boston when she'd gone to visit David for a few days? "Where's David?"

"I'm calling *you*, Joe. Can you come?" More sniffling. "What was I thinking? It's too far—"

He was already leaving a cloud of dust behind his red pickup as he peeled out of the driveway. "Don't be ridiculous. I'll be there in less than an hour." Under normal circumstances, it would take much longer to reach her, but these were anything but normal circumstances. Something had happened. Something bad. If the bad thing was between her and David, then all of Joe's dreams had finally come true. But hers had been crushed. He had to remember that. No matter what this night might bring, he couldn't forget that she'd been with David for almost as long as Joe had harbored a secret, burning love for his best friend's little sister.

On the way, he tried to keep her talking and his heart from leaping out of his chest. "You want to tell me about it?"

"No."

"You aren't hurt or anything, are you?"

"Not physically."

Oh, man. *What the hell happened?* Joe was dying to know, but he didn't ask again. He drove as fast as he dared and was stymied half an hour later by traffic in Providence.

"Are you still there?" she asked in a small voice. Janey McCarthy, *his* Janey, didn't have a small voice.

"I'm here, honey. I'm coming. Hang in there."

More sniffling.

Jesus H. Christ. Why the hell wasn't anything *moving*? Even knowing it wouldn't do an ounce of good, Joe laid on the horn. That earned him a raised middle finger from the guy in front of him. As his desperation to get to her inched into the red zone, he wished he could call Mac and get his take on things, but until he knew more about what had happened, he didn't think Janey would appreciate him cueing in her older brother that something was wrong.

As if she had read his mind, Janey said, "Don't tell Mac."

"Wouldn't dream of it." Traffic inched along, and Joe was certain his blood pressure had to be approaching stroke level.

Twenty minutes later, he flew across the border into Massachusetts. "Here I come."

"Good."

When he finally reached her location, Joe wanted to die when he saw her sitting in the front seat of her old blue Honda Civic, hunched over the wheel. Janey didn't hunch. She barreled through life with exuberance and optimism that brightened every room she entered.

He had to drive past her to the next exit, where he endured two of the longest red lights of his life before he was able to merge onto the southbound ramp. By the time he came to a stop behind Janey's car, his hands were sweaty, his heart was racing and he realized he had absolutely no idea what to say to her. Women in crisis were hardly his forte. He took a deep breath and got out of the truck.

She didn't seem to know he was there until he opened the door and squatted down.

Turning to him, her ravaged face was like a knife to his heart.

Tears pooled in her pale blue eyes. "Joe."

"What happened, honey?"

"He was. . . He . . ."

Joe reached up to caress her soft blonde hair. "Take a deep breath."

She gulped in air as a sob hiccupped through her. "He was with someone else. In *our* bed. In the bed I helped him buy. The bed he was going to bring with him when he moved home to the island to marry me."

"Okay, honey," Joe said through gritted teeth, not wanting to hear another word. If she kept talking, he wouldn't be able to contain the white-hot rage that possessed him, and he'd become an expert at hiding his every emotion from her. "You don't have to talk about it now."

"It's all I can see. She was on top of him, and he had his eyes closed. He didn't see me. I couldn't move. I just stood there watching—"

"Stop." Joe simply couldn't bear the raw pain he heard in her voice. He wanted her for himself. He wanted her more than he wanted his next breath. But not like this. Never like this. "Let's get you out of here." Joe slid his arms under her and scooped her out of the seat.

She clung to his neck, and in that one instant with her soft and pliant in his arms, everything was right in his world.

"I can't leave my car here."

"I'll deal with it. Don't worry."

"I'm sorry. You probably had better things to do tonight."

"No, I didn't." Surrounded by the scent of jasmine, the scent of Janey, Joe wished he could hold her and never let her go. But he deposited her into the front seat of his truck and went back for the bag she'd packed to spend a few days with David. Joe wanted to hunt down that son of a bitch and teach him a lesson he'd never forget. But he figured Mac would take care of that when he heard about what David had done to his sister. Right now, Joe's top priority was Janey.

Before he joined her in his truck, Joe called for a tow truck to get her car. The operator asked for a contact number, and Joe rattled off his. He ended the call and rested his hand on the door handle, taking a moment to summon the courage he needed to get her through this—to get them both through it.

"I didn't even ask if you were busy," Janey said, swiping at the dampness on her cheeks.

"I wasn't. I'm glad you called me."

"I didn't know who else to call."

He reached over and rested his hand on top of hers. Even though it was summer and damn near eighty degrees, her hand was cold and trembling. "You can always call me. Anytime you need me. That's what friends are for." Her normally robust complexion was pale and wan, her eyes and nose red from crying, and looking at her in that condition, Joe discovered it was possible to feel someone else's pain almost as acutely as they were feeling it themselves.

She ran her free hand over her face. "I must look horrible. I didn't know it was possible to cry so much."

Tucking a strand of her thick ash-blonde hair behind her ear, he resisted the urge to draw her into his arms. "You're as beautiful as always. He's a fool, Janey. Anyone who would disrespect you that way doesn't deserve you."

"Thirteen years," she said, shaking her head. "I've spent thirteen years of my life waiting for something that's never going to happen now." She gasped. "Oh, God, the wedding. I have to cancel everything." A shudder rippled through her petite frame, and he wondered for a second if she was going to be sick.

"You don't have to think about any of that today. Right now, let's just focus on getting you home."

A panicked look crossed her expressive face. "I can't go back to the island. Everyone will know. I can't—"

Joe couldn't resist any longer. He brought her into his arms and ran a hand over her silky hair. "You don't have to do anything until you're ready." Swallowing hard, he pushed the doubts and worries and despair from his mind. "You can stay with me for as long as you need to." The words were out before he could stop them. His mouth, it seemed, was operating on autopilot.

"I can't do that. It's too much of an imposition."

God, if only she knew. . . "Would you do it for me? If I needed a place to hide out for a while, would you let me stay with you?"

"Of course I would. You know that."

"Then why can't I do the same for you?" Even as he said the words, Joe questioned the wisdom of opening his home to her. She'd stay a few days and recover enough to go on with her life, but her essence would linger in his home and heart forever. Well, he could always move, if it came to that.

A deep rattling sigh, the kind that followed a serious cry, echoed through her. "You really don't mind?"

"No, Janey," he said with a deep sigh of his own. "I really don't mind."

Janey focused on getting through each minute. Breathe in. Breathe out. Don't think. Don't remember. Don't go there. But despite her best efforts, the sight of her fiancé writhing in ecstasy beneath the enthusiastic hips of another woman was burned indelibly into her memory. He'd had his hands full of breasts that were much larger than hers. Had they been the draw? Or was it simple availability? Was it the first and only time? Or had there been others? Oh, God, she'd been such a fool!

She'd never suspected for one second that he'd cheat on her. He was always so busy with his internship and his life as a doctor. And she'd just accepted his many excuses because she wanted to be supportive and not add to his stress by nagging him for more of his time and attention.

All the lingering doubts from the last thirteen years came roaring back to remind her that there had been plenty of warning signs, and she'd chosen to ignore every one of them.

Like when he'd discouraged her from going to vet school. The loans will kill us, he'd said. Only one of them should go to medical school, he'd argued, because island practices won't generate enough income to pay off all those loans with enough left over to support them and the four kids they'd planned to have.

Like the fool she was, she'd gone along with him, settling for a job as a technician at the island vet's office when she'd had the undergraduate grades to get into a top veterinary school. Six years of cleaning up dog poop and grooming poodles, killing time until the day she'd be the wife of the island's only doctor and could stay home to raise their children: David Jr., Anna, Henry and Ella. They'd named them when they were just seventeen.

A sob erupted from her throat. All her dreams crushed to dust in one unbelievable moment.

Tuning into her misery, Joe unbuckled her seat belt and drew her over to rest her head on his shoulder.

For reasons they'd never discussed or acknowledged, he was probably the very last person she should've called. However, with her brother, parents and closest friends all on the island and her other three brothers out of state, there hadn't been much choice. Resting her head on his strong, dependable shoulder, Janey knew she could count on his discretion, even if she was putting him in the difficult position of serving as her knight in shining armor.

"I'm sure it doesn't seem possible right now, but you'll get through this, Janey. I know you will."

"I wish I was so sure."

"You deserve so much better than someone who leaves you alone for years and then cheats on you."

His gently spoken words reduced her once again to tears. Just when she thought there couldn't possibly be more, there were.

"I'm sorry," he said, sounding mad with himself. "I shouldn't have said that."

"S'okay," she said between sobs. "It's nothing I haven't already told myself."

He ran a comforting hand up and down her arm, and Janey sank into the warmth of his embrace.

"Hang in there. We're almost home."

Where was home now that David was no longer a part of her life? What would she do? Where would she live? Who would she lean on and make love with and laugh with? They'd had so many plans. . . Her head ached and her eyes burned, but still the tears continued to cascade down her cheeks.

The best part was that he didn't even know she'd seen him. He had no idea their life together was over. Would he even care when he found out? Did he still love her? If so, how could he sleep with someone else? How could he do that to her? To *them*?

Janey had never before wished so strongly for a switch she could flip to shut off her tired brain. Her eyes burned closed, and she didn't try to fight the darkness. In fact, she welcomed it.

Joe gnawed on his bottom lip until the taste of blood caught his attention. Tension coiled in his neck and back as he held her close to him. He suspected Janey had fallen asleep, which was just as well. She needed a respite from the pain, and he hoped she'd find it in dreamless sleep.

Twenty minutes later, he pulled into his driveway just as the moon was rising over Shelter Harbor. He sat there for a long time pondering the implications. Bringing her here was a huge mistake. A mistake, in fact, of epic proportions. Just being around her was sheer torture, and now she'd be under his roof for who knew how long. Heartbroken and shattered and unaware of all he felt for her.

He gritted his teeth and accepted the inevitable. He'd offered her a place to stay, and he couldn't undo the invitation. Besides, even if he could, he wouldn't. Perhaps he was some sort of masochist after all. Having Janey, even in her current condition, was better than not having Janey. A tiny spark of hope glimmered just beneath the surface of his current quandary, reminding him that he was the worst kind of fool—a man who'd spent a large chunk of his life in love with a woman he couldn't have.

But she was here now—in his truck, in his arms and in his house. Maybe this was all he'd ever have of her. As he lifted her gingerly from the truck and carried her inside, he told himself it was enough.

Other Contemporary Romances Available from Marie Force:

The Treading Water Series
Book 1: Treading Water
Book 2: Marking Time
Book 3: Starting Over
Book 4: Coming Home

The McCarthys of Gansett Island Series
Book 1: Maid for Love
Book 2: Fool for Love
Book 3: Ready for Love
Book 4: Falling for Love
Book 5: Hoping for Love
Book 6: Season for Love
Book 7: Longing for Love
Book 8: Waiting for Love

Single Titles
Georgia on My Mind
True North
The Fall
Everyone Loves a Hero
Love at First Flight
Line of Scrimmage

Romantic Suspense Novels Available from Marie Force:

The Fatal Series

Book 1: Fatal Affair

Book 2: Fatal Justice

Book 3: Fatal Consequences

Book 3.5: Fatal Destiny, the Wedding Novella

Book 4: Fatal Flaw

Book 5: Fatal Deception

Single Title

The Wreck

About the Author

Marie Force is the *New York Times, USA Today* and *Wall Street Journal* bestselling, award-winning author of more than 25 contemporary romances, including the Green Mountain Series, the McCarthys of Gansett Island Series, the Fatal Series, the Treading Water Series and numerous stand-alone books. While her husband was in the Navy, Marie lived in Spain, Maryland and Florida, and she is now settled in her home state of Rhode Island. She is the mother of two teenagers and two feisty dogs, Brandy and Louie. Visit Marie's website at marieforce.com. Subscribe to updates from Marie about new books and other news at marieforce.com/subscribe/. Follow her on Twitter @marieforce and on Facebook at facebook.com/MarieForceAuthor. Join one of her many reader groups! View the list at marieforce.com/connect/. Contact Marie at marie@marieforce.com

What Others are Aaying About Marie Force's Books:

"*Treading Water is a definite must read! Treading Water creates an emotional firestorm within the reader. It shines the light on the good and the bad in life and proves that one moment can change everything and it's never too late to find love. Marie Force grabbed my heart and squeezed every ounce of emotion out of it but most importantly her monumental story left me blissful. Treading Water may be fiction but it gives me hope; hope in everyday people and happily ever after. I cannot wait for the next book in this trilogy, Marking Time.*" —Joyfully Reviewed, a "Recommended Read" for November 2011!

"*It's a rare treat that you get three gorgeous romances in one story but Marie Force has achieved that with Georgia On My Mind. Ms. Force has seamlessly woven these stories into one magical novel. Each couple is drastically different with their own issues and smoking hot chemistry. This story has a bit of suspense, plenty of humor and lots of romance. Georgia On My Mind is a keeper!*" —Joyfully Reviewed.

"*Georgia On My Mind*" *meets real life issues head-on. It will easily touch your heart with a variety of emotions. If you love a book, in spite of any flaws it may suffer, it's a keeper. This one meets that test. You'll laugh and you'll cry. Most importantly, I'm betting you'll have a satisfied smile on your face when you reach the end.*" —Romance at Random gives Georgia on My Mind an "A."

"*With its humor and endearing characters, Force's charming novel will appeal to a broad spectrum of readers, reaching far beyond sports fans.*" —Booklist on Line of Scrimmage.

"*LOVE AT FIRST FLIGHT by Marie Force is most definitely a keeper. It is an astounding book. I loved every single word!*" —Wild on Books

18211435R00140

Made in the USA
Charleston, SC
22 March 2013